NOBODY'S WIFE

LAURA PEARSON

AGORA BOOKS

ABOUT THE AUTHOR

Laura Pearson has an MA in Creative Writing from the University of Chichester. She spent a decade living in London and working as a copywriter and editor for QVC, Expedia, Net a Porter, EE, and The Ministry of Justice. Now, she lives in Leicestershire, where she writes novels, blogs about her experience of breast cancer (www.breastcancerandbaby.com), runs The Motherload Book Club, and tries to work out how to raise her two children.

* * *

www.laurapearsonauthor.com

facebook.com/LauraPAuthor

twitter.com/laurapauthor

instagram.com/LauraPAuthor

ALSO BY LAURA PEARSON

Missing Pieces

LAURA PEARSON
NOBODY'S WIFE

First published in Great Britain in 2019 by Agora Books

Agora Books is a division of Peters Fraser + Dunlop Ltd

55 New Oxford Street, London WC1A 1BS

This book is for my sister, Rachel, who made a suggestion back when it was a short story that allowed it to grow into a novel.

PROLOGUE

After the glasses had been emptied and discarded, lipstick smeared on their rims, after the polite chatter had stalled, and the well-worn stories had been told, the guests set off for home and just three remained. Emily sat with the two people she loved the most, trying not to choke on the silence, as night found its way into the room and kept falling.

She started to trace her way back through the past year, to pick through the broken promises and mistakes and betrayals. But it was more than she could bear, on that longest of days. She wanted to say she was sorry. She wanted to scream it. To Josephine, to Michael, and to Jack. But it wasn't enough, and it was too late.

Because of the four of them, only three remained. And there was no going backwards from there.

CHAPTER ONE

Emily woke on the morning of her wedding with a voice in her head telling her not to do it. She was surprised, and she wasn't. She'd felt anxious for weeks, but she couldn't pin it down. Michael was never going to be the man who turned up outside her work with a passport and a packed bag and took her to Paris. He was never going to be the man who made her forget where and who she was when he kissed her. But he was the man she could trust with her life. The man who made her laugh, who understood and accepted her. While she was getting ready, her dress hung high on the wardrobe door and her shoes still in their box, she thought about telling her sister Josephine how she was feeling but found that she couldn't say the words. It was nothing, she decided. It was nerves.

A few hours later, Emily peered into a room where everyone was still and silent, the rustlings and the whispered conversations hushed by an announcement of her arrival. A thick slice of light was falling through the high windows, brightening the faces of the people gathered there.

As she walked down the aisle towards Michael, she tried not to look at the front row where her mother should have been. If her mother had made the long journey to be here, would Emily have told her about the anxiety she'd swallowed down like a shameful secret? Perhaps. There was no way of knowing for sure. Her mother lived on the other side of the world, in Sydney. Quietly and without fuss, she'd removed herself from her daughters' lives.

When she reached Michael and stood beside him, Emily felt calmer. He'd always had that effect on her. Soothing. He was as solid as she was flighty. She took his hand, felt its slight shake, and was surprised. This day was something Michael had wanted for a long time. She hadn't expected him to be nervous.

Do you take Michael George Spencer? And do you take Emily Anne Johns? Do you promise to love? In sickness and in health? I do, I do. Emily tried to concentrate on the words, to really feel their meaning. She ignored the tight knot in her stomach, and she promised forever. When it was time for Michael to kiss her, she lifted her head to look at him and remembered seeing him for the first time. And she remembered how she had said yes, without pausing to think, when he had asked her to have dinner with him. And she felt amazed that his asking, and her saying yes — such small things — had led them to this.

After the ceremony, while the guests were drinking wine and catching up, Emily went outside to get some air and to find her sister away from the whirlwind of family and joy. Sometimes when happiness was concentrated like that, she found it almost frightening.

'Can I have a cigarette?' Emily asked.

She saw Josephine try to hide her surprise as she took two cigarettes from her bag, lit both, and handed one to Emily. It was something they'd done together years before, and Emily felt young and light as they repeated it.

'So it's done,' Josephine said, and then she started to say something else but stopped abruptly and lowered her head.

'What?' Emily touched her sister's arm, silently giving her permission to go on.

'I just can't believe Mum missed it.'

Emily shrugged. 'It doesn't matter now.'

They both knew that wasn't true, but what Emily didn't say was that the upside, for her, of their mother's absence, was that it had drawn her and Josephine even closer. She wasn't sure they would have come to rely on one another quite so much if Alice had stayed in London. And now, Emily was married and this beginning for her and Michael was an ending of sorts for her and Josephine.

They walked back inside arm in arm, and then there was Michael in front of them. He reached for Emily's hand and turned to Josephine. 'Can I take her?'

'She's all yours.'

It felt real, then, for Emily. More real than being pronounced man and wife, or the kiss, or the ring on the finger. Finally, after false starts and missed chances and long years, Michael was hers, and she was his.

They made their way to the hotel's restaurant, with its slightly shabby white-painted furniture and enormous windows. And there was something about all that light and the looks on the faces of the people she loved that made Emily catch her breath. She gripped Michael's hand a little tighter as they made their way to the front of the room.

As she took her seat, Michael's brother leaned across the table and touched Emily's hand. 'Welcome to the family,' he said. His smile was warm, genuine. Emily thought about what he'd said as the waiters darted between the tightly packed tables, serving the first course. Thought about belonging to a new family. She'd never known her father, and had lost her mother to a new man and a new life in Australia a handful of years earlier, so for a time there had only been her and Josephine. And Michael, of course. But Michael still had both parents, and a brother, and his brother's wife. A complete set that Emily was now, somehow, a part of. They were near strangers to her, and yet they had been welcoming, accepting. Would they become important to her, in time? Not a replacement for her own parents, but something significant nonetheless. It was an aspect of the marriage that she hadn't considered.

With all the food they had carefully chosen placed in front of her, one course after another, Emily found that she couldn't eat. She pushed things around her plate, knowing that Michael would notice, yet still hoping he wouldn't.

And then he took her hand under the table. 'Are you okay?' he whispered.

What was the answer to that? I love you, but something about this day doesn't quite feel right?

'Yes. I'm just not hungry.'

Michael smiled and kissed her cheek. 'Me neither.'

Emily looked at his plate and saw that he had barely touched his food, and she hoped it didn't mean anything — that neither of them wanted this first meal together as a married couple. And then one of the waiters came to take their plates and she was relieved, as though she had escaped the discovery of a secret.

Once the champagne glasses were filled and fizzing, Ben stood up and tapped his spoon against his glass, calling for quiet. Having no father, Emily had asked Ben to walk her down the aisle and to make a speech. She didn't want there to be a cavernous silence where everyone expected the father-of-the-bride's speech to be.

Ben was a year younger than Emily, and two years older than Josephine, and Josephine couldn't remember his arrival in their lives, but Emily could, just about. She could still feel her mother's hand gripping hers as they stood on their new neighbours' doorstep, ready to welcome them. She could see the flash of Ben's sandy hair as he dashed behind his mother's legs when the door was opened. According to her mother, Emily and Ben had looked at one another solemnly for a moment before Ben had emerged from behind his mother and reached out to touch Emily's face, trying to wipe away her freckles. She didn't remember that part.

'I'm Ben,' he said. 'And I've known Emily since she was four years old, when my parents and I moved into the house next door to her family. I haven't known Michael quite as long, but I've grown very fond of him over the last few years. Of course, when Emily first introduced us, I was ready to tell her he wasn't good enough.'

Emily didn't know how much truth there was in this. Despite being younger than her, Ben had always acted like a protective older brother to both her and Josephine, and he'd scared away a few of their early boyfriends with folded arms and a firmly set jaw. But by the time Michael came along, it had been different. The first time Emily introduced the two men, Ben had taken her to one side and told her he liked Michael, that he trusted him.

'But the truth is, much as I once wanted to break the two of them up and keep Emily all to myself, I couldn't do it because they're simply too good together. So I'd like to propose a toast to the happiest and most suited couple I know: Emily and Michael.'

The guests stood and raised their glasses. Emily took a sip of champagne and felt the bubbles rush on her tongue. She sought out Ben's eyes and mouthed her thanks, and there were tears in her eyes, and she wasn't sure whether it was the champagne or the speech or the emotion of the day catching up with her. She sat down and blinked them away. And then Michael stood and she looked up at him, waiting.

* * *

MICHAEL ROSE, and the buzz of conversation that always starts up between speeches slowly dulled to a murmur and then silence in that high-ceilinged room. He hadn't written a speech. He didn't want his head to be filled with words that day. There wasn't space. So when he stood up and listened to the hush descend on the room, he didn't know exactly what he was going to say.

'I'd like to say a few words,' he said, stalling.

He remembered that at every wedding he'd ever attended, the groom had thanked the guests for coming. 'Thank you for being here for a day that has been a collection of the happiest moments I've known.'

Michael paused and closed his eyes, trying to picture the moment she'd appeared at the end of the aisle. When he'd turned and seen her, he'd had to catch his breath. The girl he'd loved and longed for, there she was, walking towards him in an ivory dress she'd kept hidden from him for months. There she was, her red hair loose and long, her gait confident and sure. She looked no more and no less beautiful than she did when she woke up and turned to kiss him in the morning. But that day, he thought, at long last, she looked like a bride. And then he remembered hearing something he hadn't noticed at the time.

'Thank you for that quiet intake of breath you all took when my wife appeared in the room this morning.'

He looked down at Emily and saw that she was looking back up at him, her eyes wide and bright with tears. 'And thank you to Emily for saying "I do" — she may never know how much those two words meant to me, but I'll spend every single day trying to show her.'

As he raised his glass for the toast, Michael looked at Emily again, but her eyes were on Josephine's. For a moment, he felt frustrated. He'd accepted a long time ago that he'd always have to share Emily with her sister, but he hadn't expected to share her on their wedding day.

Michael drank from his glass and took his place beside Emily. Josephine leaned across the table towards him, and he saw that there were tears in her eyes too.

'That was beautiful,' she said.

And with that, his anger was gone, drowned in the love he felt for Josephine at that moment. She'd been there at every stage of their relationship: introduced on their third date, sharing roast dinners at the flat, leaving out books she'd enjoyed for them to pick up, taking Emily shopping for her wedding dress. It had always been the three of them.

Even at this late stage in the day, Michael could hardly believe it had really happened. They were five years into their relationship, and Michael had known he wanted to marry Emily after their second date. He was older than her, and he knew how to read the signs, how to tell whether something was going to be good and lasting. Or, rather, how to tell if it wasn't. But Emily was new to it all back then, just twenty-four when they met. He had tried to give her all the time she needed, tried not to rush her. He hoped he had got that right.

When he'd finally proposed, a part of him thought that if she wasn't ready then, she never would be, and that he'd have to move on, move out. And a part of him thought that he'd wait for her as long as it took, that he'd ask her to be his wife every day for the rest of his life if he had to.

Michael's father approached him at the end of the dinner. He shook Michael's hand firmly. 'Well done,' he said. 'You know we've always been proud of you, your Mum and me.'

'I know,' Michael said. This wasn't the kind of talk they usually had.

'Seeing you today, with Emily, you just look so happy.'

'I am, Dad.'

'Well, good. I'm pleased. So pleased.' He went back to his seat, sat down heavily.

The last few times Michael had seen his parents, he'd noticed old age creeping over them like a shadow. He wished, then, that he had made more time in his life for his parents in recent years, shown them more of the man he was now, and of Emily. They lived in Yorkshire, and it was too easy to stay in London and call them to catch up rather than making the trip.

When it was time for the dancing, Josephine made her way to the grand piano and began to play, and Michael took Emily in his arms and let his chin rest gently on the top of her head. He hadn't really wanted to do this — to have all the eyes in the room on them once again while they danced as husband and wife for the first time. But at the strangest times, the traditionalist in Emily shone through, and despite the low-key venue, she had wanted speeches and cake-cutting and a first dance.

Just before the guests joined them on the dancefloor, he leaned to whisper in her ear. 'Happy?'

She tilted her head upwards and nodded. He wished she'd spoken but felt he couldn't ask again.

If only he could go back to those early days when they'd first met and she was so unsure and he was so convinced, and he had tried so hard not to call her too often, not to scare her away. He wished he could go back and tell himself that this day would come. Be patient, he would have said. She'll be yours.

CHAPTER TWO

It was getting late by the time Josephine sat down with Ben. They'd been dancing for hours and Josephine was starting to feel the dull beginnings of a headache. The kind brought on by drinking champagne in the day. She took off her shoes, and Ben pulled her left foot on to his lap and rubbed it.

'That feels amazing,' Josephine said. 'Will you marry me?'

Ben laughed. 'I can't believe it's over, Jo. When they picked the date, it seemed like it was so far in the future.'

'It's been lovely though, hasn't it?'

'Perfect.'

They were silent for a moment, reflecting. Josephine wouldn't have said *perfect*, she thought. She'd imagined that it would be, as she'd always thought of Emily and Michael as the perfect couple. But a couple of times that day, she'd caught sight of Emily looking unsure. And she didn't know why. Perhaps that was just how it was, when you undertook something as enormous as a marriage. Josephine wouldn't know.

'She's the first of my close friends to get married,' Ben said. 'It makes me feel old. Or at least like I should be in a real relationship.'

Josephine knew what he meant. She couldn't imagine having what Emily and Michael had. It was something she wanted.

'To love,' Josephine said, raising her half-empty glass. 'To us finding some.'

'Well, you know what they say about weddings.' Ben chinked his glass against hers and laughed.

Josephine looked around her as Ben lowered her foot to the ground and picked up the other one. 'Hmm. I think we've missed the boat.'

Years before, Josephine had thought that perhaps she and Ben might end up together. She had been obsessed with him as a teenager, but she'd convinced herself it was because he was close by, and he was older, and he was always nice to her. Once, when she was home from university for a weekend, they had got drunk and kissed. But it had never happened again and they'd never spoken about it.

'I've met someone,' she said. And then she was surprised she'd said it. She'd been sure that she wouldn't while she was still trying to work out what this thing was. She tried to calculate how many glasses of wine she'd had.

'Go on,' Ben said.

'His name is Jack.'

'Jack.' Ben took a long gulp, finishing his drink. He nodded a couple of times. 'Have you been on a date?'

'A few.'

'So why isn't he here? Does Emily know?'

Josephine paused, trying to decide what she should say. 'She's been so caught up with the wedding, and it's so new, I thought I should wait. No one wants "that guy Jo went on a few dates with" in the wedding photos.'

'So it's nothing serious?' Ben asked.

'I don't know. He isn't my type, but there's something. I just don't know.'

The first time she'd seen him, he'd helped her find a book for her friend Sarah's birthday. She hadn't written the details down and by the time she arrived at the shop, she could only remember the author's first name and some details she'd read about the plot. Jack had shrugged off her apologies, asked questions. And a few minutes later she was out on the street, the book safely tucked under her arm. And that afternoon, while she was teaching a piano lesson, she had thought about him, pictured his soft brown eyes and his height, the way he had stooped a little to talk to her, the way he had pushed his long hair out of his eyes.

'Who cares about types? If you like him, you like him. I hope it works out. You never know, in a couple of years we could be doing all this for you and Jack. Another?' He held up his empty glass.

'I'll get them.' Josephine slipped her shoes back on and headed to the bar.

While she waited for the drinks, she thought about what Ben had said. He was drunk, but he was right, in a way. So what if this man was different to her previous boyfriends? Her relationships with those boyfriends had all ended. Perhaps it was time for things to change.

'What about you?' she asked on her return, placing Ben's beer down carefully.

'What about me?'

'Any dates lined up?'

'No. I'm tired of it all, Jo. First dates. They're exhausting. I think I'm ready to settle down. I just don't have anyone to settle down with.'

Josephine was surprised. Ben had a constant string of relationships, overlapping and jutting up against each other, and she'd never thought too much about the fact that they never lasted. 'Poor Ben,' she said.

'Don't worry about me, I'll be okay. I always am.'

Josephine pushed her half-finished glass of wine to the side and stood up. 'I think it's time for me to go to bed. I've been up since six. Are you coming?'

'Not me,' said Ben. 'My parents are still dancing. I have to wait them out, or I'll feel even older.'

'Okay. Goodnight.' Josephine leaned down and kissed Ben's forehead.

After she had crawled into bed, Josephine lay awake for an hour or more, her body tired but her mind refusing to stop. The previous night, Emily had been in this room with her, and they had talked until one. And now, she was alone. Emily was still her sister, of course, but they would probably never have another night like that, just the two of them. It seemed like something she'd always had was gone, and Josephine wasn't sure how she felt about it.

She looked at the clock, worked out that she'd been up for almost twenty hours, and forced herself to stop thinking. Finally, she was calm, and her breathing slowed until she was asleep.

A COUPLE of rooms away from Josephine, Michael lowered his body on to Emily's. She let out a tiny gasp and kissed him with a force that was almost frightening, and when he pulled his mouth away from hers he tasted the salty tang of blood on his lip.

Michael opened his eyes and took in Emily's naked body. The smoothness of her skin. The jut of her hips. The soft curve of her belly. Her hair covering the pillow like a spill. He wanted to keep this image with him, to store it alongside the others he'd saved. Emily, wrapped up in a sheet, or bending to fasten her shoe, or lying beneath him in shadow. These were the things he wanted to have, in case something went wrong. In case, one day, he didn't have her.

And then he closed his eyes and tasted her. Her mouth hot and fleshy, her teeth sharp. That soft skin, slightly dry at her elbows and heels. He moved on to his side and pulled her around to face him, tracing the ridges of her spine with his fingers, and all the time she clung to him, her eyelashes brushing his cheeks, his neck.

They took a long bath together.

'I don't want to go to sleep,' he said. 'I don't want it to be over.'

Emily smiled a half-smile, her face flushed from the steam and her arms wrapped around her knees. She took a deep breath and slid backwards until she was submerged, her hair, darkened by the water, swimming around her. Michael waited for her to emerge and when she did, she took a few quick breaths and her hair pasted itself to the sides of her face.

'The wedding is over,' she said. 'Now it's just the marriage.'

Just the marriage. They'd spent so long planning this day, Michael had struggled to see beyond it.

Emily stood, and the water slid off her like a discarded sheet. 'Let's open the cards,' she said.

'It's late. Shouldn't we do it tomorrow?'

'No. Anyway, you said you didn't want to go to sleep.' Emily used both arms to sweep up the stack of cards from the desk, dropped them on the bed and climbed in, a damp towel wrapped around her body.

Opening the cards was like dissecting the day, which was always one of Emily's favourite activities. It served as a reminder of who had been there, who had been missing. Sometimes, Michael found it hard to believe that Emily had essentially lost both of her parents. He felt guilty for having two and for taking them for granted. Michael was surprised, as Emily read messages aloud to him, how many people he'd barely spoken to, how many he didn't remember seeing at all.

'Hang on,' he said, more than once. 'They weren't there. Were they there?'

Emily tapped him on the head with the card. 'Of course they were there. She was wearing that gorgeous green dress. They were sat with some of your work people.'

It was fading, already. They were still in the hotel, with many of these people sleeping in the same building, and he was forgetting things. He wanted to see the photographs. Or go back and do it again.

'I'm too tired,' he said. 'I give up. It's over.'

Emily kissed him on the mouth and shook the sheet, letting the cards fall on to the floor. 'Sleep well, sweet prince.'

'That's a misquote,' he said. 'It's actually goodnight, sweet prince.'

Emily rolled her eyes and turned away from him, and he gave in to sleep.

MICHAEL DREAMED HE WAS A TEENAGER, that night. He dreamed that he and Emily were at the same school, in the same classes, passing one another in the hallway. Emily was a more awkward version of herself. Michael had seen enough photos from her teenage years to bring her to life. At fifteen, she hadn't yet grown into her beauty. Boys mocked her and girls were indifferent to her. She was too tall, too thin, and she wrapped her hair into a bun and tried to cover her freckles with poorly applied makeup.

In the dream, Michael loved her. He loved the harsh whiteness of the skin at the back of her neck, the quiet singsong lilt of her voice. But she didn't want to have anything to do with him. After lessons, he would follow her, but she never turned. He would watch her eating her lunch, her long legs kicking against the legs of the table she sat on, or walking home, her head down. She was always alone, and yet she ignored his attempts at conversation.

When Michael woke the next morning, his eyes blurry from too little sleep, the dream was vivid for a moment or two. And that girl who had shunned him had grown into the woman lying next to him, her back curved like a shell. And she was his wife.

CHAPTER THREE

Josephine wasn't used to the flat being empty. She'd got home from work early that afternoon. She taught piano at various schools and privately, so her hours were a bit erratic. Michael and Emily were on honeymoon, and when they came back they'd be moving out. She didn't really want them to go, and she felt childish for minding. She pushed the salad she'd made herself to one side and picked up the phone to call Ben.

'Jo,' he said. 'What's up?'

'I'm bored, Ben. Do you fancy a drink?' She heard some muffled sounds, thought for a moment that she'd lost him, but then his voice was back on the line, as clear as if he were sitting beside her.

'Sorry Jo, I can't tonight. I'm stuck at work. I think I'm going to be here for a while.'

'No problem. I'd better let you get on with it then.'

'Sorry,' he said again.

Josephine tried to picture him at his office where he spent so many hours. He worked for a large insurance company and, although he'd told her countless times, she didn't fully understand what he did there.

'Wait, Jo, what about Jack? How's that going?'

'It's okay.'

'So go for a drink with him. Got to go. See you soon.'

Could she call Jack and ask him to meet her? She hated these early days of a relationship, when you weren't sure what classed as being too eager and what was reasonable. She didn't want to seem needy, but that didn't stop her from feeling it.

She picked up a book, but after reading a couple of pages, she admitted defeat. She wasn't really taking anything in. She thought about calling another friend, quickly ran through a list in her head, discarding them for one reason or another.

When Emily and Josephine were younger, Emily had had trouble making friends and Josephine was always part of a large crowd. In their arbitrary way, the girls in Emily's class decided she would make a good target, and they taunted her for her glasses, her eagerness to learn, her love of French lessons. Josephine used to pass Emily at lunchtimes, always alone, and although she felt sorry for her, it never crossed her mind to ask her to join the group. Josephine was three years younger, and there were lines that just weren't crossed. So she'd pretend she hadn't seen her, more often than not, turning her head to whichever long-haired, pretty girl she was walking beside. And all these years later, she was sitting in her flat, alone, while her sister was on her honeymoon in Italy. Life was funny, like that.

Josephine thought about the first time she'd spoken to Jack, how she'd gone into the bookshop where he worked three or four times before managing it. How that day she'd gone in, determined to make a move. She'd spotted Jack sitting behind the till, his face hidden by his hair, and was both relieved and terrified. He'd been alone, reading a book. There had been no one waiting to pay and no other member of staff in sight. It had been the best chance she was going to get. She'd forced herself to walk over to him, forced herself to hold her head up high, and smile. 'Hi,' she'd said.

Jack had looked up from his book, and his frown of concentration had disappeared. 'Sorry, I didn't hear you come in. Can I help you?'

Josephine had almost faltered then, almost mumbled something and turned to walk away, but she'd somehow found the courage to stand her ground. 'I'm Josephine,' she'd said.

Jack had given her a half smile, pointed at his name badge. 'Jack.'

'Jack. I was wondering whether you'd like to go out for a drink with me tonight?' Josephine couldn't believe she had said it. She'd looked down, unable to meet his eyes for a moment longer.

'Okay,' he'd said. 'Let's do that.' He'd grabbed a cardboard bookmark from a display and written a number on it, and handed it to her. 'I finish at seven,' he'd said.

Josephine had walked quickly out of the shop and hadn't looked back. She was holding the bookmark in her hand, and once she was outside, she'd stared at it. At his number and his name, printed in small, neat letters. She'd laughed, and a couple of people had looked at her as they'd hurried by, and she hadn't cared.

Since then, there'd been drinks and kisses on street corners outside tube stations, long looks and a couple of dinners and held hands and laughter. She wanted him to be her boyfriend, but she wasn't sure whether he was, and she couldn't bring herself to ask. It felt so adolescent — that need to name things, to pin them down. But how did anyone know where they stood, otherwise?

Josephine didn't call him that evening. She had an early night and thought about Emily — how all this uncertainty was over for her, for the rest of her life. And Josephine wished she could change places with her sister and be somewhere sure and solid.

* * *

JACK WAS in a bar that evening. He shared a flat with strangers and he tried to spend as little time as possible there. After work, he'd eaten a Subway sandwich on the tube and headed to a bar that was a ten-minute walk from the flat. He exchanged a quick nod with the guy behind the bar and asked for a beer, and a couple of minutes later he was sitting in the corner, scribbling in a notepad, a book about the art of the short story propped open in front of him. He wrote in furious, ten-minute sprints, sitting back with his beer and reading a few pages of the book between them.

When his phone rang, he was in the middle of one of his writing bursts, and he threw his pen down, annoyed. He'd forgotten to turn it off. And then he saw that it was his mother. His mother, who hardly ever called. Suddenly, the music that he'd barely noticed before seemed loud.

'Hello?' he said. He wondered whether someone had died or was ill, or someone was getting married, having a baby, moving away. He had a large extended family and it was difficult to keep track of what everyone was doing.

'Hello Jack,' his mother said. Her voice was cracked and thin, the sorry soundtrack of his childhood.

'What's up?' he asked, and then there was a silence, while they both considered the fact that they were not a mother and son who just called for a quick chat.

'I was just thinking about you, that's all. I thought I'd give you a call. I'm not interrupting anything, am I?'

She was, but how could he say that when she asked so little of him? When she played such a bit part in his life?

'No, I'm just in a pub.'

'With friends?'

He knew that she was fishing, that she wanted to know about his life. Whether he had good friends to look out for him, or a girlfriend. But it felt so unnatural, this small talk. He took a swig from his drink.

'Just me.'

What could you say? Jack knew that other people knew, that other people could talk easily with their families, mixing up their recent news with shared memories, layering love.

'Would you like to come for a visit?' she asked at last, and he could hear what the words had cost her.

And that question told a story too, as well as the awkward silences between them. She hadn't said the word home. She hadn't asked him if he'd like to come home.

'Maybe,' he said. 'I'll let you know.'

They pretended, as they always did when they spoke, that they didn't both know that Jack would never go back there, not while she was living with that man who was not his father. That man who made it so hard for him to love her. So they played their parts and then they hung up, and Jack sat there quietly, oblivious to the laughter and noise that was all around him, and when he looked at his watch he saw that it was almost nine, and his glass was empty, and he hadn't written a word for a long time.

He went back to the bar, leaving his book and his notepad scattered across the table.

'Same again?' the barman asked, and Jack nodded.

He was aware of eyes on him, and he turned to his right and saw a woman sitting on a barstool. She wasn't trying to hide the fact that she was looking at him, and when he met her eyes, she half smiled. She had dark hair cut into a sharp bob with a blunt fringe. Her fringe was a fraction too long and she kept having to brush it out of her eyes. She wasn't quite pretty. But she was definitely attractive, and sometimes that was more important.

'Do you want to buy me a drink?' she asked.

Jack admired her boldness. He thought of Josephine, of the handful of dates they'd had, the kisses that had promised more to come. He wasn't tied to her. Not yet.

'What's your name?' he asked.

'Callie.'

'And whatever Callie's having,' he said to the barman, who smirked and reached for a bottle of gin.

When they got back to his table, Callie gestured to his things. 'I've been watching you. Are you a writer?'

'Something like that.'

Jack had had a hundred versions of this conversation and he was bored of it. It was all just an elaborate form of foreplay, wasn't it? This woman had told him with her eyes that she wanted him to fuck her, and he was playing along because he wanted that too. It wasn't even that he wanted her, particularly, more that he wanted to feel something, some pleasure or pain or something in between. But this ritual they had to go through, he was so tired of it. He'd been taking long swallows of his beer and it was almost empty. He drained it and stood up.

'I'm going home,' he said. 'Do you want to come?'

Callie looked a little surprised, but she quickly rearranged her features to hide it. 'Sure,' she said, leaving her drink almost untouched and picking up her bag before following him out of the dark bar.

Even as they were walking to his flat, Jack was bored. He wished he hadn't started this — he should have left her sitting there at the bar and simply carried on with his work. She was wearing heels, and he was having to walk slowly to keep pace with her, and his mind was everywhere but in the present moment. Was this because of Josephine? Was he feeling guilty? They hadn't yet slept together and there had been no talk of them being properly together, and yet, he had felt that things were heading that way, had been happy to move in that direction.

'What's going on, Jack?' Callie asked.

He stopped walking and turned to face her. He wanted to say that he wasn't sure, that he'd known these kind of encounters and they left him cold, but she reached up and put her cold hands on his face and kissed him, and he let her. Jack took her home and went through the motions, and afterwards, he wanted to ask her to leave. Instead, he waited until she'd fallen asleep and got out of bed, sat for hours in the lounge with the TV on, not really watching. He didn't want this, and he didn't know why he'd let it happen. Was it just because it was easy and satisfying? He wondered what Josephine was doing. Whether, in time, he could love her.

CHAPTER FOUR

For their honeymoon, Michael and Emily travelled around Italy by train. They saw art in Florence and architecture in Rome, and they took a trip on a gondola in Venice, holding hands under a blue, cloudless sky. But for Michael, it was the train journeys he enjoyed the most. Sitting beside Emily as the countryside rushed by the window, feeling a contentment he had not been able to imagine. On their last day, on the train that would take them back to the airport, he clung to her, wishing these two weeks didn't have to end. That they didn't have to return to the drizzle and dullness of London, the routine of their lives.

'Let's not go back,' he said. 'I'm not ready.'

'I am. I can't wait to be in my own bed.'

Michael knew this about Emily. However much she enjoyed a holiday, she always loved to go home. But he could have stayed on those trains forever, his life punctuated by hours spent waiting on platforms, with Emily as his sole companion.

'Where would I be if I'd never met you?' he asked, reaching over to touch her tangled hair.

'Oh, you'd have married some other adoring fan,' Emily said, letting go of his hand to pull her hair into a loose bun.

It was a game they played. They'd met at a book signing, five years earlier. He the promising young author, she one of a handful of attendees. She confessed to him later that she hadn't read the book at that point, but the event was being held in her favourite independent bookshop, and she liked to see authors read there. On the strength of Michael's reading of the first few pages of his novel, Emily had bought the book, waited patiently for him to sign it. And then, as she turned to leave, he reached across the table they'd set up for him and touched her wrist.

'I'll be finished in a few minutes,' he said, nodding at the two people waiting to have their books signed. 'I'm going to go for something to eat. Would you like to join me?'

Afterwards, Michael marvelled that he'd found the courage. It wasn't the sort of thing he did. But he'd seen this woman as soon as he'd walked into the shop, watched her twirling a curl of that red hair around her finger, her pale face calm and expressionless. He'd known at once that he couldn't leave without asking her to go with him.

He could see that she was taken aback, but to his relief, she nodded her consent, and twenty minutes later they were seated in his favourite Italian restaurant. That night, he told her she was beautiful, and her pale freckled skin blushed deeply, and although she blamed it on the wine, he sensed she was unused to compliments.

That night was the start of Emily and Michael. It was strange, he thought, how natural their names sounded together after the repetition of them over weeks and months and years. And yet, when he said them to himself that first night after walking her home, they jarred slightly. He'd come out of a year-long relationship a few months before, and it seemed his brain wasn't ready to move on.

Perhaps that was why he didn't call her for a couple of weeks. It was a decision he'd questioned ever since. He kept her number on his bedside table, looked often at her hurried, looping handwriting. And when he did call, he heard something in her voice that he'd forgotten about in those two weeks of waiting, something girlish and excited and charming. And he had never spent two weeks apart from her since.

So perhaps that was the real start, that call. Emily counted from there, he knew that. He learned later that she had spent those two weeks reading his book and waiting for his call, had put everything else on hold. He'd hurt her with his silence, and it was a time she preferred to forget. But marking the start of their relationship from that call meant omitting that first night in the Italian restaurant, and Michael was unwilling to do that. That moment, when he told Emily she was beautiful and watched the colour rise in her cheeks, was one of his favourite memories.

'What are you thinking about?' Emily asked.

'You,' he said. 'How lucky I've been.' He opened up his rucksack then and retrieved his book. 'Do you want yours?' he asked Emily.

'I don't think I can read. I'm too sleepy. Do you want to read to me?'

Michael looked around the carriage and saw that it was almost empty. Near the other end, another couple were staring out of the window, and in the middle, an old man slept. 'Okay. But I'm halfway through. Do you want me to start at the beginning?'

'No, you don't have to do that. I'll just pretend it's a film I've missed the start of.'

'Right, I know what that means. Lots of questions.'

Emily laughed, and Michael opened the book and began to read. Before he had reached the bottom of the page, he looked across at her, and saw that she was asleep.

An hour later, as the train pulled in at the airport, Emily opened her eyes. Michael took her in his arms and kissed her. 'Time to go home,' he said.

* * *

AS PLANNED, Josephine was waiting at arrivals to drive them back to the flat. As they approached her, Emily could see that something had happened. There was a weightlessness to Josephine's expression that Emily hadn't seen for a long time. Josephine spotted them and waved, and then flung her arms around her sister and Michael in turn.

On the journey back to Clapham, light but steady rain fell against the windscreen and Josephine drove slowly, carefully, her forehead scrunched up in concentration. 'Tell me everything,' she said. 'What did you see?'

Emily, sitting in the passenger seat beside Josephine, was silent for a moment, trying to decide what she should share. She wanted to keep some parts of their trip back for her and Michael. She wanted them to have had some experiences that no one else knew about, that no one ever would. And she felt confident that Michael would feel the same. She turned her head to look at him in the backseat, silently asked for his help.

'Italy's Italy,' Michael said. 'Fabulous pasta, great wine, beautiful buildings. We'll show you the photos. Now tell us what's been happening with you.'

Grateful for this rescue, Emily saw Josephine blush slightly.

'Well, I'm sort of seeing someone,' Josephine said.

Emily was surprised. She tried to remember the last man Josephine had introduced them to. It felt like it had been a long time.

'His name's Jack,' she said, after a long pause. 'He works in a bookshop in Soho. That's where I met him.'

'And have you been on a date?' Emily asked.

'A few, actually. I met him before the wedding, but I didn't want to bother you with it when you had so much on.'

Emily frowned the way she always did when Josephine kept anything from her. 'So how did you go from seeing him in the bookshop to going on a date with him?'

'I asked him out.'

Emily tried to picture Josephine doing this, and couldn't. She tried to imagine what her sister had said. Perhaps she'd barely had to say anything. She was beautiful, after all.

Josephine braked sharply as a cat ran out into the road, and Emily saw that they were nearly home.

'Sorry,' Josephine said. 'So, I'm taking you to the flat tonight, right? When are you moving into the house?'

'Next weekend,' said Michael. 'If that's okay with you.'

'Of course. I don't have any plans. I'll help you with the move.'

Emily scanned Josephine's face for signs of anger, listened out for them in her words, but she found none. She and Michael were moving out of the flat the three of them had been sharing, and into their mother's house where she and Josephine had grown up. The house had been rented out since their mother's departure, but she'd said that either or both of them could live there if they wanted to. The mortgage was paid off, and their mum's 'new man' had plenty of money, so she didn't seem to be bothered about the house she'd left behind or what became of it.

It had been Michael who suggested they move there, and Emily had been unsure at first. But as the weeks had gone by, and Josephine had raised no objections, Emily had begun to look forward to being back in that house, with all that space, and to finally living alone with Michael.

Josephine reversed the car into a tight space and they let themselves into the flat. When Michael went back outside to fetch the suitcases, Josephine put the kettle on and opened the cupboard to find mugs and coffee.

'God, I missed you,' Emily said. 'I can't remember the last time I didn't see you for so long.'

'I know, me too. I kept wanting to tell you things.'

'What things? Tell me now.'

'Oh, I can't even remember. Just stupid things.'

'Listen,' said Emily, reaching out to touch Josephine's arm. 'It's still not too late for us to change our plans.'

'What plans?' Josephine turned to her, looking confused.

'Moving back into the house. It's your place too. I don't want to do it unless you're completely happy.'

'We've been over this,' Josephine said. 'It makes sense. And I'll have this place to myself. I'm happy, I promise.'

Reassured, Emily set about helping to make the coffees. But the house stayed on her mind as they sat down at the kitchen table to drink them. Would it look the same? She hadn't been inside for several years. They'd left it in the hands of an estate agency, hoping the pain of their mother leaving them would be wiped out by another family's laughter.

She couldn't remember which of the furniture she'd grown up with was still in there, which pieces had been discarded or sold. Would she recognise the pictures on the walls, the curtains hanging at the windows? For a few months after their mother had gone, Emily had taken a detour on the way home from work and walked past the house. She wasn't sure what she was looking for, but she only saw the tenants a couple of times. An overweight, jolly-looking woman and a tall, heavy-set man. Three children. Twin boys, dark and skinny, roughly seven years old, and a plump girl, new to walking and unsteady on her feet.

Emily had ducked behind a tree the first time she saw them, as though she were trespassing. She watched them pile into a dented Volvo, the boys reluctant and whiney, the girl tripping as she clambered in. Emily felt as though she needed to know something about how they lived their lives, how they moved between those rooms she knew so well. She imagined the boys in her old bedroom, her childhood bed replaced by bunk beds, posters of footballers on the walls. She imagined the dining room transformed into a play area, littered with toys and dolls.

As she drank her coffee and half-listened to Michael trying to describe the things they had seen in Venice to Josephine, Emily thought about where that family might be now. Were they still there, getting ready to move out to make space for her and

Michael? Or had they moved on long before? She couldn't remember the estate agency informing them about a change of tenants. Would she find traces of them as she began to make a home for herself and Michael there? A plastic toy forgotten and left at the back of one of the drawers in the kitchen? A coffee stain on the carpet in the hallway?

It was only when Emily was lying in bed that night, the covers folded back and Michael drifting into sleep, that she remembered Jack. Josephine had said nothing about him since they'd got home, and Emily couldn't remember how the topic of conversation in the car had moved away from him. They'd learned almost nothing about him, and Emily wondered whether they would ever meet him, or whether it would fizzle out in a matter of weeks like Josephine's recent relationships had done. On the edge of sleep, she remembered the way Josephine's cheeks had reddened when Michael had asked about him, and she hoped that, this time, Josephine had met someone who would make her happy.

CHAPTER FIVE

Michael hung back and let Emily and Josephine open the door and be the first inside. He knew that Emily was ready to bring this house back to life, to get rid of the smell of other people's books and other people's perfumes. What he didn't know yet, and was looking forward to finding out, was how she would make it something new and entirely theirs.

He hadn't known the house well when Alice lived there. Emily didn't introduce them for a few long months. He understood, by the time he met Alice, that Josephine was the most important person in Emily's life. And it wasn't long after they met for the first time that Alice started making plans to move away. Both sisters felt abandoned by her, but Emily had taken it the hardest. It didn't help, of course, that neither of them had a father. Michael had never understood Alice's decision to move away and start a new life without her daughters.

Michael walked through the downstairs rooms, opening windows to let out the stuffiness of the July day. The large living room with blood-red walls, daylight streaming in through the curtainless windows. The slightly outdated kitchen, with space for a table where they would eat breakfast. The compact bathroom, freshly painted in bright white. The dining room with doors through to the long garden, entirely empty and with a light-bulb hanging down a little sadly from its fitting.

Michael knew that, for Emily and Josephine, each of these rooms would be heavy with memories, but for him, the empty house was just that: an empty house. He wasn't sure whether it was worse for them, with those memories jostling for space and demanding attention, or for him, who would never share them.

Michael didn't linger long in any of the rooms. There was heavy lifting to be done, and he didn't want to leave Emily and Josephine to it. But then he found Emily in the hallway, sitting on a box of books, her head in her hands, and he took her hand and led her out into the garden. 'Where's Josephine?' he asked.

'She's gone back to the flat to load up the car again,' Emily said. 'I didn't know where you were, and Jo was gone, and I remembered the day she left…' Her voice cracked, tailed off.

'Hey, it's okay,' Michael said.

'I don't know whether this was a good idea,' Emily said, after a long silence.

'All I know is that I've heard hundreds of stories about times you've spent in this house, and almost all of them were happy. We can carry that on, make some new memories.'

Emily nodded.

'Shall we have lunch?' Michael asked.

She had packed a coolbox the night before with sandwiches, bottles of juice, and a punnet of strawberries. They took it out into the garden and sat on the grass and ate with their fingers, the plates still lost and packed. Gradually, Michael saw Emily return to herself as she bit into fresh strawberries, catching the juice that ran down her chin.

There was a swing at the bottom of the garden, a tyre for its seat. When they'd finished eating, Emily wandered over and sat on it, scuffing her feet along the dusty ground as she pushed herself back and forth.

'Was that here when you were growing up?' Michael asked.

'Yes,' said Emily. 'But for a long time we weren't allowed to use it.'

'Why?' he asked.

'You know this,' Emily said, nudging his arm. 'Jo fell off and hit her head, had to have a couple of stitches. So Mum thought it was dangerous and it was forbidden until we were about fourteen, by which time we didn't want to use it anyway.'

Michael searched his memory for the story. It sounded vaguely familiar but he didn't remember the specific details of it. He must have assumed it had happened elsewhere, at a park or a playground. 'So why didn't she have it taken away?' he asked.

'She nearly did,' Emily said. 'She looked into it and then she changed her mind. She never said why. But I think she thought it was a good lesson for us to have something that we could see but not touch, that it would teach us about not always being able to have what we wanted.'

Michael tried to imagine his own parents doing something similar but couldn't. It seemed ludicrous to him. Over the years, he'd been slowly building a picture of Alice, getting to know her through the daughters she had left behind. He wanted to understand Emily completely, to know how her ideas had been shaped. He thought it would help when they came to have children of their own.

* * *

In the late afternoon, there was a knock on the half-open door and Ben's face appeared around it. 'Hey Michael,' he said. 'I was just at my parents' place. I thought I'd see how you were doing.'

'Come in,' said Michael, and then he called Emily and Josephine down from upstairs, and they stepped forward to give Ben warm hugs.

'I won't stay,' Ben said. 'You must have loads to do. But it's so nice to see the house again.'

'Shall I show you around?' Emily offered.

Michael shifted a couple of boxes into the kitchen, a couple into the lounge, and he listened to the girls and Ben talking easily about the changes to the rooms Ben hadn't seen for the last few years. Michael heard their voices echoing through the empty house, and he was seized by a need to fill it, to make it something new and theirs.

After he'd seen every room and drunk a quick coffee, Ben got up to leave and Josephine said it was time for her to get going too.

'Jo,' Emily said, as they stood on the doorstep, 'do you want to come back and have dinner with us when we're done? Just a take-away or something?'

'Oh, I can't,' said Josephine. 'Jack's coming over.'

'Bring him.'

'Can we come another night? When you're a bit more settled?'

Michael was glad. He wanted the house and Emily to himself. He felt like they were always on show, always available, and he just wanted to settle in and be with his wife, in their new home.

'Why do you think she didn't want to bring Jack over?' Emily asked, after Josephine had left.

'I don't know. There could be a hundred reasons.'

'Maybe it's over,' Emily said.

'Why would it be over? And if it was, wouldn't she just say?'

Michael thought it was funny, how interested Emily was in other people's lives, how she wanted to know all the details. For him, it was irrelevant. Josephine and Jack would stay together, or they wouldn't. It made little difference to him, and he couldn't see that changing.

Emily stood up on her toes, then, and kissed him. Slowly, she began to unbutton his shirt.

'Here?' Michael whispered into her neck.

'Why not here? It's our house.'

There was no bed, and no sofa, and so Michael lowered Emily to the ground between the dusty boxes in the hallway and tasted the damp sweat in the crook of her neck. And Jack was forgotten.

* * *

THROUGHOUT THAT DAY OF MOVING, Josephine was adjusting to the fact that she wouldn't be back in that house, except to visit. That Emily and Michael would be there, moving through those rooms, making her home theirs.

At the end of Ben's brief visit, it became clear to Josephine that it was time to go. She left, pulling the door hard to stop it catching, as it always had, and made a promise to herself that she wouldn't go back until she was invited. That she wouldn't turn up unannounced, despite the fact that they had given her a key. She would give them the time and space to make their home.

Back at home, Josephine took a shower and washed the dirt and sweat of the long day off her. She had about an hour before Jack was due to arrive, and she was fighting a nervousness she hadn't felt in a long time. She'd lost count of the number of dates they'd been on, and they'd spent long hours talking and kissing in bars and in the street. And yet they hadn't slept together, and that night was the first time he was coming over to the flat, and she felt sure that it would happen.

Josephine wandered from the bathroom to her bedroom and then through to the lounge and the tiny kitchen, trying to see it as a stranger might. The rooms were cluttered but not untidy, with books and jewellery and shoes all on display but in the places where they belonged. There were gaps everywhere where Michael and Emily's belongings had been. She didn't venture into their bedroom; wasn't ready to see it stripped and bare.

Jack was late. Josephine had prepared a stir-fry for dinner, chilled some wine, and was sitting on the sofa reading the same page of her book over and over, unable to concentrate. He was always late, she'd learned that. It was nothing to worry about. And yet she worried. What if he'd tired of her, what if he'd decided she wasn't worth it? She was enjoying the time they were spending together, his quiet sweetness, and when he kissed her she felt a lust and a fear she hadn't known for years. That fear was exhausting: the fear that she would end up alone again, a little more reluctant to open herself up to somebody when all anyone seemed to do was take things from her and leave.

Fifteen minutes later than they'd planned, Josephine jumped at the sound of Jack's sharp knock on the door.

'Sorry,' he said, as she opened it wide to let him in. 'I was held up at work.'

She watched him take in his surroundings, but he said nothing about what he made of them. She couldn't tell whether he was nervous too, if this night was something that could frighten him. She couldn't imagine it.

Josephine led him into the kitchen and handed him a beer, and he leaned against the worktop as she started to cook the dinner.

'Good day?' he asked.

'Tiring. I was helping Emily and Michael move house.'

'Of course.' He looked at her and then away.

He hadn't kissed her. She tried to remember whether they had kissed the other times when they'd met. But all she remembered was the waiting for him to arrive, feeling anxious, her hands clammy. 'What about your day?' she asked.

'Not bad. It was pretty quiet so I had a book hidden underneath the counter.'

Josephine tried to imagine the way Jack would interact with customers, and with his colleagues, tried to remember how he had been with her on her first visit to the shop, but it seemed so long ago. He didn't say much to her and she didn't yet know whether that was just the way he was. She felt, sometimes, as though she barely knew him at all.

Jack picked at his dinner, taking long slugs of wine between each mouthful. Josephine wanted to ask whether there was something he didn't like, or he just wasn't hungry. For her part, she had felt ravenous when she'd returned from the house, but her appetite was all but gone by the time she had served the food. Before long, Jack pushed his plate to one side and lit a cigarette, saying nothing, and Josephine felt a kernel of anger starting to build inside her. She felt like asking him to leave. She went into the kitchen, taking the plates and scraping the uneaten food into the bin.

'Do you want to watch a film?' She asked the question from the kitchen, and she couldn't see him.

But then he appeared behind her and caught both of her hands in one of his and turned her around and kissed her. 'Not really,' he said.

She leaned into him, closed her eyes. And all of the difficulties of spending time with him — not knowing what he was thinking and wondering whether he was going to turn up or ask to see her again — were gone. There was something searching in his kiss, something that told her more about him than any of the few things he said. The urgency of his hot mouth on hers spoke of loneliness, and fear, and untapped passion. It was a feeling she had only ever known with him, and it made her absolutely certain that she must see him again. A feeling of being the only people in the world, of being dizzy, and lucky, and alive.

And although she was still afraid, Josephine let Jack take her into the bedroom, and she kissed him urgently and pulled at his clothes because she was sure that their bodies would fit together in the way that their mouths did.

Between hurried kisses, Josephine caught sight of a faded scar on Jack's chest. It looked to her like a sign of violence. The permanent mark left by a belt buckle or something thrown. She didn't touch it — tried not to look at it or get too close with her hands or her mouth. When Jack traced a line down her body with his hot tongue and knelt between her legs at the side of the bed, she saw another one, slightly longer and more curved, on his back.

Jack's touch was slow and sure, but Josephine's mind was filled with flashing images of how he might have been hurt. She saw him as a lost boy, a frightened adolescent, and she knew that she wouldn't come. She closed her eyes and pulled him up until he was lying on top of her, and she closed her eyes to the imagined pain while he moved rhythmically inside her. And afterwards, when he was asleep, she sat in the dark in the lounge and smoked a cigarette, trying to recall small details of the best and the worst sex of her life.

CHAPTER SIX

When Jack met Emily, a memory flashed up, unbidden. He was sure that on one of those grey school days, he'd been asked to draw a picture of someone in his family, and, discarding his mother and father, he'd made someone up. A girl-woman — half comforting, half sexual — although he hadn't known that at the time. Tumbling red curls like Botticelli's Venus, freckles and angles and curves. And now, all these years later, she was standing there in front of him, a smile playing at the corner of her lips, as though he had sketched her into life.

They had gone over for dinner, Jack and Josephine, and Emily ushered them into the warm house, pulling her sister close and kissing Jack's cheek, her movements quick and sure. Jack had been expecting a dull evening — a duty. Not this. He felt overly aware of his body. He didn't know where to put his hands.

The three of them went into the living room where Michael was sitting. 'You must be Jack,' Michael said, standing and reaching out his hand.

Jack felt as though his reaction to Michael's wife was clear to see on his face. He shook Michael's hand, feeling fraudulent.

Michael was older, Jack noticed. Older than himself and Josephine, and older than Emily. His dark hair was sprinkled with grey and there were creases around his eyes that gave him more credibility than Jack afforded himself. He also looked a little familiar, but Jack was fairly sure they hadn't met. Perhaps Michael had been a customer in the bookshop.

'We've been looking forward to meeting you,' Michael said, and Jack realised that he still hadn't spoken.

'Thanks for asking us over,' he said, feeling like a child at the end of a party.

When Emily stood and left the room, Jack had to stop himself from following her. But seconds later she was back, a bottle of wine in one hand and four glasses held by their stems in the other.

'I hope you like red,' she said, looking at him, her face a question mark.

'Very much.'

Emily set the glasses down on the coffee table and Jack watched her pour the drinks. She kept pushing back her hair, and half of him wanted her to tie it back and half of him didn't.

When they each had a glass in their hand, Josephine asked what they were drinking to, and Jack turned to her, almost surprised that she was still there. He couldn't make sense of what was happening. There he was, just starting to feel good about this new relationship, just starting to believe that he was ready. And now Josephine had brought him here, to meet her sister, and just like that, he was lost again.

'To us,' Emily said, looking at each of them in turn, including them in her toast.

'To us,' the three of them chorused.

Jack swilled his wine in the glass and took a long drink, hoping it would steady him. Knowing it would do the opposite.

Jack had been surprised when Josephine asked if he would come with her for this dinner. It seemed too soon. How long would he have to be with someone before he took them to meet his mother? It had never come up. He hoped that Josephine wouldn't expect it.

Before dinner, Jack ventured upstairs to use the bathroom. He needed a few moments away from the situation, to catch his breath, steady his nerves. But when he got upstairs, he couldn't remember whether Josephine had told him to take the first or the second door he came to. He opened the first, peered into the darkness, and saw at once that it was their bedroom.

Jack turned on the light and surveyed the room. The bed was large and unmade, and he couldn't help but imagine them in it, naked and kissing, or curled up together in sleep, or reading the paper and drinking coffee on a Sunday morning. A man's T-shirt lay on the left pillow. Almost certainly his, Jack thought, but which of them wore it? He thought of her wearing it, imagined the way it would ride up when she stretched and yawned. He felt a sharp stab of pain. What was happening here? Jack backed out of the room, trying to erase it from his memory, knowing that he would see it when he closed his eyes to sleep that night.

The house wasn't the sort of place that people he knew lived in. Everyone he knew lived in a flat, mostly shared, and barely any of them had bought one. And it was beautiful, too. Large and high-ceilinged and bright. He wanted to know how Emily and Michael had this. He felt like he'd stepped into a different city, a different life. This was the sort of Friday night he could imagine in his future. Two couples having dinner, maybe a couple of kids sleeping upstairs. Wine and food and conversation. But not now, at thirty. If it wasn't for Emily, he would be ready to flee.

When Jack returned, they moved to the kitchen for dinner. It was a long room with a small table at one end. Michael filled their glasses while Emily served the food. Jack watched her take the dish from the oven, her face flushed, and sweep over to the table with it.

'It's just enchiladas,' she said, shrugging. 'Help yourselves. But be careful, the dish is really hot.'

She brought over a large bowl of salad, and then went back to the drawer to get the servers. Finally, they were seated. Michael was beside his wife, Jack opposite her. He tried not to look at her too often, but he couldn't remember how to be natural.

'What do you do, Jack?' Michael asked.

It was a question that had never bothered Jack. But that night, he didn't want to answer. He saw his life from a different angle, and it looked makeshift and childish. 'I work in a bookshop. And I do some freelance writing.' Jack glanced at Emily to see what she made of his life. Her expression remained fixed, but he thought he could sense disapproval.

'Michael's a writer,' she said, her tone neutral. 'What kind of writing do you do?'

'Just bits and pieces. Book reviews, travel articles. Whatever I can find.' Jack wished the conversation would move away from him. 'I write short stories too,' he added, and then wished he hadn't. He caught Josephine's eye and saw the surprised expression on her face and realised that he hadn't told her that.

'What do you write?' Jack asked, turning to Michael. He was surprised by this revelation about Michael's job. Writing didn't buy this kind of house. Not unless you were very successful.

'I write for an online magazine,' Michael said. And then he got up to retrieve another bottle of wine — the third, or fourth — as if he was unwilling to say any more on the matter.

And it was then that Jack remembered why Michael looked familiar. He was Michael Spencer, the author of a book Jack had read a few years earlier. Jack had seen him read at a bookshop once. Jack wondered why he didn't mention the novel but decided against bringing it up.

Once the awkward small talk was out of the way, the women dominated. Jack sat back and listened, and at one point, Michael caught his eye and shrugged. It was as though they had their own language, Josephine and Emily. They didn't look much alike, but their gestures mirrored one another and they talked fast, weaving in and out of stories and memories, names and places that were unfamiliar to him. Jack knew that, even without the cloudiness caused by the wine, he would be lost.

Emily told stories about her work. She was a primary school teacher, and the brightness in her eyes spoke of how much she loved her job.

'Did I tell you they made me a card, for the wedding?' she asked. 'I'll show you.'

She went to the drawer and came back with a card, which she passed to Josephine. Jack looked over at it. It showed a crudely drawn man and woman, both dressed in white, and someone had written 'Happy Wedding Day' across the top in a rainbow of colours. Around thirty messages were crammed inside.

'So sweet,' Josephine said.

'Luke, he's my favourite.' Emily turned to Jack. 'I know I shouldn't have a favourite, but I always do. He cried when I told them I was getting married. He said he was going to ask me, but he was waiting until he was old enough.'

Emily and Josephine laughed, and Emily flicked her eyes away from Jack's, and Jack tried to think of something to say to bring her attention back to him.

When he stood up after dinner, Jack felt very drunk. He turned to Josephine, and, seeming to understand him completely, she told Emily and Michael that it was probably time they went home.

Jack thanked them, and in the hallway, he shook Michael's hand. And then he leaned across to kiss Emily's cheek and caught the scent of her perfume. Fresh and clean, like spring flowers. For a dreadful moment, he thought that he might stumble and fall against her, but he regained his balance, and as she turned away from him her hair brushed across his face.

'So what did you think?' Josephine asked as they covered the short distance back to her flat.

It was a perfect mid-summer evening, and he stopped for a moment, grabbed Josephine's shoulders. 'Look at that sunset,' he said.

The sun was blazing, melting on the horizon, and the sky was all purples and pinks. It was like a photograph you couldn't quite believe in.

'It's beautiful,' she said, but then she turned away from it, back to him. 'What did you think of my sister, and Michael?'

Jack shrugged, unsure what his response should be. 'They're nice. They made me feel welcome.'

Josephine smiled tightly, and he knew he had said something wrong, but had no idea what she had wanted. She was silent for the rest of the way, and he tried to conjure up an image of Emily. But, just moments after he'd seen her, he couldn't fit the pieces together in his mind. He hoped he wouldn't have to wait too long to see her again.

* * *

WHEN JACK and Josephine had left, and Emily had shut the door on the night, she turned to Michael. 'What do you think of him?'

Michael shrugged. 'He seems like a nice enough guy.'

Emily was frustrated. Michael didn't play this game well — the dissecting of new people. It was a game she was more used to playing with Josephine, but she couldn't do that this time, not with her sister's new boyfriend.

She'd been surprised when she had opened the door. Jack was standing behind her sister, almost lost in the shadows of the porch. And when he stepped into the house, she saw that he was nothing like Josephine's previous boyfriends. She hadn't considered that Josephine had a type before, not until she met this man who was so far from it. As Emily and Michael finished off their wine, an old Nina Simone album playing softly in the background, Emily catalogued Josephine's exes.

There was James, when Josephine was sixteen. He was charming and confident, the school's football captain. The perfect boyfriend for one of the most popular girls at school. The relationship had lasted throughout the rest of school and a little bit beyond, despite the two of them going off to different universities. Josephine in Manchester, and where was James? She wasn't sure. Somewhere southern. She remembered Josephine calling her in tears when James told her it was over, that he didn't want to spend his time at university travelling up and down the country to spend his weekends with her. The call came the night before one of Emily's final exams when she had more revision left to do than hours left to do it in. But Emily had put her books aside, tried to say the things that she thought Josephine needed to hear.

But Josephine's tears never lasted too long. A few months later she'd met Andrew, a fellow music student. Andrew played trumpet in the university's orchestra, a fact that always surprised Emily a little. Secretly, she thought of university orchestras as the home of outcasts, but Andrew was popular and sure of himself. Josephine had thrown herself into that relationship — almost to the point where it had cost her her degree, and she had spent long hours telling Emily that this was it. In her more wistful moments, after a few glasses of wine, she had sometimes spoken of a wedding and children.

Andrew left Josephine when she was in her final year, studying for her own final exams. He was sleeping with a cellist, Emily remembered. By then, she was with Michael and she could truly empathise with her sister because she'd tasted the fear of something similar happening to her.

Since then, there had been a few dates, a few brief flings, but nothing lasting. And now, the first time in years that Josephine seemed to really like someone, she had brought them Jack. A tall man with pallid skin and unbrushed hair. With dark clothes and hypnotic eyes and a voice like music. The sort of person Josephine and her popular friends wouldn't even have noticed in their school days.

Lying beside Michael in bed, Emily brought him up again. 'I'm not sure about him,' she said. 'I don't think it will last. Do you?'

'Who's to say?' said Michael. 'You never really know about other people's relationships.'

Emily felt restless, unable and unwilling to sleep, and she couldn't pin down why. Something about Jack had ruffled her. Something about the way he'd looked at her, when he thought she wasn't looking. Emily leaned across and kissed Michael, pulling him towards her. He responded, but she could tell his heart wasn't in it. He wanted to go to sleep. But she did not. She ran a hand down his back, pushed her body against the length of his, kissed him harder. She would have her way.

'Hey,' Michael said, pulling back. Emily had bitten his lip. She hadn't meant to.

'Sorry,' she whispered.

'I'm pretty tired,' Michael said.

Emily felt pushed away, frustrated. She had a higher sex drive than him, and they joked about it sometimes, but he rarely turned her down.

'I want you,' she said, and it sounded loud in the darkness of the room.

Michael turned to face her. He ran a finger down the side of her body, stopped at her hip. And then they were kissing again, and his hands were in her hair and she was pulling at his boxers. When he was inside her, she felt her frustration start to ease.

But there was still something untapped. And she woke in the middle of the night and knew, with a sudden clarity, what it was. It was the fact that Jack was the sort of man she had always fallen for, in the days before Michael. Long-haired, a little stooped, a little shy. Always living slightly outside of the rules. Helpless and daring and moody. All through her adolescence and early adulthood, Emily had longed for men like that. A string of them had passed through her life, and not one of them had kissed her. And now, here was another one, another link in the chain. Just when she had thought it was broken.

CHAPTER SEVEN

Jack arrived at work a little late and smiled over at his boss, Tim, who was checking the till. Fridays were his favourite of the four days he worked at the bookshop. It was always quiet and he and Tim were always on the shift together, and they'd spend the day catching up with one another, going over their plans for the weekend.

'The fashionably late Jack,' Tim said, once Jack had dropped his bag off in the staff room and put on his work T-shirt.

'Sorry.' Jack thought that perhaps his frequent lateness was becoming a problem, and Tim's jokey tone was masking annoyance. Earlier that year, Tim had made Jack the shop's assistant manager, and he was grateful for the extra money. He would sort himself out, he decided. Set his alarm a little earlier, take a shorter shower.

'Now that you're here, I'm going out to get a coffee. Want one?'

'I'd love one. Thanks. And I'm sorry I was late.'

Jack walked around the shop, straightening books on the tables, topping up the piles where necessary. He could see what had sold well during the week, what had remained untouched. He picked up a couple of books and skimmed the back covers, and he put aside one that he wanted to buy. And while he was doing all this, and waiting for Tim to return with their morning coffees, he thought about Emily, and about Josephine, trying to decide what was going on. Had Emily felt the way he had, or even a fraction of it? He wanted to believe there was something there, that his attraction was reciprocated in some way, but he wasn't sure.

Just then, the bell above the door chimed and when Jack looked up, Josephine was there in front of him.

'I was nearby,' she said, hurriedly. 'I thought I'd call in to say hello. I hope you don't mind me turning up.'

'No,' said Jack, and he gave her a quick kiss.

Josephine looked down at the books on the table where they stood, picked one up and turned to the first page.

'Why don't you read the back cover?' Jack asked.

She shrugged. 'I never do. Ever since Michael told me that the author doesn't usually write the blurb. He wrote a novel, you see. I think you can get more of an idea from the first page.'

Jack nodded. 'I think the first page is often over-edited. I sometimes look at the start of the second chapter.'

Josephine put the book back in its place and flashed Jack a smile. And he found himself considering really being with this woman, maybe even living with her, storing his books alongside hers. It took him by surprise. He hadn't thought about a woman like that for a long time. Emily had been all over his thoughts since they'd met but then, he pushed her into a corner of his mind, and hoped she would stay there.

Tim appeared in the doorway and handed a large coffee cup to Jack. 'There you go, mate.' He raised his eyebrows, silently asking who Josephine was.

But before Jack could introduce them, she turned to go. 'I should let you get on,' she said. 'And I've got a lesson.'

'Okay. Do you want to do something later?'

'Yes,' she said. 'I think so, although I'm not sure what time my last lesson is. I'll call you.'

'So,' said Tim, the moment the door was closed, 'who's the girl?'

Jack gave Tim a long look, and then he took a seat on a high stool behind the counter, took the lid from his coffee and blew on it. And then he told the story of how he and Josephine had met and what had happened since.

Tim had married his university girlfriend when he was just twenty-two, and now, ten years later, Jack sometimes thought he detected a sense of regret in some of Tim's words and expressions. He liked to hear the ins and outs of Jack's love life, his one-night stands and awkward dates and chance encounters. Perhaps he was happy, Jack thought. Perhaps he just liked to live vicariously through him a little, but really he preferred his solid, settled life.

Every few minutes, the bell chimed and a customer wandered in from the streets, blinking to adjust to the shop's darkness. And Jack paused in his telling of the story, and Tim stopped asking questions, and together they ensured that they found the required book or simply let the customer browse in the silence that book-browsing requires. And then the customer came to the till to pay, or left empty-handed, and the story of Jack and Josephine continued. Jack enjoyed the role of narrator, and he relegated Emily to the sidelines. In telling Tim about Josephine, he tried to convince himself that it was simple.

'Where are you going to take her tonight?' Tim asked, as the door closed behind a stooped old man who had been looking for a rare book on military history.

'I don't know. Maybe dinner somewhere.'

'Have you taken her to your Soho place yet?'

There was a restaurant in Soho that Jack loved. It was hidden away, so that tourists never stumbled across it, and the food was cheap but really good, and the waiters knew Jack's name and the wine he liked to drink. Tim knew that Jack didn't take women there often. Jack had once told him that he had to be sure about a girl before he took her there, because he didn't want the place to be filled with women he'd once dated and their new boyfriends. So when Jack answered Tim's question, they both knew what it meant. 'I haven't,' he said. 'But I think I will.'

THAT EVENING, Jack and Josephine met outside the Soho restaurant. Jack was there first, early for once, and he watched her walking towards him down the street, unsure of her surroundings, looking this way and that.

'Thank God,' she said, when she saw him. 'I don't know this street. I thought I was lost.'

Jack could see why she would hate to be lost, this clever, strong woman who was always so in control, so together. He took hold of both of her hands and pulled her close to him, and he kissed her for a long minute and then led her inside.

'I've had a shit day,' she said, once they were seated.

'What happened?'

'Oh, nothing major. My lessons were just arranged horribly, so I kept going back on myself. And then in my last lesson, one of my favourite students told me she was giving up the piano. She's going to do gymnastics instead.'

'Did you slap her?'

Josephine laughed. 'I was so disappointed. She's pretty good. Well, she isn't, but she could be. Her mum told me afterwards that she was sorry — she can't seem to settle on anything. First it was ballet, then tennis, then piano, now gymnastics. The poor woman seemed a bit frantic, like she was really hoping that this one would stick. Anyway, how was your day?'

'I spent most of it talking about you, actually.'

'Me?'

'Yes. Tim — that's my boss — he wanted to know who you were after you came in this morning.' Jack shrugged. 'It was a slow day. I told him all about you.'

Just then, the waiter brought over a bottle of Jack's favourite red wine without having been asked, and Jack wondered whether that was the kind of thing that would impress her. He suspected it wasn't. But when the food arrived, it seemed like she had shrugged the weight of the day off her and it was easy to read her, as though she was a window that had just been wiped of condensation.

'Wow,' she said. 'This is fantastic.'

Jack smiled, feeling pleased that he had brought her somewhere new, somewhere good.

'How did you find this place?' she asked, looking around as though she was noticing her surroundings for the first time.

'I've been coming here for years,' he said. 'I can't really remember the first time.'

Jack looked forward to going home with her, as they shared a slice of baked cheesecake for dessert and finished off the wine. He thought about being pressed against her all the way home in the tube's late-night crush, and the way they would smile at one another, in anticipation.

It was dark when they left the restaurant, when they emerged from that winding staircase into the lamp-lit street outside. Josephine took Jack's hand as they made their way towards Leicester Square.

'Thank you, Jack,' she said. 'That was lovely.'

And when they had dodged the crowds who were lingering around the station and were standing at the entrance, she leaned across to kiss him.

'Do you want to come home with me?' she asked.

'Yes.'

They walked together down the steps and through the ticket gates and onto the escalator. Their bodies pressed together in the chaos of the Friday night tube journey. And though he didn't want to, Jack found himself thinking about Emily, about how an evening with her might have ended.

CHAPTER EIGHT

Josephine was pleased when Ben called and invited her over. Jack had an article to finish, and she wasn't sure what she was going to do with her evening. It was funny, she thought, how she'd spent so many evenings alone in her life, and yet after a few weeks with Jack the idea seemed so foreign.

'I've asked Emily too,' Ben said. 'I guess you could come over together. About seven?'

And so Josephine and Emily met on the corner near the house and took a bus over to Brixton where Ben lived alone in a ground-floor flat.

'Come in, come in,' Ben said, taking the bottles of wine they held out to him and putting one arm around each sister for a hug. 'I've made risotto.'

They moved into the kitchen, where Ben poured them large glasses of wine and stirred the food. 'How's the new house?' he asked Emily. 'Well, new old house.'

'We're settling in,' she said. 'It doesn't seem like the same place somehow.'

Josephine bristled at that. She wanted it to seem like the same place. She'd thought that, although she didn't have any parents around now, she would always have that house. She knew that they had asked her, time and again, whether she was all right with them moving in, and she had told them that she was. She didn't have any right to feel upset, or jealous. But she did.

'Michael's made one of the bedrooms into a study,' Emily continued, 'so he finally has somewhere to work, which is good.'

'Which room?' Josephine asked.

'Yours,' Emily said. 'I hope you don't mind. It's just that my old room's a little bigger, so it makes more sense to have that as the guest room.'

'No,' Josephine said. 'It's fine. That makes sense.' And it did make sense, but it wasn't quite fine. She hoped that, in time, it would be.

'So,' Ben said then, smiling over at Josephine. 'Emily tells me you're still seeing Jack.'

'I am,' she said.

'So what's he like?' Ben turned to Josephine.

'Well, Emily's met him. What did you think, Em?'

Josephine felt a little awkward asking this and she wasn't sure why. It was quite possible, Josephine thought, that Emily didn't like Jack. She tried to think about him objectively, to imagine how she would react to him if he was introduced as someone else's new boyfriend, but it was too hard. She couldn't separate the Jack she thought she might be falling in love with from the Jack she had first met.

After a pause that was slightly too long, Emily spoke. 'He's great. But I've only met him once. There's not a lot I can say. That's your job, Jo.'

'It's ready,' said Ben, and Josephine wanted to know whether he had picked up on a slight tension between her and Emily. Had there been? Or had she imagined it?

And so they moved into the living room, and Ben presented them with bowls of steaming risotto and chunks of freshly baked Italian bread, and he filled up the glasses of wine that they had barely started drinking. 'I want to hear everything,' he said, once they were settled.

And Josephine wanted to tell everything, but what was it acceptable to tell? She was full of Jack, desperate to talk about him for long hours and ask people what they made of things he had said and done. She felt like a teenager. She wanted to tell her sister and Ben about the scars she had seen on Jack's body, and how they had frightened her, and how she hadn't asked him about them. She wanted to tell them that she was having the best sex of her life, that she felt almost scared by it.

She wanted to tell them that she was happier than she'd been in years. That she might be in love. That she was almost definitely in love. That she was, at the very least, definitely almost in love. That she was terrified of scaring him off, of spoiling it, of doing something that might make him leave. That she wanted to skip through all of this uncertainty, in spite of the excitement of it, and get to the part that Emily had with Michael, where everything was safe and certain.

'I think it's real,' Josephine said finally. 'I think it's serious.'

* * *

EMILY FELT herself go a little cold at Josephine's words. She had wanted to hear her sister say that it was something and nothing, just a bit of fun, although she had known, hadn't she, that that wasn't the case? That knowledge hadn't stopped her hoping. For the truth was that Jack had awakened something in Emily, a desire that had lain still and sleeping since her adolescence. Or had it? Had it always been there since those painful days of late child-hood, somehow suppressed? Or had it gone away entirely, and returned? She wasn't sure.

A few days earlier, a Saturday afternoon, Emily had told Michael that she was going shopping. And she had got the tube to Covent Garden, knowing that she was going to look for Jack, and pretending she wasn't. She'd stepped inside the door of the book-shop and seen him behind the till, talking to a customer, and something had twisted in her stomach. An ache. A need. She had hung about in the fiction section for ten minutes before he had come over.

'Emily?'

Her name in his mouth. She'd turned and he'd been standing close behind her, so that their faces were only a few inches apart, and she had stepped back, feeling colour rise on her chest and in her cheeks.

'Hi Jack,' she had said.

She shouldn't have come. She knew that.

'Are you looking for something?'

She was looking for an escape, for an alternate life. She was looking for a way out of her perfectly happy marriage. A different path. If he was prepared to lead her down one.

'Just looking,' she had said, and then she had held up a hand in a half-wave and stepped out into the bright, sunny day.

'Say something, Em,' Josephine said. 'Aren't you happy for me?'

Emily looked up, saw that Josephine and Ben were looking at her, waiting for her to speak. Ben had a forkful of risotto resting a few inches above his bowl. 'Of course I am,' she said. 'Sorry. I was miles away.'

What was wrong with her? She remembered the way Josephine had been when she first met Michael. How she had listened to Emily talking about him and dissecting their early dates. How she had sat with Emily almost every night for those two weeks of silence after their first meeting, understanding that Emily wanted to be beside the phone, distracting her for the long days that it didn't ring. She owed her sister something. Excite-ment, understanding, time. And she couldn't muster them. Jeal-ousy sat in her stomach like a cold and heavy stone, refusing to be ignored.

'I think it's great,' Ben said, and Emily thought that his voice sounded a little hollow. Still, he'd covered the growing silence with the words that Emily should have spoken. 'In fact, I have a bottle of champagne in the fridge, and I think we should drink it.'

Josephine smiled, standing up. 'I'm just going to the toilet,' she said. 'Don't open it without me.'

Was it possible that she hadn't noticed Emily's strange reaction? She didn't seem hurt or upset. Perhaps the excitement she felt was strong enough that what Emily did or didn't say failed to matter. Or perhaps she was putting on a show for Ben's sake and would question Emily later.

The moment Josephine left the room, Ben gave Emily a look that made it quite clear that he had noticed something amiss, even if Josephine hadn't. 'What's going on?' he asked. 'You're being really weird. Don't you like him?'

'No,' she said. 'I mean, I barely know him. I'm sorry. I'm just feeling a bit strange this evening. Maybe I'm coming down with something.'

Ben looked at her closely, and she felt herself blushing slightly. She wasn't a good liar and Ben knew her too well. He didn't believe her, and she knew he didn't, and that left them in a strange, deceitful place that they'd never ventured into before.

'Well, at least act like you're happy about it,' he said at last. 'She's excited. And don't forget she's been helping you to plan your wedding for months. It's about time something good happened to her.'

And then Josephine was back in the room, and Ben and Emily went silent, and it was clear that they had been talking about her in her absence.

'So where's this champagne then?' Josephine asked.

It was late by the time Emily and Josephine got up to leave, and it had started to rain, so they decided to call a taxi. Emily felt a little drunk, a little dizzy, and was glad that they wouldn't have to negotiate the bus journey. At the door, Ben kissed their cheeks and said that he would call them, and they dashed out into the wet night and piled into the back of the waiting car. Emily turned to give Ben a final wave, but she could barely make out his shape at the door beyond the drizzle and the raindrops that ran down the window of the car.

'I'm sorry if I was a little strange,' she said, turning to Josephine. 'I'm really pleased about you and Jack. Really. It just takes a bit of getting used to, that's all.' She hadn't known she was going to say any of it, but once the words were out she hoped they would clear the air.

'It's fine,' Josephine said.

But then she turned her face away and Emily could see that she had hurt her. Emily reached out a hand, touched her sister's shoulder.

'I just really want you to like him,' Josephine said.

'We should spend some more time together,' Emily found herself saying. 'The four of us.'

'Yes, I'd really like that.'

It was what Emily wanted and what she feared. She had been looking for Jack on the street since that night they'd met. Not only the day she'd visited his bookshop, but every day. She had hoped to find him in the faces of London strangers. But perhaps it would feel different, next time she saw him. He would be with Josephine, and she would be with Michael, and things would be as they should be. So what if he reminded her of the boys and men she had fallen for years before? She was twenty-nine years old now, and she was married. She wasn't that lost and lonely girl anymore. She wasn't still crying out, inside, for someone like Jack to come along and love her.

CHAPTER NINE

Jack closed the pub's door behind him and looked around for Michael. He wasn't there. Michael had suggested the place and it wasn't a pub Jack knew. It was close to both Emily and Michael's house and Josephine's flat, a real locals' place. Floral carpet, red velvet curtains, old men sat in groups of two or three, nursing pints of ale. Jack felt a little uncomfortable, and when he saw that there were no available tables, he took a seat at the bar, hoping he wasn't crossing some unseen line. He'd just ordered a pint of lager when the door opened and Michael came inside.

Michael wasn't a tall man, but he had a certain presence. Jack waited for Michael to see him, enjoying that moment of studying him, and when Michael caught his eye, the two men smiled and nodded and Michael made his way over. On the way, he stopped to say hello to a few of the clusters of old men. He was known here. He was comfortable.

'Sorry I'm a bit late,' Michael said.

'It's no problem.'

'So how are you? How's Josephine?' Michael asked. He took a seat beside Jack at the bar, then got the barman's attention and asked for a pint of a beer Jack had never heard of.

'Good,' Jack said. 'We're good.'

Jack had been surprised when Michael had called. Surprised and flattered. He thought that perhaps Emily had had a hand in it. Jack had decided that he would like to get to know this man, and yet he was jealous of him too. He'd spent long hours since that dinner they'd had thinking about Emily, imagining what he would say and do when he saw her again. And then she had turned up at the shop, and he hadn't quite believed that it was a coincidence. He watched Michael take a long drink and tried to come up with things for them to talk about.

'You know,' said Jack. 'I've read your book.' He could tell that Michael was surprised, and he quite enjoyed seeing this man wrong-footed and unsure.

'You're part of an elite group,' Michael said, after a long pause.

'When Josephine and I came round for dinner, you looked familiar to me. I had to dig out the book when I got home to be sure.'

'I'm not used to being recognised.'

Michael laughed, but Jack could tell he was a little uncomfortable. 'I loved it,' he said. He wasn't sure whether that would put Michael's mind at ease, but it was the truth, and he wanted Michael to know.

'Well, thank you.'

'So will there be another one? Novel, I mean?' Jack watched Michael's face closely, but he wasn't giving much away.

'I'm working on it. But what about your writing? You said you write short stories, didn't you? Any success with that?'

Jack smiled at the way Michael had steered the conversation away from himself, just as he had done that night at dinner. It wasn't clear whether Michael was secretive or just shy.

'Not really. I haven't really shown them to anyone. It's just something I do. Something I've always done.'

'Always?'

'Well, since I was at school, yeah. I used to spend a lot of time up in my room writing. Mainly because I didn't get on with my stepdad.'

Michael nodded, and Jack wasn't sure whether it was a nod of acknowledgement, or if he understood. Whether he had turned to writing to escape his own childhood too.

'Maybe I could read something?' Michael ventured.

'Yes, of course.'

Jack imagined knowing, back when he first read Michael's novel, that in the future he would sit in a pub with this author. That this author would offer to read something Jack had written. It seemed impossible. But then his thoughts turned to Emily again, and he imagined taking her from Michael, this man he admired and was starting to like. Everything came back to that, in the end. And where was Josephine in this scenario that he was focusing on more and more? What would become of the two of them?

'You know,' Michael said, 'I'm really happy that Josephine's met someone.'

Jack thought that was a strange thing for him to say. Did that mean she'd been alone for a long time? He tried to remember what she'd said about previous boyfriends. 'I guess you know her pretty well,' Jack said.

'I met her really soon after I started seeing Emily. They sort of come as a pair.'

They were close — that much Jack knew. He'd pieced together this idea of the three of them. No wonder Michael was glad they'd met. He'd finally got his wife to himself. And at the thought of that, Jack felt a sudden, sharp pain, deep in his stomach, and he wanted to talk about something else, but he needed to talk about her.

'They don't really look like sisters,' Jack said, gesturing to the barman to refill their glasses, hoping his face wasn't giving him away.

'No, they don't look much alike,' Michael said. 'I guess it's because they have different fathers.'

'Oh really? I didn't know that.'

As the barman handed over their drinks and Jack paid, a variety of emotions played across Michael's face. Jack guessed that he was trying to work out whether he'd said something he shouldn't have, had revealed too much that should have stayed private. Finally, he spoke. 'They don't really talk about it much. Neither of them grew up with a father. I guess that's why.'

'Go on,' Jack encouraged.

'Well, there isn't really much to tell. Emily's father died when she was a baby. Heart attack. Very sudden. Unexpected. And then a year or so later, their Mum met Josephine's father. He was married. They had an affair, and Josephine was the result.'

'Did he leave his wife?' Jack asked.

'No. He never lived with them, as far as I know. The girls never knew him. So it was always just the three of them, you see. And then their Mum moved away a few years ago, so they only really have each other. Family-wise, I mean.'

'Family,' Jack said. 'It's never simple.'

He was back in his own childhood for a moment, curled up in his bed, jumping every time he heard a stair creak. That boy he'd been, that little boy. So frightened. And how much had he changed, really, in the years between?

Michael shook his head, cleared his throat.

A little later, after a third drink, Michael stood up. 'Listen,' he said, 'I've got some things I need to do back at home. I should head off.'

They left the warmth of the pub together and faced the blustery London streets. August was just beginning, but the summer weather had broken, making way for wind and showers.

'I'll see you,' Michael said, at the point where they parted. He shook Jack's hand.

'Yes, see you later,' Jack said. And then he stood on that corner as though he was rooted there. He thought of Michael going back to his house and his wife. He watched him, hoping Michael wouldn't turn back and see him standing there foolishly. After a few long minutes, rain started to fall in fat, heavy drops, and that was enough to get Jack moving again. He walked to the tube station and went home, aware that Josephine would expect him to go to hers, if she knew he was so close, but somehow unable to face it, with his mind so fixed on Emily.

* * *

MICHAEL WALKED HOME QUICKLY, his head down against the wind. He thought about what Jack had said, about family never being simple. It was the kind of thing people said, and yet, for him, family had always been simple. A mother, a father, and a brother. All present and correct throughout his childhood. All still alive, parents still together, brother happily married. No neglect, no violence, no adultery, no abuse, no addiction, no unemployment, no fear.

At moments like this, Michael was reminded of how lucky he'd been, and was thankful. He remembered the faraway look on Jack's face when he'd made that comment and wondered what secrets his past held, what experiences he'd lived through that made him say something like that. He would probably never know.

As he pulled his key from his pocket and let himself in, Michael felt tired, and he was glad that he was coming home to a warm house and to Emily. He'd lied to Jack, about having things he needed to do. He had just wanted to go home.

Emily was curled up on the sofa, her feet tucked neatly beneath her, a paperback book in her hands and a frown of concentration on her face. She held up a hand as Michael entered the room, a sign he knew well, a sign that meant that she was finding a suitable place to stop. He went into the kitchen and made two mugs of coffee, and when he returned, the book was facedown on the arm of the sofa.

'You'll crease the spine,' Michael said, lifting the book and looking around for something to use as a bookmark. 'How many bookmarks have I bought for you?'

'A lot,' Emily said, and shrugged. 'I lose them.'

Michael tore the corner from the previous day's newspaper and closed the book around it.

'So,' Emily said. 'How was your evening?'

'Exhausting,' said Michael, taking a seat on the sofa beside her. He lifted her legs and pulled them across his knee, rubbing her feet. 'I'd forgotten how tiring it is to spend time with someone you don't know.'

'What's he like, though?'

'Hard to say.'

'You're useless,' she said.

Of the two of them, Emily was the sociable one. Michael often envied her the ease with which she gathered new people up and into their lives. It was something Emily and Josephine both had, although Emily hadn't always had it, he knew that. So maybe it was something that could be learned, after all.

'I think the four of us should go out for dinner,' Michael said. 'It'll be much easier with you and Josephine there.'

'Why all the interest in him?' Emily asked, blowing on her coffee before taking a cautious sip.

'He seems like a nice guy, and Josephine seems pretty serious about him, so we should probably get to know him.'

'What makes you think it's serious?' Emily asked, her voice changed, slightly higher pitched.

Michael smiled. He understood Emily was worried that she'd lose her sister to this man. 'She was always going to meet someone, you know.'

Emily flashed him a sharp look, pulled her feet away and

tucked them beneath her again, closing up. 'I know that. I just don't think it will last, with him. He doesn't seem like her type.'

Michael didn't know what to say to that. He didn't know what Josephine's type was. She'd been single all the time he'd known her, except for a few brief flings, and he'd never met any of the men involved in those. He found himself hoping that this time it would be different, that this relationship would be lasting. And he realised that it wasn't just for Josephine's sake, or just because he wanted more time alone with Emily, although both of those things were true. There was something in Jack that he liked, something about his manner. He felt confident that, once she had got used to the idea of him and knew him a little better, Emily would feel the same way.

'I love you, Mrs Spencer,' he said.

Emily laughed. She was in the process of changing her name, had sent off her passport and talked to the bank, and it made Michael happy to say it.

'I can't get used to it,' she said. 'It just sounds so strange. Like an old woman's name.'

'That's what you are, now you're married.' Michael tickled Emily's feet, wanting to hear her laugh again. She shrieked and wriggled, breathing hard, begging him to stop. When he did, she was red in the face and her hair was wild, and he wanted to take her to bed.

CHAPTER TEN

Emily could tell that Josephine hadn't picked the restaurant. Jack had led the four of them through the maze of Soho streets to a green door with no sign, and then they'd gone downstairs to a dimly lit basement room. Emily thought it was a miracle that anybody ever found the place, but it was packed with people. She turned to Michael, and he gave her a quick smile and she tried to imagine what he might be making of the place. It wasn't like anywhere they'd ever been together. Jack signalled to a thin, fast-moving waiter, and he came over and took Jack's hands between his own in a warm, friendly gesture. He led them through the crowded room to a small, round table at the back, and they took their seats. Emily sat with Josephine on her left and Michael on her right, Jack opposite. His face was partially obscured by the tall candlestick, and she didn't look at him. As long as she didn't look at him, she felt safe.

'Have you been here before?' Emily asked Josephine.

'Yes,' she said. 'A few times. Jack's been coming here for years.' Josephine opened her menu and held it towards Emily. 'They do great pasta.'

The waiter returned with a bottle of red wine and a jug of water.

'Oh,' Emily said. 'We haven't ordered drinks yet.'

The waiter smiled at her as he opened the bottle and poured a little for Jack to taste. 'Jack's a regular,' he said. 'We always make sure we have a bottle of this in for him.'

Emily watched Josephine smile and reach for Jack's hand across the table, as though he'd done something that had made her proud.

Who was he, this man who knew all the right people and places? Emily felt a petulance rise up in her, and she reminded herself of the girls in her class, the way they were when they didn't get their way. The way they stamped their feet and pouted.

'I'd like a glass of white, please,' Emily said. 'Dry.'

She knew it was childish, and Michael looked at her questioningly, knowing she almost always drank red, but something in her didn't like the assumptions that were being made.

'Right away,' the waiter said and shot off towards the kitchen.

'You know,' Michael said, swirling the wine in his enormous glass. 'This is a really good wine. You should try it, Em.'

'I'm fine with white, thanks,' she said. And she noted, not for the first time, that something about this man of her sister's was making her act strangely. She'd tried and failed to deny the attraction she'd felt to him that first night that Josephine had brought him over, and she thought about him often. She thought about him when she was alone, in the shower, at work. And when she saw him, and he looked at her, she felt as though he knew.

Emily turned to Josephine and tried to smile. 'So what's been happening? I haven't seen much of you lately.'

'Nothing much,' Josephine said. 'I saw Ben last week; he told me to say hi. And I've been spending a lot of time with Jack.'

'What's happening at work?'

'I'm teaching at two new schools,' Josephine said. 'In Dulwich.'

'That's great,' said Emily, genuinely pleased. She sometimes worried about Josephine's erratic working hours, about schools being able to get rid of her at the drop of a hat. As far as she knew, Josephine didn't share those worries, and it sometimes annoyed Emily that she was saddled with them. But they'd always differed in that way: Josephine bold and Emily more cautious.

Other than at the wedding, Emily hadn't heard her sister play for a long time. When they were growing up, she'd loved to listen to her from her bedroom. The piano was in the living room, directly beneath Emily's bed, and she would lie there with a book, the sound drifting through the ceiling and up the stairs until it reached her, muffled and quiet but quite, quite beautiful. Sometimes she would go downstairs and stand in the living room doorway, watching Josephine's fingers dance over the keys, hoping she wouldn't sense her standing there, and falter.

After their mother agreed to Josephine having lessons, they'd both learned for a while. Emily was a clumsy player, without grace. She remembered sitting on the piano stool at their teacher's house, the room hot and her legs sticking to the leather of the seat, while Mrs Grady paced up and down beside her and made her play the same scale over and over. The fact that Josephine was a natural made it harder. While she progressed to classical pieces, Emily was stuck on the simplest of nursery rhymes. Before long, she gave up.

'Any future stars?' Emily asked.

'Some of them are doing well, but none of them practise enough to ever be really good. It's frustrating, but what can you do? I only see them for half an hour each week. I can't make them do it.'

Emily understood Josephine's frustration because she had never had to be forced to practise. Despite her hordes of friends and social engagements, she had always found time for the piano. Emily thought that probably most of the kids Josephine taught were a lot like Emily as pupils and felt sad for her sister.

The food arrived and a second bottle of wine was brought,

with a second glass of white for Emily.

'This is great,' Michael said, after tasting his food.

He was right, Emily thought. She wanted to ask how Jack knew about this place, this secret haven beneath some of London's busiest streets. And she looked at him then, for the first time that evening, and she saw that he was looking at her, quite openly, with an expression on his face that was not quite a smile.

What did he make of her? This was only the third time they'd met, and the second time, in the bookshop, had been a matter of minutes, and she wasn't sure what kind of an impression she had made. Did he just see her as Josephine's older, married sister? She wanted him to see something different, something more. Whenever she thought of him, in secret, she dared herself to believe that he was attracted to her, but now, here, sitting opposite him, the idea seemed laughable. Emily dipped her head and concentrated on her food, wishing for the evening to be over just as fervently as she had wished for it to start.

* * *

JOSEPHINE LOOKED AT EMILY, confused. Her sister had always been so easy to read, but lately she had been frustratingly incomprehensible. First she had failed to react to Josephine's relationship with Jack, and now she was refusing to drink the wine Jack had chosen. When Emily said that she hadn't seen much of Josephine for a while, Josephine felt sure it was a dig. They knew each other well enough that they rarely had to raise their voices to hurt one another.

Josephine was aware that she'd been spending very little time with Emily. It was almost the end of September, and she hadn't asked Emily about her new class, and she didn't know much of how Emily had spent her long summer holiday, other than settling into her new home. Josephine and Jack had been holed up at her flat, and going out on dates, establishing themselves as a couple. They'd watched each other's favourite films, and recommended books to one another, sitting side by side on her sofa, their feet touching. Since the new school year had begun, Josephine had been reluctant to leave the flat to go to work, and each night she had hurried home, hoping that he would call.

While they were eating dessert, Josephine noticed that Jack and Michael were in the middle of their own conversation, their heads bowed slightly towards each other. She wasn't sure when it had happened, when the group of four had split into pairs. She had wanted the four of them to form an easy alliance, like the one she had always shared with Emily and Michael. And she had wanted Emily to learn more about Jack over this dinner, to start to see a little of what Josephine saw. Nothing was going to plan.

And then, under the table, Jack reached out and rested his hand lightly on her thigh, and it seemed to steady her.

'Jack's been telling me about his writing,' Michael said.

'The freelance stuff?' Josephine asked.

'No,' Jack said, a little sharply. 'My own writing. My short stories.'

Josephine knew that Jack wrote short stories, but she hadn't read them. She hadn't known whether to ask. Would he welcome the request or turn it down flat? Some nights, he told her that he couldn't come over, that he needed to write, and she tried to picture the process, but she couldn't.

'I'd like to read them one day,' Michael said.

And Josephine saw a flicker of pride in Jack's face, and she wished that she had asked to read them. But perhaps it wouldn't have had the same effect, she reasoned. Michael was a writer, a published author. Perhaps his offer to read Jack's work meant much more than hers would have done.

'How's the day job, Michael?' she asked. 'How's Sarah getting on?'

Josephine's friend Sarah had just started a new job at the magazine where Michael worked.

'God, she's a lifesaver,' Michael said. 'We're short of a music reporter, and Sarah was too new to take it over, so we've been doing it together. We're always going to hotels to interview bands I've never heard of, and they all look about fourteen. Sarah briefs me on who everyone is on the way there.'

'What kind of music?' Jack asked.

'The kind I'm too old to listen to. The other day, we were in some hotel room in Covent Garden, and the guy we were supposed to be interviewing wouldn't get out of bed. His management said he'd got the flu, but the room was full of empty vodka bottles, and I'm sure I could see a syringe on the bathroom sink out of the corner of my eye.'

Josephine laughed — Emily and Jack were smiling too. She wanted to keep this togetherness going. 'So what did you do?'

'We had to sit on the edge of his bed while he lay there with a towel over his face giving us monosyllabic answers to our questions, and his manager was pacing up and down the room, answering phone calls every thirty seconds. I couldn't wait to get out of there, but Sarah told me afterwards that she'd loved it. I give her two weeks before she's running the show.'

'Let's have another round,' Jack said.

Josephine nodded eagerly. At last, there was one conversation going on, a chance for Emily and Jack, the two most important people in her life, to learn a little about one another.

'I'm pretty tired,' Emily said.

And Josephine felt it all slipping away. But then Emily must have seen the disappointment on Josephine's face because she agreed to stay for one more. A waiter was summoned and four glasses of port were brought out.

'Emily,' Jack said, 'what do you make of Michael's novel? His second one, I mean.'

Josephine was surprised. She knew how much Jack admired Michael's work and hadn't expected him to bring up the novel that had been causing Michael so much difficulty. He must have been emboldened by the drinks. She hoped Michael wouldn't take offence at the question. Everything seemed a little precarious, ready to tumble and fall.

'I haven't read it,' said Emily, shrugging. 'He never lets me read anything until it's finished.'

'And when will it be finished?' Jack asked, turning to Michael.

Michael shifted a little in his seat and Josephine sensed his discomfort.

'Soon, I hope. It's more personal than the last one, I think that's the problem. And the critics were kind to me last time, too, so I know they'll be ready to pounce on my next one and rip it to shreds. Especially when it's taken so long.'

It was the most Josephine had heard Michael say about the matter. It was the closest he had ever come, in her presence, to admitting he was afraid. She thought that perhaps they'd all had too much to drink.

And yet, still, Emily hadn't really joined in the conversation. It was as though she was sitting at a different table, present but absent from the group. She had nodded and smiled, and answered questions that were put to her, but she hadn't volunteered anything.

When the bill came, Emily took it from the waiter and said that she'd like to pay.

'Don't be silly,' Josephine said. 'We'll split it.'

'No, really,' Emily said. 'I'd like to.'

And so she did, although Josephine caught the slightly puzzled look that Michael gave his wife. What was she paying for? Josephine wanted to know. Was it an apology for her silence, for her refusal to spend any time getting to know Jack? And did she think that buying them dinner made her distance any easier for Josephine to accept?

That night, after they had split into two pairs, Josephine and Jack returned to her flat.

'I'm not sure whether your sister likes me,' Jack said.

Josephine looked at him, trying to detect whether this admission had cost him anything, but his face was in shadow. 'I like you,' she said. She pushed him against the kitchen counter and kissed him.

'You know what, Jo? I'm pretty tired. Let's go to bed.'

Josephine lay awake that night. It was the first time Jack had stayed over and they hadn't had sex. And she thought about what he'd said, about thinking Emily might not like him. Eventually, she fell into a restless sleep, full of nonsensical dreams and visions, and when she woke, Jack was up and dressed and on his way out of the door.

CHAPTER ELEVEN

When Jack called and asked her to meet him, Emily was overly aware of her heart beating a little too fast. She'd been waiting for this, wishing for it. She felt she couldn't breathe as he said the words she'd simultaneously hoped for and dreaded.

'Emily, it's Jack. Listen, can I see you? Can we meet?'

'Yes,' she said, without thinking.

There was never any question of not going. Despite the inconvenience, the deception, not going wasn't an option she considered. Jack didn't say what he wanted to see her about, and yet an unspoken agreement was made somewhere during that short call that she would not tell Michael about this. She wondered about it afterwards, about how she knew that this was not the kind of meeting you mentioned to your husband. She tried to tell herself, that evening, that he might just want to ask her something about Josephine. Her sister's birthday was coming up and she reasoned that he might be organising a party or trying to pick a special present. But she knew, all along, that that wasn't the case.

He suggested a café near the bookshop he worked in, and she agreed, although it seemed too risky, too central. He suggested the following day, at ten, and she agreed, although it would mean missing work. That evening, Emily made roast chicken, one of Michael's favourite dinners. She supposed it was an apology of sorts.

The next morning, she lay in bed, preparing lies. She was usually the first to leave the house, but if she wasn't going to work, she had nowhere to go.

'Shouldn't you be in the shower?' Michael asked, reaching an arm across the bed and resting it on her waist.

'I'm going to the dentist,' Emily said. 'Nine thirty.'

Michael frowned. 'Don't you usually arrange those things in the school holidays?'

Trust Michael to know and remember that kind of thing. 'I do, but one of my wisdom teeth has been hurting a bit, on and off. I thought I should get it checked before it gets worse.'

'You never said.'

Emily felt tired from the lying. It was like this, she thought. One and then another and soon you were so lost and confused that you gave yourself away.

'I didn't think to mention it. It's not that bad. I'm just being cautious.' Emily turned onto her side, away from Michael, hoping that would put an end to the questions. She picked up her book from the bedside table and tried to read, but she couldn't focus.

Once he'd showered and dressed, Michael would go down for breakfast, she thought. That was his routine. She kept looking at the same page of the book while he pulled on his clothes, and only put it down, propped open on her chest, when he came to kiss her goodbye. Their eyes met, and Emily felt sure he knew. Not necessarily that it was Jack, but that she was doing something she shouldn't. Meeting someone she shouldn't.

'Let me know how it goes,' he said. 'At the dentist.' He leaned down to kiss her forehead and Emily held her breath, waiting for him to question her further. But of course he didn't. She wasn't sure he would, even if he did know. He wasn't impulsive. He wasn't reckless.

After Michael had left, Emily called her boss. This was only the second time Emily had called in sick in her three years of teaching, and the first time she'd been stuck in bed with the flu. This time she had a meeting — a date? — with her sister's boyfriend. As she dialled the numbers, Emily felt slightly sick, as if by considering this deception she was bringing on the illness she was about to feign.

'David Simpson.'

'David, it's Emily.' She stalled for time, realising she had not picked out an illness in advance. She couldn't be suffering from a cold or flu, she reasoned, because you could hear that sort of thing in a person's voice. She considered toothache, a migraine, an upset stomach. Emily had always been healthy, and she felt unsure of exactly which illnesses would warrant a single day's absence.

'Emily, hi. How are you?'

Of course, it didn't have to be an illness. People took a day off for all sorts of reasons. Family crises, bereavement, any number of personal matters. But she discarded all of these in a moment, feeling somehow as though it would be tempting fate to claim she had problems at home at a time like this, when she was on the verge of creating a crisis. 'I'm not too good, David. I've been up half the night with a migraine. I'm sorry, but I don't think I'm going to make it in today.'

David was a reasonable man, a good boss. Emily felt confident that he would be sympathetic about this, which made things slightly easier, and slightly harder.

'I'm sorry to hear that. Awful things, migraines. I used to suffer. Do you get them regularly?'

'Not really,' she said. 'Now and again.' Emily had never had a migraine. She felt hot, and wanted to get off the phone as quickly as possible. She couldn't listen to the kindness in David's voice.

'You stay in bed,' David said then. 'We'll sort everything out here. I'll see you tomorrow if you're feeling better.'

'Thank you,' Emily said and then flung down the phone as if it had burned her.

Emily took a long bath, letting her hair float in the water around her shoulders. And then she dried her hair straight, and wasn't sure why she had. It was something she almost never did, preferring to let it dry naturally and give in to its tendency to curl. She didn't know what she should wear, but she knew that if she let herself think about it for too long she would try on everything she owned and have to rush to get there on time, leaving a colourful mess of rejected items on the bed and the floor. She forced herself to choose quickly, put on a simple black dress and ankle boots.

As she dressed, Emily thought about what she was doing, what she was risking, and she felt sick again. But when she went into the bathroom and stood over the toilet, her hair gathered in one hand, nothing came. Jack, it struck her, would probably just leave the shop for half an hour. He wasn't having to make the same sacrifices. But she hadn't said any of that when he called, so he couldn't be expected to know that she was thinking it. Every question he had asked her, she had answered with a yes.

JACK GOT TO WORK EARLY, hoping that he'd have a chance to talk to Tim alone before the rest of the staff arrived. When he walked into the staff room, Tim was sitting on the battered leather armchair — the favoured seat of all members of staff — with a mug of black coffee. He looked at his watch and frowned.

'Jack? At this time? Am I seeing things?'

Jack pushed his bag into his locker and then checked whether there was enough water left in the kettle for another coffee. There wasn't, so he filled it up halfway and put it on to boil again. 'I wanted to have a quick word, actually,' he said.

'Sounds serious,' said Tim, as the kettle started to whistle.

'No, it's nothing,' said Jack, trying to keep his breathing steady.

The kettle's whistle rose to a shriek and Jack flicked it off, unable to bear the sound a moment longer. He kept his back to Tim as he made his coffee, stirring the sugar in for longer than was necessary. 'I just wanted to take an early lunch. At ten if possible.'

'Is that all?' Tim asked. 'That's no problem. Helps me cover the lunch period.' He patted Jack's back as he turned on the tap to rinse out his mug.

Jack flinched, almost, but not quite, imperceptibly.

'Hey,' said Tim. 'Are you okay? You don't seem yourself.'

'I'm fine,' Jack assured him, still not turning to face his boss. 'Fine.'

THE HOUR between the shop opening and Jack leaving to meet Emily dragged by. He was on the customer services desk, which meant helping people to identify books they wanted from the most obscure part of the title or author's name, or sometimes the wrong information altogether. Jack normally enjoyed this job, liked the investigative nature of it, and he was good at it. But that morning he was irritable and just wanted to tell the customers to come back when they had the right information. This was how he'd met Josephine, he recalled. If he hadn't met her, things would be simpler, in one sense. But then, if he hadn't met her, he would probably never have met Emily either.

A couple of minutes before ten, he slipped out of the door, nodding at Tim as he did so, and walked over to the café he'd suggested. It was somewhere he rarely frequented, which is why he'd picked it. At the coffee place just around the corner, they knew his name and his usual order, and Josephine's too.

A quick scan of the place confirmed that she hadn't arrived yet. He was relieved, wanting to take a minute to catch his breath and try to work out exactly what he wanted to say. He was the one who had summoned her, after all. It was up to him to steer this meeting.

'Coffee,' he said, when it was his turn at the counter. 'Large.'

'Latte? Cappuccino?' The girl behind the counter was smiling, but there was an irritability behind her eyes, the same irritability he'd felt with his customers that morning. She was used to customers who knew exactly what they wanted.

'Just a normal coffee,' he said. 'White.' Should he get one for Emily? He didn't know how she drank her coffee, or whether she preferred tea, and there seemed to be an insurmountable sum of things to learn. He picked out a quiet table by the window, and felt a jolt of worry as he sat down. What if she wasn't coming? It was a few minutes past ten now, he saw, checking his watch. What if she'd changed her mind?

But she hadn't. She appeared at that moment, bursting through the door, that hair and those eyes and something else that he couldn't quite get to grips with. When she wasn't there in the same room as him, he couldn't picture her. He knew all the facts — the size and shape and colours of her — but the image his mind created wasn't quite right. And then every time he saw her, he tried to memorise her, feeling sure that next time he'd get it right. He lived in fear of never seeing her again and not having a mental picture to cling to.

'Jack,' she said, her voice level but her eyes pleading.

'Emily,' he said, standing. 'Can I get you something? I didn't know what you would want.'

She waved her hand and sat down. 'Just get me anything,' she said. 'It doesn't really matter.'

Jack chose a latte and a slice of carrot cake. Both large, as if he believed that not having finished her coffee would keep her there if she wanted to go.

* * *

EMILY FELT self-conscious eating cake in front of Jack. She pushed the plate to one side, trying to pretend that it wasn't there, that it wasn't her favourite. She tried not to take that as a sign that he knew her, that he understood her cravings and her pleasures. She took a sip of her coffee, burned her tongue and tried not to show it, as she waited for him to speak. There was something adolescent in her physical attraction to him, and it was embarrassing, and exciting. Had she ever felt that way with Michael, that desperation to touch him, to have him touch her? She knew she hadn't. And she'd thought it was because it didn't happen when you'd passed that stage of your life. But she'd been wrong.

Jack shifted uncomfortably in his chair. 'It's hot in here,' he said, pulling his jumper over his head.

Emily watched as his T-shirt started to come with it, and saw the line of hair stretching up and down from his belly button. She had to stop herself from reaching across and stroking it, and that was when she knew, for certain, that she was in danger of starting something terrible, and wonderful, and wrong. That she would start it, if he gave her the opportunity. She glanced around the café for people she knew, or people who might be watching them, listening in. But all she saw were strangers, their heads buried in books or bent close together in conversation.

'I've been thinking about you,' he said finally.

That was all it took. A small admission of what was happening here. Emily felt her throat constrict and her eyes well up, and when the first tear fell, she just let it roll down her cheek and drip from her chin, and he didn't reach to wipe it away.

'Emily,' he said, as if in pain. He covered her hand with his long fingers and she pulled it back, held it in her lap with her other hand, terrified of the warmth and strength of that small gesture.

'How's Josephine?' she asked defiantly, wiping her eyes.

'She's fine,' Jack said.

Emily noticed him flinch before he answered, and she was

pleased. She stood up, without knowing she was going to. 'I shouldn't be here,' she said. 'I'm supposed to be at school.'

'But you came,' he said, his voice gentle and quiet. He reached out and put a hand on her wrist, and she was annoyed that he was confident she wouldn't leave, confident enough to remain seated. But there was a pull, of sorts, in that, too. He was straddling that line between confidence and arrogance, and he was just about on the right side. She sat down again.

'Yes.'

Jack drained his coffee then, and looked at his watch. 'Look,' he said. 'I have to be back at work in a few minutes. I don't know what to say. I called you because I've been thinking about you, and I had to see you.'

'Why?' Emily asked, feeling uncharacteristically bold.

'There's something here,' Jack said. 'Between us.' He pointed at her and then at himself.

There was, Emily agreed. There was something. It felt scary and unstoppable.

'I know it's not ideal...' Jack said.

'Not ideal?' Emily asked, incredulous. She saw an old woman turn to look at her and lowered her voice. 'You're with my sister. And I'm married. It's about as bad as it could be.'

Jack laughed, almost a scoff. Was it an indication that he thought things could be much worse? That he'd known much worse? In spite of herself, Emily was intrigued.

Jack placed his hand over hers again and this time she didn't stop him.

'I have to go,' Emily said. She waited a moment for him to plead with her, to ask her to stay. He didn't. He stood, and there were inches between their bodies, and he smelled of something Emily couldn't place. Something musky, earthy. She longed to touch him, to feel the solidity of his body against hers. To see how they would fit together differently from her and Michael. It was almost a need, and she was surprised by the strength of it.

They walked to the door, him behind her, and on the street, they parted abruptly. They did not embrace and they did not kiss. But Emily knew that none of that mattered. She had gone there, and she had let him take her hand and say those things, and nothing could change that now.

CHAPTER TWELVE

That touch stayed with Emily. She could feel the warmth of it all over her body like a rash; in the gym, in the classroom, in bed at night. It was a sharp and shocking contrast to the gloomy October days. Whenever Michael reached to pull her towards him, she almost flinched. She didn't want the complication of his touch layered over Jack's.

When Michael told her that he was thinking of going away, Emily felt as though she had pushed him. She felt breathless and scared at the thought of what might happen while he was gone, what she might do. And she felt horribly excited, too. Her stomach churned and she clutched at it, afraid. They were lying in bed, only inches between her body and his.

'I've been playing around with this novel for years,' he said. 'I'm not getting anywhere. I feel like I have to have one last proper go at it.'

Emily listened, wondering whether Michael could sense the tension between them, hear her heartbeat. She felt too warm, suddenly, and she pushed the covers off her. Michael reached for her hand in the darkness, and she let him take it. 'Of course,' she said.

'I need to get away, to do it properly. You know it's set up in Yorkshire. I think I need to be up there for it to work. Just for two or three weeks, maybe a month.'

Emily propped herself up on her elbow. 'So you'll stay with your parents?'

'Yes. I don't see them enough anyway.'

'What about work?' Emily grappled for something he might not have thought of, something that might mean he had to stay. But when he said he'd spoken to his boss, arranged a period of unpaid leave, she was mostly relieved. 'When will you leave?'

Michael laced his fingers through hers, propped himself up on his elbow so that their bodies mirrored one another. 'Next week, probably. But listen, I won't go unless it's okay with you.'

For a moment, Emily questioned what he was saying. He had already arranged this with his boss, must have been mulling it over for a while. She knew that he would stay if she asked him to. But she didn't. 'You should go,' she said.

He thanked her and she heard his voice crack. And she had to turn away and pull her knees up to her chest, tell him that she was tired, because she couldn't bear his belief in her. His belief that she was supporting his dream and accepting the necessary sacrifices, when all she could think about were the possibilities that lay in front of her during this unexpected time alone. She lay there, almost foetal, and tried to slow her breathing so that he would think she was already asleep.

THE FOLLOWING DAY, Emily felt restless, distracted. She couldn't settle to anything — not her book, or her emails, or the documentary Michael was watching. She flitted about, making cups of tea and then forgetting to drink them, starting odd jobs she knew she wouldn't finish.

'What time are we leaving?' Michael asked, mid-afternoon, and she looked at him, her face blank and questioning.

'Where are we going?' She'd pictured a leisurely dinner, maybe a bottle of wine, and an early night.

'Emily,' Michael laughed. 'What's the matter with you? We're going over to Josephine's, for her birthday dinner.'

Emily sat down on the edge of the sofa, fearful that her legs were about to buckle beneath her. How could she have forgotten? She'd spoken to Josephine only the day before, wished her a happy birthday, made arrangements to go over at seven the following evening. Her sister's presents — a silver necklace and matching earrings she'd admired on a recent shopping trip — were wrapped and waiting on the kitchen windowsill, the card propped up behind them. Emily had even bought a new dress.

'Of course,' she said, collecting herself. 'I don't know what's wrong with me. It must be this going away thing — it's thrown me. I said we'd be there at seven.' And she hated herself for lying. For using Michael's imminent departure as an excuse for her strange mood.

Upstairs, Emily took a shower. She washed her hair, shaved her legs, used a scrub all over her body that made her feel raw. She dried her long hair, pulling a brush through it again and again to tame her curls. In the mirror, she looked flushed, her pale skin pink, the colour hiding her freckles.

Her new dress was hanging on the wardrobe door. It was emerald green, daringly short, silk. She hadn't told Michael how much it had cost because when she'd seen it in the window of the boutique, she had known that she would buy it, regardless of the price. She could already feel it against her skin, clashing beautifully with her hair, skimming her thighs. She slipped it on and then applied her make up more carefully than she had for months, lining her eyes and her lips, curling her eyelashes.

'Wow.' Michael was stood at the door, watching her in the mirror.

Emily hadn't heard him come in. She put her mascara wand down and watched him approach her, then felt his strong arms around her waist. She pulled away. 'You'll crease it,' she said, quietly.

Michael turned her around gently, held her at arm's length, appraised her. 'Can I crease it later?' he asked.

Emily smiled and nodded, lowered her eyes, embarrassed at the naked desire in his.

'Well,' Michael said. 'I was going to go like this, but I suppose I'd better change. I don't want to disgrace you.'

Emily sat on the end of the bed and watched Michael get ready. He moved around the room with quick movements, knowing where everything was and what he needed to do. The movements of a man comfortable in his home, with his wife. Confident and sure. She looked at his body as he undressed. Everything about him was strong and solid — his hands, his legs, his stomach. She tried to imagine what Jack would look like naked. He was thinner than Michael, and a little pale. But there was something about his hands that made her imagine them on her body. He wouldn't hold her the way Michael did, folding her against him and making her feel small and protected. And yet, there was a dull ache of excitement at the thought of being held by someone new. At feeling less protected, less comfortable, but more alive.

* * *

JOSEPHINE LOOKED AT HER WATCH.

'They'll be here,' Jack said. 'Stop worrying.' He was sprawled on the sofa, holding a book open in mid-air with one hand, reaching out to turn the page every minute or so.

'I know. I just thought she might be early. I need her help with the starter. It's her recipe.'

'It's just friends coming. No one's judging you.'

No, Josephine thought, but they will be judging you. Ben and Sarah would be meeting Jack for the first time that night. Separately, they had both teased her, saying she was hiding him away, keeping him a secret. They had guessed at why she might be doing so. But the truth was that she just hadn't felt like spending time with anyone else. Winter was coming, and it was as if she was hibernating, curling up in a ball with Jack, unwilling to come out or let anyone else in.

And then there was the fact that Jack was so different from her previous boyfriends. She wasn't sure what her friends would make of him, and she didn't want them to circle him, asking him questions, finding faults. She didn't want to face them afterwards, to defend him and tell them what she saw in him. Because Josephine still wasn't sure herself what it was about Jack that made her feel so strongly. She had questioned it, tried to pin it down, but all she really knew was that she felt excited when she was with him. She was terrified of someone she loved telling her that that wasn't enough.

'Are you going to get changed?' Josephine asked. She had been ready for an hour or more, in her favourite navy-blue dress and matching heels, her hair pulled back neatly.

Jack put his book face down on the armrest of the sofa. 'Won't I do?' he asked.

He looked a little hurt, and Josephine wasn't sure whether it was genuine or for show. There were things she didn't know yet, hadn't learned. Jack was wearing worn jeans and a black shirt. It was one of many almost identical outfits. She reasoned that, if he changed, he wouldn't look any different. 'Sorry,' she said. 'You look fine.'

She walked across to the sofa, bent to kiss him. And then the doorbell rang, and she jumped slightly before striding out into the hall to let in her sister and Michael.

'Wow,' Josephine said, when she answered the door.

Michael laughed. 'That's exactly what I said.'

There was a change in Emily, subtle enough for only Josephine to see. She looked fabulous in that bold dress, her legs long and slim, her hair falling down her back and around her face. But that wasn't it. She seemed edgy, a little nervous. Her fingers were in her hair, smoothing her dress, never still.

Josephine took them through to the kitchen and poured out glasses of wine, and Jack followed them in.

'Jack,' Michael said. 'Good to see you.'

Josephine watched the two men shake hands, and felt proud. Michael didn't warm to everyone. He chose people carefully, and it looked as though he had chosen Jack. And then she watched Jack move across to kiss Emily's cheek, and she saw that edginess in her sister again, and questioned for the hundredth time whether Emily didn't like him. Of everyone, she desperately wanted Emily to like him.

'Let's get this starter under way before the others arrive, birthday girl,' Emily said.

Jack and Michael retreated to the lounge, leaving the sisters to their preparation, and Josephine started to get things out of the packed fridge and forgot about the strangeness she had seen in Emily.

Sarah was the next to arrive, and she joined the women in the kitchen. She was one of Josephine's oldest friends — they'd lived together throughout university. She came armed with a bottle of champagne and a bunch of tulips. 'Michael let me in,' she said. 'So where's this Jack I've heard so little about?'

'I'm here.'

Josephine turned to see Jack entering the room, crossing to the fridge to get a refill. She tried to imagine seeing him through Sarah's eyes, seeing him for the first time. Tried to imagine what Sarah would make of him. Sarah, who was all designer clothes and manicured nails. She would think he was scruffy, Josephine decided, and probably unsuitable.

Jack brought the bottle of wine over and filled Josephine and Emily's glasses, reached up to get a glass for Sarah. Josephine watched his shirt ride up to show his pale back. Finally, he presented Sarah with a glass and kissed her cheek. 'Pleasure to meet you,' he said. And then he was gone, just as quickly as he'd appeared.

'Nothing like I expected,' Sarah said, once he was out of earshot.

Josephine listened out for disapproval, but she didn't hear any.

Ben arrived half an hour late, and the six of them sat down at the table in the corner of the living room. 'So Jack,' said Ben, as he took his seat. 'Tell us all about yourself.'

Josephine was already halfway out the door, Emily ahead of her, on their way to bring out the first course. She wanted to go back, sit down, listen to what Jack would say. She lingered for a moment.

'What do you want to know?' Jack asked.

And then Emily called Josephine from the kitchen and everyone's eyes turned to her, and she left the room.

Later, over dessert, the talk turned to Jack's writing.

'Jack and I are going to be working together when I get back from Yorkshire,' Michael said.

Josephine saw Emily's head snap up at Michael's words. 'What do you mean?' she asked.

'I've been writing some short stories,' Jack said. 'Michael's going to take a look at them, maybe do some editing, and then try to help me find a publisher.'

Josephine was pleased, excited at the prospect of Michael helping Jack to make something of his work.

'I didn't know you were going away, Michael,' Sarah said.

'Oh yes. I'm taking a bit of time off work, trying to get my novel sorted out. You'll have to handle all those musicians on your own, I'm afraid. But don't worry, I'll teach you everything I know before I leave. It'll take about half an hour.'

JUST AS JOSEPHINE was settling into the evening, starting to worry less about what everyone thought of Jack, the dinner was over, and Sarah stood up to leave.

'Sorry to break up the party,' she said, blowing a kiss to Josephine. 'I've got a cold coming; I need my bed. Don't get up. I'll let myself out. Happy birthday.'

The rest of them had a coffee, but there was a sense of the evening winding down, and within an hour, Josephine was left alone with Jack. She went to the kitchen to start clearing up, but then Jack appeared behind her and kissed the back of her neck.

'Leave that,' he said. 'I'll do it in the morning.'

She let him take her through to the bedroom and undress her. The worry she'd felt, that night after their dinner with Emily and Michael when they hadn't had sex, seemed ridiculous at that moment. Jack stroked her hip and took her nipple in his mouth. While they'd been swapping books and films and music, they'd learned each other's bodies, too. Jack knew what she liked, what she needed. And there was something in his touch that drove her quietly wild. She had never wanted someone so much.

Afterwards, Josephine smiled a secret smile in the darkness. She was pleased that Ben and Sarah had met Jack, pleased that Jack was there, beside her. It was the happiest birthday she could remember.

CHAPTER THIRTEEN

As Michael stepped off the train on to the platform at Leeds, the cold hit him straight away, and he pulled his coat tighter around him, wishing he'd brought a scarf. He'd forgotten how much colder it could get up there. And that reminded him, once again, of how long it had been since his last visit. A year, or more?

His father was waiting in the car park, the engine of his Toyota running, his arm out of the wound-down window to wave at Michael. 'Hello,' he said, once Michael had put his case in the boot and opened the passenger door. 'Good to see you.'

Michael reached across to give his father a hug, but their position was awkward, and the gearstick pushed uncomfortably into Michael's hip. 'Hi Dad, it's good to see you too. Really good.'

It was a half hour drive to his parents' countryside house. Michael took in the familiar sights and smells and spoke little.

'How's Emily?' his father asked, after a long silence.

'She's great.'

'You know, we thought that maybe there were something wrong, when you said you were coming up for so long.'

Michael looked across at his father, saw that it hadn't been easy for him to bring this up. 'Dad, I told you, I'm here to do research for my book. Nothing's wrong.' Michael imagined his parents discussing this, but he wasn't angry. He knew that they would always worry about him, about his happiness.

His mother had made a pot of tea and put out a plate of biscuits. Michael held her close and then pulled away, looked at her. She looked older, he thought, a little frailer. He considered what would happen when one of his parents was left alone. They coped all right, supporting each other, but he wasn't convinced that either one of them would be able to survive without the other.

He considered talking to Emily about moving up there, knew immediately that she couldn't be happy away from the buzz of London, away from Josephine. And him? Could he be happy there again?

'Such a treat,' his mother said. 'Having you here for so long.'

The three of them sat down and Michael's mother poured the tea, fussed over her two men, just as she had always done.

'Will we see Emily, while you're here?' Michael's mother looked at his father pointedly, as if silently asking whether he'd already broached this subject in the car.

'She might come up for a weekend,' Michael said. 'But it's only for a few weeks. And as I've already told Dad, there's nothing wrong. I just need to be here to do some research.'

'But won't she be lonely, rattling around in that big house?' Michael's father chipped in.

'She's busy with school, and she's got Josephine.'

'Oh yes,' his mother said, holding out the plate of cakes. 'Maybe her sister will move in while you're away, keep her company.'

'Probably not,' Michael said. 'She's got a new boyfriend.'

'Oh, has she? I am glad. I always worried about her, on her own like that. And such a pretty girl.'

Michael's parents smiled at him, pleased that the matter was settled. His marriage was not in trouble, Emily would be okay on her own, and Josephine was no longer lonely. They were reassured.

Later, upstairs in his childhood bedroom, Michael sat down at the desk. It was where he'd done his homework, studied for long, silent hours for his GCSEs and A levels. His parents, not vaguely academic, hadn't really understood his desire to be educated, but they had supported him, bringing him cups of coffee and bowls of soup, sometimes finding him asleep at the desk, his head resting awkwardly on an open textbook.

Michael pulled out his laptop and checked his emails. There was nothing from Emily, but one from Jack, with several attachments. *Michael*, he read. *I really appreciate this. I've attached seven of my stories, and look forward to hearing what you think. Jack.*

Michael hadn't expected Jack to send so much, so quickly. He checked the email again. Jack had sent it the morning after Josephine's birthday dinner. Had he done the right thing, offering himself up as a mentor like this? He wasn't sure whether he had the time for it. But he was curious about this quiet man of Josephine's. There was a sureness about him, almost an arrogance. Michael was keen to find out whether his work would live up to it. He opened the first attachment, moved over to the bed, and settled down to read.

Michael had no intention of reading all of Jack's stories in one sitting, but that's exactly what he did. He was transfixed by them. There was a lyricism to Jack's narration that should have sat uneasily alongside his stark plots and sharp dialogue, his troubled, fragmented characters, but somehow it came together beautifully, and seemed so right that Michael was scared to suggest any minor changes for fear of upsetting the balance. Jack wrote of unhappy relationships, warring families torn apart by abuse and neglect, damaged protagonists making their way, unsuccessfully, in an impossible world. And yet all the time, he used language so deftly that, more than once, Michael was almost moved to tears.

Michael wanted to know how much of Jack's own life had found its way into these sad tales, thought again about Jack's throwaway comment in the pub about the complexities of family. He tried to push the jealousy he felt of Jack's talent to one side. To remind himself that their work was so different he could hardly compare it. Stronger than jealousy, he felt a sense of privilege. He was grateful for the opportunity to read this work, to be among the first to see it. He felt almost euphoric, as though he had discovered something. As though the part he might play in getting these stories seen by the right people was almost as important as Jack's role as creator. His own writing forgotten for the time being, Michael reopened the first attachment and started to read each of the stories again in turn. Savouring them this time, letting them take him somewhere he had never been.

That evening, Michael's brother came over for dinner with his wife. The two brothers, Michael and Charles, shook hands at the door and then Charles's wife, Ann, stepped forward and hugged Michael warmly. They sat in the kitchen and Michael watched as Ann chatted easily to his mother, helping her with the roast dinner, stirring the gravy and setting the table. He barely knew this woman, who Charles had been with since his schooldays and married to for fifteen years, and yet she spent more time with his parents than he did. He watched the two women, their heads bent together and laughter in their voices, and he felt a pang of something like regret.

'Dad tells us you're here for a few weeks,' Charles said, once they were all sat around the table.

'That's right,' said Michael. 'Three or four weeks, probably.'

'What about work?'

Michael tried to make out what his brother was asking, tried to determine whether he'd heard a note of disapproval. He explained that he'd arranged some unpaid leave, and Charles went back to his dinner, apparently satisfied.

'You'll have to come over to us one night,' Ann said. 'It's been ages since you saw the house.'

'Oh, you'll hardly recognise it,' his mother said. 'They've worked wonders.'

It was arranged for Saturday. Michael hoped his parents would come too, unsure that he and his brother and sister-in-law would find enough common ground to pass a whole evening.

They'd been close once, Michael and Charles. It seemed like a lifetime ago, but they'd passed their childhood and adolescence side by side. There was only eighteen months between them, a fact that allowed them to enjoy the same pastimes and share the same group of friends.

Charles was the older brother, and he had left school at sixteen, as expected, and taken his place beside their father behind the counter of the tailors that had been in their family for four generations. He had taken over when their father retired, but Michael wondered then, for the first time, what would happen to it when Charles himself reached retirement age. Charles and Ann were childless, though not, Michael suspected, through choice.

'How's Emily?' Ann asked, jolting Michael out of his thoughts.

'Very well,' he said.

He felt like he was being tested in some way, by all of them, but what else could he say about Emily? She was well, and they were happy. Perhaps Ann, who didn't work, thought it was strange that he had come up here alone, left his wife in London. Perhaps he was required to justify this temporary separation.

'She's busy at work. There's a chance she might be made Deputy Head. And she can't take time off during the term.' Michael trailed off, slightly irritated at feeling the need to prove his marriage was a happy one, once again. The comment about a possible promotion was a lie. It had been there, that chance, just less than a year before, but Emily had been passed over for someone who'd been at the school longer. He wasn't sure why he'd said it, but something about being at home and being scrutinised like this made him behave like someone else.

Michael called Emily from the privacy of his room, once Charles and Ann had gone home. 'I miss you,' he said.

He heard her laugh, her voice light and clear despite the miles that lay between them. 'Already?' she said. 'You've only been gone a day.'

Was there something in her voice that had changed? She didn't sound quite like herself. If he were there, next to her, he would pull her into him for a kiss. But he wasn't, so the best he could do was tell her. 'I don't belong here anymore. I belong with you. You know,' he added, 'they all think there's more to it than research, me being here.'

'And is there?'

He was shocked into silence. He had thought she would laugh, that they would laugh together. That it would be them against his family, with their silly concerns. Something clenched in his stomach, and it felt like fear. 'Of course not. Why would you ask that?'

'I don't know,' she said, and he thought he heard a slight crack in her voice.

'Emily, is something wrong? You can tell me, you know.'

He held his breath while he waited for her to speak.

'No,' she said. 'Nothing. I have to go. I'll call you tomorrow.'

He heard the click as she hung up, and he felt very alone. He was displaced, there in his childhood bedroom, his parents bustling about downstairs, his brother a few minutes' walk away, and yet so far from home.

CHAPTER FOURTEEN

For three days after Michael left, Emily didn't go out except to go to work. She jumped whenever the phone rang, and tried to pretend, when it was Michael, that she wasn't hoping it was Jack. She hadn't heard from him since they'd left one another on the street, but she knew that couldn't be the end of it. On the second evening, Josephine called to invite her round for dinner. Emily told her she thought she was coming down with something, tried to make her voice sound a little muffled, a little croaky. On the third evening, Josephine turned up on the doorstep with a bunch of flowers.

'How are you feeling?' she asked.

'Not bad,' Emily said. 'Maybe it wasn't a cold after all.'

Josephine stepped inside and handed the flowers to Emily, shrugging off her coat. Emily wondered how long she was planning to stay and hated herself.

'And Michael,' Josephine said, 'how's he?'

'Fine. Missing London, I think.'

'Missing you, probably.'

Emily shrugged.

'Em,' said Josephine. She said it tentatively, as though unsure of what she was about to ask. 'Is something going on? You haven't seemed yourself lately.'

'I'm fine,' said Emily, forcing a smile. 'Coffee?'

It wasn't until they were sitting in the lounge, coffees steaming on the table, that Josephine broke the news. 'Something's happened,' she said.

Emily looked closely at her sister's face to determine whether it was something good or something bad. Was it Jack? Had they split up? Josephine looked tired and anxious, but not heartbroken. Emily gazed at her sister, nodded, encouraging her to speak.

'I've had a letter,' she said. 'It's from my dad.'

Emily went cold. They didn't have fathers, either of them. They never had. It had always been the two of them and their mother, in that house, full of oestrogen and open doors, and the silent courage of women going it alone. But no, that was years ago, before she had brought Michael home and before their mother had left them for a different life. And now there was Jack. Jack, with his eyes like heavy clouds.

So things had changed, and why shouldn't there be a father? Hers was dead, torn from her before she had ever really known him, but Josephine's wasn't. They'd always known that. So why had she never considered this possibility — that he might enter their lives like this, through a side door, when he was least expected?

'I don't understand,' Emily said.

'He's been trying to find me,' said Josephine. 'He's divorced now, so...' Her voice trailed away to nothing.

Where Emily had been born into young, strong love, Josephine had been the product of an affair between their mother and a man they'd never known. It was a year after Emily's father had died, and Alice was lonely. That's what she'd told them. This man, this married man, had appeared in her life and she'd been flattered by his attentions. And then they'd created Josephine, unwittingly, and he'd gone back to his wife and his children, and she had just carried on.

Emily wondered, as she had before, whether Josephine felt the pain of this abandonment. Death was one thing, of course, but betrayal quite another. 'What does he want?' she asked.

'He wants to see me, to get to know me. I don't know what to do.'

And then Emily saw that Josephine was crying, and she moved over to the sofa where her sister was sitting, lost among the cushions, and she held her sister tightly, wishing she knew what to say, what to do.

'I talked to Jack,' Josephine said, through her tears. 'But he doesn't really understand. He doesn't get on with his family at all, never sees them, and he thinks I'm probably better off without him. He says I've managed without him for all these years, and there's a chance that he'd let me down again if I got to know him. But I don't know. Everyone wants to know where they come from, don't they? And even though you've never had a father, you've got all those pictures and stories. I don't have that.'

Emily kept her father in a box under her bed. It was a heavy wooden box with ornate carvings on the top, and inside, there was a wedding photo, and a picture of him holding her as a baby a couple of months before he died, and letters he'd written for her mother. It wasn't much, and she didn't look through it often, but it was something. And here was Josephine, with the chance to have more than that, with the possibility of future birthday cards and holidays and smiling photographs. Out of nowhere, Emily thought that, when she married, Josephine might have someone to give her away, to walk her down the aisle.

'I think you'll always wonder, if you don't meet him,' Emily said.

Josephine nodded.

'Have you talked to Mum about it?'

Josephine shook her head. 'I feel like she'd be angry with me, somehow. I'm not sure why. I wouldn't know how to bring it up.'

Emily rarely spoke to her mother now, and she knew it was the same for Josephine. She understood, how hard it would be to deliver this news.

'Where does he live?'

'Brixton. All these years, and he's just a few minutes' drive away, a bus journey. I could have passed him on the street.'

And then a new thought struck Emily. Their mother had told them the story, saying that he'd gone back to his wife and children. And children. Half-brothers or half-sisters of Josephine's. A whole other family. Would she lose her sister to this other clan? No, she told herself, calmly. She wouldn't lose Josephine that way. But she might just lose her if she fell in love with her boyfriend. If she took him.

'I'm going to call him,' Josephine said. 'Do you mind if I do it now, here? I want someone with me.'

'Of course not. Do you want me to go into the kitchen?'

Josephine smiled crookedly, nodded. 'Yes please.'

Emily didn't hear the conversation, and she didn't ask Josephine to repeat it afterwards. The facts were that they had arranged to meet on neutral ground, at a restaurant in Brixton, the following evening. Josephine was elated, her fear dispersed for the time being. 'Thanks Em,' she said. 'I couldn't have done it without you.'

Josephine stepped forward to give her sister a hug, and Emily let her, hoping that Josephine's glow would spread to her, take away the darkness she was holding inside.

On the doorstep, Josephine turned back. 'I forgot to say, Michael loved Jack's stories. Did you hear?'

Emily hadn't heard. Why not? Had Michael sugar-coated his real thoughts, out of politeness or family loyalty? No. That wasn't the kind of thing Michael would do.

When Josephine had gone, Emily thought about Jack's stories, wishing she knew what he wrote and how, and whether he wrote about love. Could she determine, if she read them, what he thought about love?

The following morning, as she was getting ready for work, and just when she had stopped expecting it, Jack called.

'Can I see you?' he asked. 'Tonight?'

She liked the way he asked for what he wanted, nonchalant and brave. 'Yes,' she said.

And all day at work, she thought about Josephine preparing to take a huge step that evening, meeting the father who had abandoned her, and how, while it was happening, she would be at home with Josephine's boyfriend. She thought about how, just as Josephine was gaining something, she would be losing something else, and how she, Emily, had the power to stop it.

When Emily opened the door that evening, Jack stepped inside and closed it behind him. Emily had spent a long time making sure her face and her hair and her body were ready for this encounter. But Jack looked just as he always did. A little scruffy, a little lost. Emily took a deep breath and looked up at him, knowing that he was going to kiss her and feeling so terrified and so full of desire.

They looked at one another, neither saying anything, and Emily considered that it was still possible to stop this. But she didn't want to. She didn't want to. Jack kissed her, there in the hallway, his hands in her hair and his lips on her mouth, her neck. She started to speak and he put a finger to her lips. Knowing, as she knew, that if they talked about what they were doing, they wouldn't do it, wouldn't dare. He tasted like cigarettes. And something else, something sharp, almost metallic. He tasted nothing like Michael, and Emily was grateful, and afraid. She took his hand and led him up the stairs, almost opened her bedroom door and then changed her mind, walking past it and into the spare room. It was only later that she realised she had taken Jack to the bedroom she'd had as a teenager.

Without a word, Jack undressed them both, and then he picked Emily up, stronger than he seemed, and laid her on the bed. He looked at her, all of her, as though drinking her in, and she wanted to pull the covers over her body, to shield herself from him, but she didn't. She looked back at him, feeling as though she might disappear if he didn't touch her soon. And then he was on top of her, inside her, and she gasped at the shock of it, so soon, so unexpected.

Afterwards, she couldn't look at him and she couldn't look away. She heard the phone ringing distantly and knew that it was either Michael or Josephine, both of them needing her in their different ways. And there was Jack, lying beside her. Did he need her too?

'Leave it,' Jack said.

She didn't notice that she was crying until he reached over and brushed away her tears with his long finger.

'Don't,' he said. 'It was always going to happen.'

Was it? Was it always going to happen? It felt that way, but was that just a way to excuse the devastation they were about to cause? Emily corrected herself. The devastation had already been caused. But she wasn't sure whether it counted, if Michael and Josephine didn't yet know.

'Will we tell them?' she asked.

Jack sat up, reached out of the side of the bed and retrieved his cigarettes and a lighter. He looked around for something to use as an ashtray.

'There,' Emily said, pointing at a glass that had been left on the bedside table.

He lit a cigarette and held it out to her, his eyebrows raised. She took it and he lit another for himself. 'I don't know, Emily,' he said. 'I haven't been with Josephine very long. I'm not involved the way you are.'

Emily winced at the sound of her sister's name, at the thought of him touching Josephine. 'I'm married,' she said, as though reminding herself.

Jack started to speak, and then stopped. And then he stood up and began to put his clothes on, and Emily fought against a desire to ask where he was going, and lost.

'Are you going to Josephine's?'

'I have to,' he said. 'She's meeting her father tonight, she wanted me to be there when she got back.'

'She'll know,' Emily said.

'No, she won't.'

Emily was still lying naked in bed, wrapped in sheets, and he leaned across and kissed her lightly, almost carefully.

'When will I see you?' she asked, wondering whether she should have left that to him, let him chase. But it was too late for that. Even she could see that they were both already caught.

'As soon as I can,' he said. 'I'll call you.'

And then he was gone, back to Josephine, to support her with the joy or the disappointment of her first meeting with her father. And Emily was alone, unable to answer the phone as it rang again, sure her voice would speak of everything she had just given away.

CHAPTER FIFTEEN

Josephine took a deep breath and pulled open the door to the restaurant. Despite forcing herself to sit and read her book until she was sure she would be late if she didn't leave the flat, she had arrived ten minutes early. The booking was in her father's name — Peter Barker — and the waitress told her that he hadn't arrived yet and showed her to a table by the window. Peter Barker. She tried the name out, silently. It was unfamiliar, meaningless. Ben had said it sounded 'suitably Dad-ish' and she had laughed. She couldn't recall the words ever coming from her mother's lips. Josephine ordered a beer and watched people pass by outside, searching for men of the right sort of age, her heart beating fast every time someone slowed or stopped in front of the restaurant. But then they would pull out a phone, or a cigarette, or simply carry on, and she would let out a breath she hadn't known she'd been holding.

He arrived a minute or two late. Josephine watched him walk in, and could tell from his obvious nervousness that he was her man. And such an ordinary man. Average height, average build, tidy grey hair, dressed in brown corduroy trousers and a cream shirt. She didn't know what she'd been expecting. But it wasn't this.

The same waitress who had seated Josephine guided him to the table and Josephine forced herself to look straight at him as he approached. He smiled, and she saw her own smile within it.

'Josephine,' he said, sitting down, as the waitress walked away. 'Thank you so much for coming. I've been waiting so long to meet you.'

'It's funny,' she said. 'All the years I was growing up, Mum never mentioned you asking to meet me.'

He bowed his head, and she hoped that he felt ashamed. She hadn't known she was going to do that until the words were there in the space between them. She hadn't intended to be bitter and hard. It wasn't the side of herself she wanted to show him. But it was too late.

'I'm sorry. I made a lot of mistakes.'

There was a moment of silence then, and Josephine didn't know how to start asking all the questions that she had, that she'd been piling up for years. There was no obvious starting point, no easy way in. But he must have sensed them, she thought, because he held his arms out in a gesture of openness and told her she could ask him anything.

'Did your wife know about me?'

'No.'

'And are there others? Other children, dotted around London? Are you doing the rounds now that you're divorced, gathering them all up?'

'God, no. Look, Josephine, I understand why you're angry and upset. And I'm happy for you to take it out on me. I deserve that. I just want you to give me a chance to start making up for all those years.'

Josephine wished that Emily were there with her, or Jack. She felt as though she needed to hold someone's hand. 'Let's get some food,' she said. She called the waitress over, ordered another beer and raised her eyes at her father to ask whether he wanted one.

'Mineral water, please,' he said.

She wanted to know whether he didn't drink, or he was an alcoholic, or he was driving. Things she should know, and didn't. 'I'll have the mushroom risotto,' she told the waitress.

'And I'll have the same.'

While they waited for their food to arrive, he asked how her mother was.

'She moved away,' Josephine said. 'Sydney. A few years ago. She met a man online and fell in love, and he invited her to move out there to live with him, and she did.'

'You must miss her,' Peter said.

Josephine couldn't make out his tone or his expression. He was a stranger to her, and she didn't know his ways. Did she miss her mother? Of course she did. Did it hurt that she barely called, these days? It did. And yet she didn't need to talk to him, of all people, about that.

'Was there anyone else?' Peter asked, filling Josephine's silence. 'When you were growing up?'

'No. I never had a father, if that's what you're asking.' Josephine couldn't keep the sharpness out of her voice.

They were mostly quiet once the food arrived, and Josephine thought that someone observing might mistake it for a companionable silence; father and daughter, enjoying their meal together without any need for constant chatter. Only the two of them knew better.

Josephine thought about what kind of an impression she had made. Had he felt any disappointment, or any pride? Was it as strange for him as it was for her, to sit across a small round table from this stranger with whom he shared blood, and no memories?

Later, after the dishes had been cleared, Josephine found the courage to ask the question she'd been thinking about ever since she'd read his letter. 'You have other children, don't you? With your wife?' For a moment she felt like she was somehow betraying Emily, asking about these half-brothers or sisters. But she had so little family.

'I have two sons,' he said. 'They're quite a bit older than you. Sam's forty and Neil's thirty-eight. They both live in London.'

Josephine was hit with another set of questions. They lined up in her mind, pushing and shoving, impatient to be asked. She wanted to ask what these men who were her brothers did for a living, what they looked like, whether they had children of their own. But she didn't. There would be time for that later, she decided.

It was Josephine who made the move to leave. Peter offered to pay the bill and she let him. She was thinking of her Mum, who had endlessly supplied her food and her clothes for all those years. This meal, these beers, were the first things he had ever bought for her.

On the street, he seemed as though he might hug her, but then he didn't. He reached out and touched her arm a little awkwardly. 'Can we do this again?' he asked.

She could hear the hope in his voice. It was important to him. She was important to him. But why now? Why hadn't she been important back then? 'I'm not sure,' she said. 'I need to think. I've got your number. Goodnight.'

She walked away, letting him watch her and wonder whether it was the only evening he would spend with her. Those short, stilted hours in that empty restaurant, the only memory he would have to keep. She knew that she would call him; there was so much she wanted to know. And she felt cruel for letting him think that she might not, that this might be the beginning and the end of them, but she did it all the same. After all, she'd waited for his call a lot longer.

* * *

JACK PACED the living room of Josephine's flat, a glass of whisky in his hand, thinking about Emily. It had finally happened, and for a while, he'd felt satisfied. But it wasn't enough. Not nearly enough. He wanted to be with her, then, always. He didn't want it to be a sordid secret, the first of a thousand lies. He drained his whisky, moved through to the kitchen to pour another. He'd left her there, in bed, alone, and it had been unbearable. Michael was away, and he could have stayed the night, woken up beside her and kissed her awake and told her that he loved her. Because he did, he loved her. She was all over his mind and his heart like a spill.

And Josephine, what did he feel for her? Not that, nothing like that. He cared about her, worried about her — about her meeting her father and about the pain his own actions were going to cause her. But that wasn't love. Her presence in his life was a butterfly — pretty, distracting — while Emily's was a white-hot poker in his chest. The crux of it was that he could leave Josephine without looking back. But would he? Should he? He needed to talk to Emily. There was so much they hadn't said. He pulled his phone from his pocket and then froze as he heard Josephine's key in the lock.

Josephine was weary; he could see that. She joined him in the kitchen, eyed the bottle of whisky hungrily. He took another glass from the cupboard and poured her a large measure. And then they both sat down at the kitchen table. He was relieved that she didn't try to touch him.

'How was it?' he asked.

'It was okay. I don't know what I expected. He's just, you know, an ordinary man.' Josephine hung her head and her hair fell in her eyes, and Jack almost reached out to brush it away, but couldn't, not quite.

Josephine put down her empty glass and said she was going for a walk, asked if he would go with her. It was freezing outside: one of those clear, cold nights with a full moon hanging in the sky, and he wanted to stay inside, stay warm. But he said yes, of course. In the darkness, she wouldn't be able to see his face.

They wrapped up warm — coats, gloves, scarves. Josephine pulled on a woollen hat he hadn't seen before, and for a moment, with her hair covered, he could see a trace of Emily in her. And that made it all worse.

She took his hand and he was happy for the leather and cotton of their gloves between them. He wasn't ready for anyone else's touch on his skin.

Josephine stopped at the end of the street, and Jack thought she was deciding which way to go, but then he looked across and saw her gazing up at the sky. An icy puff escaped from her mouth with every breath. 'Look at the stars,' she said, her voice distant. 'You hardly ever see so many stars in London.'

Jack pulled her gently by the hand and they crossed the empty, silent street. 'Will you see him again?'

'Yes. I have to. I feel like I have to know him. Mum's gone, really, and there's no one else. Except Emily, of course.'

Jack felt the poker's tip twist slightly at the sound of her name, decided to try it out in his own mouth, terrified that his guilt would spill out with it. 'Do you think you'll introduce them? Your dad and Emily?'

Josephine stopped walking for a moment and looked at him, a little hurt, and he thought he must have given it away.

'Don't call him that. Not yet. It's Peter.'

'Sorry, I didn't mean…'

'It's okay. I guess they'll probably meet, eventually.'

They reached the common and walked in silence for a while, her gloved hand small in his. There was no one around. The coldness had secured their solitude. He thought of all the people, tucked away behind their curtains, their bodies warm. And he wondered whether any of them were carrying a secret like his, whether any of them loved the way he did, right then, and yet held on to someone else's hand.

'I've got two half-brothers,' she said.

'Really? What did he tell you about them?'

'Nothing really. Just their names. And that they live in London.'

'So you might meet them too?'

She sighed. 'I guess so.' And then she turned to look at him. 'Let's go home. I want you to take me to bed.'

He kept hold of her hand as they walked back, but he couldn't meet her eyes. He couldn't leave her, not like that, and yet he knew he couldn't be what she wanted. She would want to be held, want him to kiss her, to make love to her, and it was more than he could give.

That night, as soon as they got into bed, Jack turned away from her. Josephine nestled behind him, threw a cold arm around him and let it rest on his chest, and he lay very still, very quiet, waiting for sleep.

'Jack,' Josephine whispered, into the darkness. 'Will you move in with me?'

CHAPTER SIXTEEN

The second time Jack went over to Emily's, everything was different. There was no hurry, no rush. They knew what was going to happen and they didn't have to talk themselves into it, or out of it, or pretend that it wasn't true. Everything was slower, as though this was a legitimate seduction. So that was why, when Jack undressed that night, Emily saw the scars she hadn't noticed the first time. There were two, one on his back and one on his chest, faded but undeniably real. And before she could stop herself, Emily thought about what Josephine had made of them. Had she asked about them? Were there things about Jack that she knew, that Emily did not? She reached out, a little unsure, and traced the silvery line that ran beneath his left nipple with her finger. She saw him flinch, but she decided to speak anyway.

'How did you get this?' she asked, trying to make her voice as gentle as possible.

'It doesn't matter,' he said. But then he pulled his shirt back on and sat on the bed and she wasn't sure what to do next.

'You know,' she said, 'if something happened to you, you can tell me.' Even to her own ears, it sounded inadequate. The kind of thing a teenager would say.

'I said it doesn't matter.' Jack stood and left the room and Emily heard him padding down the stairs in his bare feet.

After a moment, she followed him. 'Are you leaving?'

'I don't know.' He was sitting at the kitchen table, checking his phone for messages.

'Let me get you something,' Emily said. 'A beer? A coffee?'

'No thanks. I think I'm going to go. I'll call you.'

'No,' she said, following him into the hallway. 'Don't go, please. I'm sorry I said anything. You don't have to tell me.'

'No,' he said. 'I don't.' But he paused, there in the hallway, and Emily thought that he might stay after all.

And then her phone rang, and she answered it without thinking. 'Hello?'

'Em, it's me.'

It was Michael. She didn't know what to say.

'Em, is everything okay?'

Emily stood there, silent, watching Jack watching her. And she saw him turn, pull open the door, and leave without looking back. 'Sorry Michael,' she said, trying to keep her voice level and calm. 'I couldn't hear you properly. Bad reception.'

She thought about the lies this thing had caused her to tell already. To Michael, to Josephine, to her boss, to Ben. She was getting better at it, and that made her uncomfortable.

'Is someone there?' Michael asked. 'Am I interrupting something?'

'No,' she said. 'There's no one here.' She sank down onto the third step of the stairs and tried to think of things she could tell her husband. She was aware of how wrong it was that she had to filter her thoughts and her news, deciding what he should know and what he shouldn't. She would focus on work, she decided. She would tell Michael about the capital cities projects her class had handed in that day, about how good they were. The topic had been Michael's idea. He'd said that it would be good to get the kids thinking about other places, how other people lived. It was the kind of thing he helped her with.

'How's your writing going?' she asked.

'Well, I think. I was right about needing to be up here. Everything's flowing much more easily. But I miss you. I miss hearing about your day. Tell me about your day.'

And so she did. She ran through her day, omitting the past couple of hours and the fact that Jack had been on her mind every second.

When Michael had hung up, Emily sat on the sofa and thought about all the secrets and parts of her life that Jack knew nothing about, and all the things he kept hidden from her, or that she simply hadn't yet found out. She didn't know the intricacies of his past. When she closed her eyes, she could still picture the scars she'd seen on his body, and she wished she knew what had happened to him.

She knew nothing about where Jack had come from, where he'd spent his years. His voice — low, neutral — gave no clues. She knew that he lived with flatmates, somewhere in south-east London, but she hadn't been there. She couldn't picture him in his home, how he would spend his time there or what his furniture and his belongings might look like. And she knew nothing of his family either. Was he cut adrift, like her, with barely anyone to call his own? Or did he have people scattered here and there, people he could go to?

Emily's mind shifted to Josephine then. She wanted to know whether Josephine had made any more plans with her father. Ordinarily, she would have called to ask, but how could she, when Josephine's boyfriend had just dressed and left her house? She could feel her sister drifting from her, and she was aware that she could stop it at any time she wanted. Or she could have stopped it, before. But now, whether she ended things with Jack or not, it would always be there, hanging between them. There would be a distance between the sisters that Emily could not cross.

All of it rested on what people did or did not know, she thought then. All of those things she didn't know about Jack that Josephine might know. And all of the things that Josephine and Michael did not know about what had been happening between her and Jack. There was power in knowing things.

Only at midnight, Emily noticed that she had been sitting in an entirely darkened room. The curtains were still open and the streetlights were shining through the window. She had been sitting there on the sofa, quite still, with no television and no music and no food, and the night had fallen around her without her noticing. She was about to get up and go to bed when her phone rang. And she reached for it, hoping that it was Jack. And it was.

* * *

'I know it's late,' Jack said. 'Can I come back?' He hoped she couldn't hear the shake in his voice.

'Of course.'

Jack hadn't gone far. He'd been walking around the common, wondering whether he should go home. But he couldn't face his flat, and he couldn't face Josephine, and the one person he could go to, that he wanted to go to, was Emily. So within ten minutes of the call, he was back on her doorstep, and when she opened the door he didn't say anything, he just stepped into her arms. And they stayed there, in the hallway, for a couple of minutes. It was where they had first kissed. It was where he had first seen her. It was where it had all started.

'Do you want anything?' Emily asked, when he finally pulled away.

'Do you have any whisky?'

She nodded, gestured for him to go into the living room, and appeared in the doorway a minute or two later with a bottle and two glasses.

'I'm sorry about earlier,' he said.

'You don't have to be. I shouldn't have asked. It's not my business.'

It was the truth and it wasn't the truth. It shouldn't have been her business, but Jack wanted it to be. He wanted to know everything about this woman, and he wanted her to know all there was to know about him. Even his ugly, unhappy past. Especially that.

'I haven't told Josephine any of this,' he said. 'I haven't told anyone.' And it was true. There had been girlfriends who had asked, and girlfriends who hadn't, and he had walked away from their questions or their silence. Josephine hadn't asked, and sometimes he resented her for it, and sometimes he was relieved.

Emily handed him a glass. 'Do you want to tell me?' she asked.

'Yes,' he said. He found it hard to look at her, although he could feel the weight of her eyes on him.

'You know, everyone has secrets,' she said.

'Did you and Michael?' he asked. 'Before this, I mean? Before us?'

'Of course,' she said, but she didn't offer an example.

It was hard to get started. Would she judge him for what had happened to him, all those years before? He decided to just tell it, the simple truth.

'My dad left when I was young. And a few years later, my mum met this guy, John. He moved in pretty quickly, and she was happy because she'd been lonely. But I wasn't very happy about it because it had just been me and Mum, and I'd got used to that. So I started skipping school, stealing things, just trying to get attention really.'

He paused and Emily didn't say anything, just waited for him to start speaking again. When his glass was empty, she poured him another drink.

'One night the police brought me home because they'd found me drinking in the park with a friend. I was twelve. My friend was a bit older, and he'd managed to run away when the police got there. So they dropped me off at home and told Mum and John what I'd done, and I remember John saying, "We understand, Officer. We take this very seriously. We'll make sure it doesn't happen again." And so the police officers left and my Mum was crying and then out of nowhere, John took off his belt and hit me. I think Mum was as shocked as me. There was all this rage on his face that we hadn't seen before. He was like a completely different man.'

Jack stole a glance at Emily to see how the story was affecting her. She had been completely silent, but she hadn't taken her eyes off him. As he caught her eye, she gave him an encouraging smile. He was back there, as he told it. Even as he was sitting in that room with Emily, he was back in that house, a child, feeling the pain all over his body and in his heart.

'After that, it happened all the time. And Mum just turned a blind eye to it, pretended she didn't know it was happening. I used to go to her, begging her to leave him, for it to go back to just being the two of us, and she just used to look through me and say that John had been very good to us, and that he'd helped us out financially, which was more than my father had done. I used to hate her. Sometimes I still do. They got married when I was fourteen. I didn't want to go, but Mum cried that morning and said that she'd never forgive me if I wasn't there, so I went. And I wished that he just wouldn't turn up, even though I knew how hurt she would be.'

Jack thought about Josephine, just starting out with her father, and about Emily, never having one. Since Peter had come into Josephine's life, Jack had felt himself pulling away from her, pulling closer to Emily. The two of them were adrift in the same way, he felt. And perhaps they could be one another's family.

'I used to think that as I got older I'd be able to fight back, but he was a big guy, and I've always been skinny. I was no match for him. I just tried to stay out of the house as much as possible, but then he'd beat me for coming home late and treating the house like a hotel. I used to worry that once I was out of the way he'd turn on Mum. I'd never seen him hit her, but I wouldn't have put it past him. But it wasn't enough to keep me there once I was sixteen. She'd known what was going on and she'd married him anyway.

'I moved out and I haven't been back since. They're just a couple of hours away, in Nottingham. I look at the train times sometimes. But I won't go to see her while he's still there.'

Jack stopped talking there. He looked at Emily again, for longer this time, and he could see in her eyes that she wanted to ask him a question, so he nodded, telling her it was all right.

'Are you in touch with your dad? Does he know about any of it?'

'No. I never heard from him again after he left. He could be anywhere. Mum said he was thinking about making a fresh start somewhere. America, I think.'

She didn't ask anything else. Jack was sure she could tell how hard the confession had been. Strange, he thought, to think of it as a confession, as though he was the one who had done something wrong.

'I don't know what to say,' Emily said. She reached for his hand and laced her fingers through his. 'I've never had to cope with anything like that.'

'You don't have to say anything,' Jack said. 'I'm pretty tired. Let's just go to bed.'

That was the first whole night they spent together. They didn't have sex, but they didn't sleep much either. Jack lay awake, his eyes on the ceiling, and he knew that Emily was awake too, but he didn't touch her and he didn't speak. He thought about how his revelation would change things between them. He considered whether she could ever love him when she knew how damaged he was.

CHAPTER SEVENTEEN

As his trip was nearing its end, Michael called his friend Alex.

'Hey Michael, it's been a long time. How are you? How's the book coming?'

Michael and Alex had studied together in Brighton, shared a house. And then Alex had started working for a literary agency and Michael had written a book, and it seemed that everything had worked out perfectly. Except that now, all these years down the line, Michael's second novel wasn't finished and he couldn't talk to his old friend anymore without being asked about it. 'Not too bad,' he said. 'But that's not what I'm calling about. I've got these stories, by this guy I know — my sister-in-law's boyfriend — and I think you should take a look at them.'

'I can't get stories published,' Alex said. 'You know that. Not unless they've been written by Stephen King.'

'But they're really good, I'm telling you.'

'It doesn't matter how good they are. He should try entering them in competitions or something.'

Michael was surprised to hear Alex sound so hard. Had it

always been there in him, innate? It hadn't seemed like it. Not when they'd known one another properly.

'Listen,' Alex said. 'How many words have you got? I keep talking you up to publishers, but it's not going to work unless we can finally get something to them.'

'Fifty thousand, give or take.'

'What? Didn't you have sixty thousand before this trip?'

Michael winced. 'I sort of went in a different direction.'

'Yeah, backwards.'

Michael thought about trying to justify himself, about telling Alex that he'd found the heart of the story now, that he was really making progress. 'Look, Alex, I've got to go. I'll call you when I'm back in London. Maybe we could go for a drink.' He hung up, doubting that he would call Alex before the novel was finished. His unwritten words hung between them, their friendship, and Alex couldn't see past them.

Downstairs, Michael put the kettle on, stuck his head round the living room door. 'Cup of tea?'

'Lovely,' his mother said, and his father looked up and nodded, smiling.

'Have you finished for the day?' his father asked as Michael set the steaming mugs down on the coffee table.

'Yes. Early finish.' He watched them, side by side on the sofa, content. They were watching a quiz show on television, the volume turned up loud. Michael didn't understand how they filled their days. Even after three weeks. He'd spent long hours in his room, the door closed, only coming down for refills of coffee. Just like he'd done when he was at school, or home from university in the holidays. He was torn between feeling proud of the way his writing had come on and guilty for having spent so little of this time with them. 'I think I'll head home tomorrow,' he said, testing out the words.

Their heads tilted across to him in an echoed movement.

'Oh?' his mother said, surprised. 'It seems like you only just got here.'

'It's been three weeks. It's time to go back to work, and to Emily.'

His father nodded. 'You get back to her, son. It's been lovely having you.'

On the phone, Emily sounded surprised too. 'I thought you were making progress,' she said.

'I am. I have. I can do the rest from London.' He twisted the cord of his parents' old-fashioned phone around his fingers, wishing he'd called from his mobile, upstairs. He hoped his parents couldn't hear him from the living room. But no, the television was turned up too high, and anyway, they weren't listening in. He'd told them when he first arrived that everything was fine with Emily, and they believed him. For the first time, he questioned whether he'd been right.

'As long as you're sure.'

'Is something wrong?' he asked, suddenly tense. 'I thought you'd be pleased.'

'I am pleased. Of course I am. I just don't want you to get back here and then wish you'd stayed longer, written more.'

'I won't.'

He packed his things after dinner, tidied his room, collecting up the coffee mugs he'd left scattered everywhere. And then he went to bed, but he couldn't sleep. Staring at the ceiling, he watched the minutes and hours tick by. Midnight, one, two. Had he made a huge mistake, going up there? Had he caused some sort of problem with Emily?

He thought about the wedding, and the months that had passed since. He'd never been happier. But was she? He'd thought so; she had seemed to be. But this trip, this distance, had made him less sure. Their phone calls had been short and infrequent, and he'd put it down to them both being tired. But was that all it was? This was the longest period they'd spent apart since they'd met.

Michael couldn't wait to be back there, touching her, talking to her properly. There was something about phones that made him clam up, made him speak to everyone in a stilted way, like a stranger. He was much better in person. He closed his eyes and Emily was there, behind his eyelids. And he promised her, there in his childhood bed, that if he'd hurt her by going away, he would make up for it. He would stay by her side, as he'd promised to do, and spoil her. In his head, he made plans, for trips to the theatre, home-cooked dinners, weekends away. And then he slept, finally, and when he woke up, it was time to go home.

THE NEWS that Michael was coming home came as a shock to Emily, although it shouldn't have. She'd been living a different life, those three weeks, snatching time with Jack where she could. And every night that she'd slept alone, she'd thought of Jack sleeping beside her sister. And not of Michael. She'd been pretending she was someone else, someone free. That they were both free, and that this thing they were doing, which felt so inevitable, wasn't a betrayal of the two people she loved the most.

On the day of Michael's return, Emily walked to school with questions buzzing in her mind. Would this be the end of it, now that her husband was coming back? Was it over? She felt her stomach tighten at the thought of it, at the dread of never being with Jack again. Of seeing him across dinner tables and at her house and Josephine's flat, and never once touching him.

Since that night, when he'd laid bare his past for her — the raw pain of it — everything had changed for Emily. She had thought, before, that perhaps it was only lust. Her own teenage lust, catching up with her and taking over. But watching him as he told her his secrets, she had known that it was more. That it wasn't going to evaporate or even fade. She was in love with Jack. With the enigma and torture of him, with the way he fucked her and the way he held her so gently afterwards, as though she might break. And she might, she thought, if it was over. She might break.

Emily headed for the staff room and made herself a cup of coffee. The room was deserted, all the other teachers busy in their classrooms, planning their days. Emily considered the possibility of Michael knowing. She'd been so busy pretending that it hadn't crossed her mind before that moment. She had never taken Jack to the bed she shared with Michael, but perhaps he would sense it somehow when he went into that spare room, or he would be able to see it on her face, or trace the touch of another man on her body. She worried that they might have left something in the room, tried to remember whether she had opened a window to clear the air of the smoke from Jack's cigarettes.

The day was a blur of activity — twenty-eight children working noisily through their maths textbooks, cutting and pasting for their history projects about the Second World War, doing gymnastics in the school hall. She was exhausted by their endless energy. But by mid-afternoon, an hour before they were due to go home, she had them all sitting quietly, cross-legged, at one end of the classroom, books in their hands. The final hour of the day was always reading time, and the children took it in turns to come and sit with Emily and read aloud to her.

She called Jessica over first. Jessica was a quiet, thoughtful girl, small for a seven-year-old, but quick to learn. Emily let her read, not really concentrating too hard on the words on the page before them, knowing that Jessica rarely needed her help.

She thought about the moment when Michael would appear in the doorway, what he might be wearing, what he might say. He would take her in his arms and hold her tightly against him, and would she stiffen? Would she give herself away in that first moment? And later that night, in bed, would she be able to touch him, to let him touch her? She realised with a jolt that she couldn't remember how Michael kissed. It was as though her three weeks with Jack had wiped her mind and body clean of him.

Jessica was looking up at Emily, the story finished. 'That was great,' she said, and watched Jessica pick her way through the legs and knees, back to her spot on the floor.

'Taylor,' she said. 'You're up next.'

Emily forced herself to concentrate for the remainder of the reading hour, hearing stories from three more children, her ear listening out for the bell. And when she finally heard it, she watched the kids pack up their bags, shoving books and pencils in their drawers in their hurry to be free, and she understood their impatience. Despite the rain that had been coming down heavily for most of the day, she couldn't wait to leave this classroom, to be off-duty, to allow all these thoughts and questions the space they needed in her mind.

Michael called when she was on her way home to say that he'd be back at around eight. She felt more and more nervous as the minutes ticked by, as though she was preparing to go on a first date or about to lose her virginity. With ten minutes to go before eight o'clock, she was sitting at the kitchen table, a cup of cold tea in front of her, and when her phone beeped, she jumped. It was a text from Jack, asking if he could come over that evening, and she realised that she hadn't told him. And it was so clear to her that she wished Michael wasn't coming back. She felt a cold wash of dread. She wished she could say yes to Jack, and then wait for his arrival, excited and expectant as a teenager.

She called him. 'Jack, I'm sorry, Michael's coming back tonight.'

He was silent for a moment and she thought he might be angry. But he'd known, hadn't he, that this was her situation?

'So that's it?' he said.

'No, I didn't say that. I just...he's coming home. This is his home.'

'Josephine's asked me to move in with her,' Jack said.

Emily hadn't been expecting that. She didn't know what to say. She wanted to say that she couldn't bear it if he took that step. But how could she, when she couldn't offer anything in return?

'And?' she said, eventually.

'I think I will. I hate my place.'

Was he doing it to punish her? Or had she misunderstood how he felt about her?

And then she heard a key turning in the lock. 'I have to go.'

'Emily?' Jack's voice was a little cracked.

'I have to go.' She hung up.

She wasn't sure whether to stand and greet him in the hallway, or let him find her sitting there in the kitchen. She stood, then sat again, and then stood and strode out of the room before she could change her mind. He was there, in the doorway, wearing a familiar smile and looking tired, but happy.

'I missed you so much,' he said, dropping his case to the floor and pulling her to him.

She sank into him. And then he held her away from him for a moment, looked at her face as though reminding himself, and he kissed her. And she wanted to curl up and hide from it all. Because with that kiss, she knew for certain that Michael wasn't the man she wanted.

CHAPTER EIGHTEEN

J ack, too, had put off thoughts of Michael's return. Had let
himself believe that it would always be like it had been for
those three weeks. Those slow hours they'd spent at Emily's
house, learning each other's touches and tastes. He was lying on
his bed when she called, and her words had brought reality
crashing back in. He'd cleared his evening, told Josephine he had a
book to finish for a review. He'd bought Emily flowers — orange
lilies — that had made him think of her hair and her freckles.

Emily took her wedding ring off whenever they went to bed. It
was automatic, something she did before they undressed. She
would leave it on the bedside table, and Jack would find himself
picturing it when he closed his eyes. He thought perhaps it was a
conscious thing, that it made her feel that what they were doing
wasn't quite so bad. He wanted to ask her what it meant.

Jack thought about Michael, about this man that he barely
knew. Some emails had gone back and forth between them while
Michael had been away, but Jack had detached Michael from
Emily in his mind. Pretended that this was someone else,
someone entirely unrelated, who was reading his work and trying
to help him with it. Michael had expressed a genuine interest in

Jack's stories, had understood the heart of them in a way that other friends who'd read them had failed to do. Jack wondered whether it was because he was a writer or if he just understood things that other people didn't. Whether he understood Jack, and the type of person he was, and the type of stories that surged into him, demanding to be written almost faster than he could type them.

Jack had been longing to write about Emily, but he was terrified that he would lose her in trying to get her down on the page and make her someone else entirely. He often based his characters on people he knew, and because of this, he had started to think of people he met as potential characters. He could write Josephine, he knew that. And he thought that he could probably write Michael, if he knew him a little better, understood his motivations and his fears. But he knew, without thinking, that he would fail if he tried to capture Emily. There were too many sides to her, too many angles.

With his evening unexpectedly free and his housemates not at home, Jack ran a hot bath and sank into it slowly, feeling his muscles relax. As he lay there, he felt sure that something had to be done. Michael's return had made it clear that things couldn't simply carry on. And he couldn't bear for it to be over with Emily, so what else was there? There was Josephine, of course. He knew that he should end things with Josephine, stop lying to her, hurt her once to avoid hurting her over and over again. That was the right thing to do, whether it would lead to Emily leaving Michael or not. But he was afraid of being left with nothing — neither the quiet, certain comfort he'd found with Josephine nor the intensity of every moment with Emily, discovered again and again in those lost weeks when Michael was away, when they'd pretended things were different. And then he'd mentioned moving in with Josephine to hurt Emily, and he'd wished, almost instantly, that he could take it back. But maybe he needed to do something like that to push her, to make her understand how it was for him, with her spending every day and every night with someone else.

Jack tried to remember what had drawn him to Josephine in the first place. She was pretty, there was no denying that. That blonde hair, those slim hips and slightly sleepy-looking blue eyes. And then they'd spoken, and he had been charmed by her, by her wit and her kindness. But it wasn't love. Not on his part. He'd thought, for a time, that it might grow into love, but then he'd met Emily and known that it never would.

HE LONGED to speak to Emily, to be lying beside her, whispering in her ear, asking her what he should do. If he'd had more warning about Michael coming home, he might have had the chance to do so. But now, as it was, he felt as though they were miles and miles apart and he had no idea when he would be beside her again. And the pain of that, of not knowing, was like nothing he'd ever experienced. It was how he imagined a knife would feel, sunk into his stomach, and twisting slowly.

After his bath, Jack thought about making himself something to eat, but he couldn't quite make himself get up from the sofa to do it. Instead, he sat there, thinking about everything that he and Emily would never have. He thought about the unfairness of the situation, the fact that she had met Michael before she had met him. That she had promised to be with another man for the rest of her life. That this person, the only woman he'd ever been able to imagine sharing his whole life with — his ugly past and his scattered present and his unknown future — would never be entirely his. That the only way this awkward situation could possibly end was badly.

Jack thought about calling his mother. Emily was with her husband, and he didn't know what he could possibly say to Josephine, and he needed to hear the softness of a woman's voice. He needed someone who would protect him, care for him without judging. He got as far as picking up the phone, but then he could hear his mother's voice in his head. What would he tell her? How could he break years of silence with a story like this? She wouldn't understand. She'd never understood.

As an only child, Jack had always felt that he was in the way while he was growing up. That he was a mistake his parents — who didn't seem to like one another very much — had inadvertently made and then had to live with. When his father left, a few weeks after Jack's seventh birthday, he thought he and his mother might become closer, but instead he watched her retreat into herself, and he lived almost alone. And then there was John, and with his arrival things got steadily worse.

Jack didn't quite understand the closeness that he had witnessed between Emily and Josephine, having never known what that sibling relationship was like. The closeness that he and Emily were in the process of destroying. Would it ruin the two of them forever, this thing that had happened? Did he, Jack, who had grown from that silent, lonely child, have the power to rip apart something that seemed so strong?

Jack had known many siblings, seen many close sisterly or brotherly relationships, but what he had seen in Emily and Josephine — and what he had gathered from things the two of them had said to him, independently — was different again. It was something he'd never known. Lately, he'd seen a distance growing between them. He would never know how much that was down to him. He wasn't innocent — far from it. But Josephine had just gained a father, something neither she nor Emily had ever had. That might have damaged them somehow, regardless of Jack's involvement. But when he was being entirely honest with himself, he knew that he was the main cause of their drifting. And that there was the potential for them both to blame him for it, in time. It was something he tried not to think about.

When Jack finally admitted to himself that he couldn't bear to be alone that night, with the walls seeming to close in around him more and more with every breath he took, he made his way over to Josephine's flat on the bus. Where else was there, after all? He felt ashamed as he stood on the doorstep, but there was nowhere else to go, no one else to go to.

'Jack,' she said, surprised, as she opened the door. 'I thought you had things to do.'

Jack shrugged, feeling tired. 'I finished early. I thought I'd see if you were in.'

'What a nice surprise,' she said, reaching out to pull him inside and into her arms. 'I was just about to make some dinner. Are you hungry?'

He was hungry. He hadn't noticed it. But at some point on his way over to her flat, the sadness in him had given way to hunger, and her words acted as a trigger to make him feel it. Just a few minutes later, Josephine set a hot bowl of pasta down before him and handed him a beer from the fridge. He ate quickly, speaking little, and a feeling started to wash over him, one of safety and of comfort. And that was when he really saw what Josephine was to him. Not a lover, not a partner, but a mother figure. The mother figure he'd never really had.

'What are you thinking about?' she asked. 'You're quiet.'

'Sorry,' he said. 'I'm just tired.'

And so Josephine led him up the stairs to bed as soon as he had finished eating. She gave him a towel and reminded him where she kept the spare toothbrush he sometimes used when he stayed over, unplanned, and hadn't brought his things. And Jack was grateful and ready to give himself up to sleep, but he could tell, without her having to say a word, that Josephine wanted him. And wasn't it the least he could do, after all she had done for him? And didn't he want to be held close, too? So Jack made love to her that night. Slowly, carefully. And she did not smell or taste like Emily. Afterwards, he spoke.

'I'd like to move in, if you still want me to.'

Josephine smiled in the darkened bedroom, and he could see

how much it was going to hurt her when he broke her heart. She fell into a deep, easy sleep and Jack lay awake beside her, wondering whether Emily and Michael had been having sex at the same time as him and Josephine. He felt a rush of nausea and slipped out of bed and down the hallway to the bathroom, thinking that he might be sick. But he wasn't sick, just so jealous that he felt it like a clutch around his heart. Squeezing and twisting. Of course they would have slept together, Jack reasoned, once he was back in bed, staring at the ceiling. Michael had been away for three weeks, and he was her husband. Of course they would have. She isn't yours, he whispered inwardly. Never forget that she isn't yours.

Not yet.

CHAPTER NINETEEN

It was the day before Christmas Eve, and Michael was preparing a beef stew in a rented house on the south coast. Since Emily and Josephine's mother had left, they'd always gone there, the three of them. That year, for the first time, Jack was with them.

Out of the corner of his eye, Michael watched Josephine, who was standing quietly beside him, chopping vegetables and washing up the implements he used. Knowing how precise he was when he cooked, she was letting him take the lead.

They were alone. Jack had said that he needed to do some last-minute shopping and Josephine had laughed, saying it was typical of a man to be so disorganised, and Michael had pretended to be offended by her comment, and Emily had offered to drive Jack to Southampton, saying there were a couple of things she still needed herself.

'How's the novel?' Josephine asked. 'Or shouldn't I ask?'

'No, you can ask. It's actually going pretty well. I got on the right track while I was up at my parents'.'

'That's great. I've been waiting a long time to read it.'

Michael felt at peace. There, in the kitchen, creating a meal with his sister-in-law that the four of them would sit down to enjoy later, with some music in the background and a couple of bottles of wine on the table. It was cold outside, and he was happy to be there, away from London, with the fire burning in the living room. He could feel the year closing in, and it didn't scare him, as it sometimes did, the thought of a whole new year beginning, because his writing was going well, and he knew that the novel would be finished the next time they were gathered together in that house.

'I'll give you a signed copy next Christmas, or maybe the one after,' he said. 'That is, if anyone wants to publish it.'

Despite his words, Michael was confident that the book would be published, that it would be well received. He was more proud of it than he'd been of his first novel, which dealt with student life at the end of the nineties, and had a love story woven in. This time, he was writing about his family, his background, his home. And although he'd cast different characters in the parts of his family members, he felt that he was on solid ground, and that his confidence came through in the writing. The love story, this time, felt more real, more believable, because he knew exactly what love was. He hadn't, before, all those years earlier, not long after he'd finished being a student himself. He'd thought he had, of course, but he'd been wrong.

Michael took the meat and the vegetables Josephine had chopped and emptied them into a large dish.

'What's next?' she asked.

'We're done. It's ready to go in the oven.' Michael looked at his watch. 'Listen, shall we go and join them? See if they need any help?'

Josephine liked the idea, and they rushed around finding their boots and coats before heading out in her car.

'Have you read any of Jack's stories?' Michael asked her as she drove, realising that he didn't know.

'No,' she said. 'He won't let me. He's very secretive about them. I was amazed when he sent them to you, but then he told me how much he'd enjoyed your novel, so I suppose it's different with you.'

Jack, and others, had told Michael how they felt about his first novel, and it still surprised him. Had he somehow captured more in it than he thought? Perhaps he couldn't take it all that seriously because he'd read it over and over again while he'd been editing. He couldn't imagine what it was that someone like Jack had found in it to admire, someone whose own writing was so beautiful.

'He's really very good,' Michael said, aware even as he spoke that his words weren't sufficient.

'Have you told them we're coming?' Josephine asked as she pulled into a multi-storey car park. 'Sent a text?'

Michael pulled his phone from his pocket. 'I did, when we first got in the car. But there's no reply. I'll give Emily a call.'

He held the phone to his ear, listening to it ring. Emily often had it in her bag and didn't hear it. He tried Jack. Same thing. Josephine was stamping her feet and pulling her scarf tighter around her neck.

'Let's go into the shopping centre and keep trying,' she said.

When they'd been calling for another ten minutes or so, Michael felt the cold finger of panic in his chest. Could something have happened? Josephine seemed more irritated than worried, so Michael kept his fear to himself.

'He's so bad with his phone,' Josephine muttered. 'He just forgets about it, leaves it places. I bet it's back at the house.'

Coming into town to surprise them like this had seemed like a good idea but now it was tainted. It felt foolish, absurd. 'Let's find somewhere to have a coffee,' Michael said.

As they were cutting through the crowds to go into a café, Michael thought he saw them. A woman with the exact same shade of hair, a tall man. He put a hand up to wave to them and then saw that they were holding hands, and he pulled his hand back down, confused. He put his hand on Josephine's arm, and when she looked at him, he pointed.

'What?' Josephine asked, and then he watched her as she saw them, really focused on her face.

'Jack!' Josephine called.

And then the woman turned her face to one side and Michael saw that it wasn't Emily at all. She was younger, almost still a teenager. And Michael almost laughed at the strangeness of it.

His phone rang. 'Emily?' he asked, and he found that he was breathless.

'We're on our way back,' Emily said. 'I'm so sorry we missed you.'

Michael wanted to ask why it had taken her so long to check her phone, but it seemed petty. He sighed. 'We'll see you back at the house, then,' he said, and Josephine's face changed to a frown.

On the drive back, he remembered Josephine and Jack's arrival at the house, remembered the bags he'd helped carry in from the car, bags loaded with wrapped presents. Surely they couldn't all have been Josephine's, he thought. But then they were driving through the gate and Emily was opening the door for them, and he forgot all about it.

* * *

EMILY DROVE. Jack was calling out directions, his hand resting heavily on her thigh.

'I've booked us a hotel,' he said, an apology in his voice. 'I didn't know where else we could go.'

As they checked in, Jack saw that Emily couldn't look at the woman behind the reception desk, and he felt a pang of regret that he had done something that made her feel ashamed. But then they were up in the room, and it was forgotten because they were closing the door and pulling at each other's clothes, their hands and mouths all over one another's skin.

In the weeks leading up to Christmas, in the midst of all the parties and the gatherings and the shopping, they hadn't found much time to spend together. It had been three weeks since they had had sex, two weeks since they had kissed — a hasty, hidden kiss — and he had felt as though he would go mad. And he could hardly believe that they were there, together, and that this room was available to them for the whole night, but they couldn't stay. Jack could count the number of times he'd spent a whole night beside Emily on one hand, and it wasn't enough. It wasn't nearly enough.

There were so many things he wanted to tell her. That this was more than a fling, an affair; that this was it, for him. That he had never believed he could love like this, after being hurt so much and for so long. That she had saved him. But he didn't tell her any of those things. Instead, he held her head in his hands and kissed her fiercely. And he savoured the feel of her skin on his; the warmth and comfort of it.

When he was inside Emily, Jack felt entirely at peace. He felt as though he was finally where he should be, after years of running. He stopped moving for a moment, let his hips rest against hers, their bellies touching.

'What is it?' Emily asked.

Her voice was soft, a little breathless, and there was a small bead of sweat at her hairline.

'Nothing,' he said. And he kissed her forehead and rolled them over so that she was on top of him. He lay still as she moved her hips slowly and her hair fell over his face, obscuring his view of her pale body.

JACK LAY with his head on Emily's chest, her heart beating steadily in his ear. Fast at first, and then slower. And he dared to imagine that things were different, that she was his and his alone, and there was no hiding and no lying and no pretence. He imagined holding Emily's hand on trains and in restaurants and at the theatre, with no price to be paid for doing so. He imagined her sleeping next to him night after night and finding her way into his arms in sleep.

Her phone rang first, and they ignored it. Then his. They looked at one another, knowing it must be either Michael or Josephine. And still, neither of them moved to find their phones in the tangle of clothes they'd left, discarded, on the floor. But the ringing carried on, over and over, until Emily stood up.

'Jesus!' She found her phone and stared at it.

'What? What's happened?'

'They're coming into town, Michael and Jo. They're coming to meet us.' Emily looked at him, her expression pure anguish.

'Shit, tell them we're on our way home.' Jack got out of bed and started to pull his clothes on. There wasn't time for a shower.

When they got back to the house, Josephine's car wasn't there. They let themselves in and Jack kissed Emily in the kitchen, slipping his hands inside her clothes. She moaned, pushing him away and then, a moment later, pulling him towards her so their hips met. And then they heard the crunch of gravel and Emily pushed him away properly and went to the door, and Jack left the room, not ready to see them and pretend he was happy.

Later, when they were eating the stew Michael had made, Jack watched Michael reach across to brush a strand of hair from Emily's face. And it was clear, to Jack, that this was a man who would never jeopardise what he had. Not for the first time, Jack wondered what he would do when he found out. Because he would find out. And Jack knew that Michael would not let Emily go without a fight.

Emily was quiet at dinner, and Jack tried to draw attention away from her silence by filling any pauses in the conversation. He told jokes and made up stories, and he could hear that his voice was a little too loud. A couple of times, Josephine reached across the table for his hand and her eyes asked why he was acting strangely, but he couldn't stop it because he was watching Emily noticing them touch.

Finally, Emily rose from the table and said that she had a headache and was going to have an early night, and Jack was able to relax. He went up to the bathroom a few minutes after she had gone, and they met on the landing, stood there, face to face, in silence. He could smell the toothpaste on her breath.

'Shall we try to get away tomorrow?' he asked.

'No,' she said. 'We can't — not again.'

Jack took her wrist and pressed the palm of his hand against hers. Her skin felt cold. He knew that what she said was true, that there was no feasible excuse for them to leave the house together two days in a row. And yet he couldn't bear the thought of the nights to come, sleeping in the same house, a few feet and thousands of miles apart, without the promise of another snatched hour or two. He kissed her, then, with all the urgency of those earlier kisses, back at the hotel. And she pushed him gently against the wall, put her cold hands inside his shirt and moved her fingers up and down his chest. He gasped, grabbed her hips, pulled her body closer to his. She was wearing a long T-shirt and he pulled it up, took in her nakedness, ran his hand up the inside of her thigh.

There was a sound from downstairs and they sprang apart, listening, breathing heavily. They heard Michael and Josephine move from the dining room to the lounge, heard the TV being switched on. Emily kneeled down before Jack, unzipped his flies and took him in her mouth. He looked at her long legs, tucked neatly beneath her, watched the shadows move across her face. He made a low sound as he came, and she stood up, put a finger to her lips.

And then she slipped through the door to the room she shared with Michael and was gone, and Jack felt, for a moment, as though he'd imagined the entire exchange. He stood there for a minute or two in the darkness of the landing, and then he checked his clothes and his face in the bathroom mirror, and went back downstairs to join the others. Sure that they would know what had just happened — at least half of him hoping they would know.

CHAPTER TWENTY

When she got back to London, on New Year's Eve, Josephine called Peter. 'I hope you had a good Christmas,' she said. She knew that he had seen both of his sons, and their wives and children, but that he had spent Christmas Day itself alone. He had told her that Sam and Neil felt they should be with their mother, as it was the first Christmas since the divorce. Josephine had thought of him on Christmas Day, had felt sorry for him, but she hadn't called.

'It's lovely to hear from you,' he said, not answering her question.

'I'm sorry I wasn't around for Christmas,' she said. 'I was wondering whether you'd like to spend tonight with us. With me and Jack, I mean. And Emily and Michael. They're having a party.'

Josephine heard him take a long breath.

'I would love that,' he said.

She gave him the details and hung up the phone. She was looking forward to seeing him. To seeing in the new year with him; a year in which she was sure they would continue to get closer.

Josephine and Jack got to Emily's house early. Josephine wasn't sure how many people were coming, and she didn't want Peter to arrive and find a busy house full of unfamiliar faces. She wanted to greet him at the door, and introduce him.

She had told him to come at around eight o'clock. When the doorbell rang, at dead on eight, she was standing in the kitchen with Jack, filling up bowls with crisps and nuts. She knew it was him. 'Come with me,' she said to Jack, tugging at his hand.

She felt as though she was constantly introducing people to one another. First Jack and now this man who didn't yet feel like a father. She felt as though her life was a series of puzzle pieces, and she was shifting them, trying to make them fit together.

Peter looked a little lost, standing there on the doorstep, a bottle of sparkling wine in his hands. Josephine didn't know whether he'd ever been to this house when he was seeing her mother. It hadn't crossed her mind when she'd given him directions over the phone earlier.

'I thought,' he said, and then his voice trailed away. He held out the bottle to her. 'For midnight.'

'Come in,' Josephine said, stepping forward and giving him a slightly awkward hug. They hadn't yet mastered a comfortable way to greet and leave one another. 'This is Jack, my boyfriend. Jack, this is Peter.'

Jack took Peter's coat and shook his hand. Josephine looked at the two men; polite, a little unsure. She thought of past boyfriends who had never had to go through this with her, who had only had to meet her mother, who was always welcoming and sweet from the outset. And now there was Jack, who might never know her mother, but who was meeting her father instead.

Before the other guests began to arrive, the five of them sat in the living room with glasses of wine. Josephine didn't say much. She watched Peter and Emily talking, saw how easy they seemed with each other, and felt a stab of jealousy. Was this hard for Emily? Did it dredge up difficult thoughts about her own father? If it did, she didn't let it show.

It wasn't long before the house was alive with talk and laughter. Josephine didn't know everyone, and she stayed close to Peter. She felt protective of him, somehow. Jack flitted about. Josephine saw Michael introducing him to people, and at one point, she saw him talking to Emily in a corner. Their heads close, their faces earnest. She wished she knew what they were talking about. She looked at Peter then, and saw that his eyes had followed her gaze.

'He seems nice,' Peter said.

'Jack? Yes. He is.'

'How long has it been?'

'Six months.' Josephine wanted to say more, to talk about how she had seen him from afar and known that she wanted him. How she had found the courage to ask him out. But it didn't seem right to share such intimate details with him, not yet. She was drawing lines, guessing at what was normal and what wasn't.

'Oh? I'd assumed it was longer. He seems very at home here.'

Josephine went to the kitchen to refill their drinks, and she thought about what Peter had said. He was right. Jack did seem at home in this house. Tonight especially. And although that was what she had wanted all along — for Jack to be close to her sister and Michael — the realisation made her feel a little uneasy, and she didn't know why.

When Josephine returned to her father, he was talking to Ben. She hadn't seen him arrive.

'Ben,' she said, putting her arms around him, 'this is Peter.'

'We've met,' the two men said, simultaneously, and then they all laughed.

'It's nice to meet you,' Ben said. 'Josephine is one of my oldest and dearest friends.'

Josephine felt proud to hear Ben describe their friendship in that way, in front of her father. For reasons she hadn't really addressed, she wanted Peter to know that her life was full of people who loved her — that she was busy, happy; that she was having to make space for him rather than letting him fill a gap.

Josephine looked at her watch and saw that it was a couple of minutes to midnight. She was surprised. The evening had passed quickly. Instinctively, she scanned the room for Jack, but she couldn't see him. She felt disappointed. It was their first New Year, and she had wanted to hold his hand during the countdown, feel his lips on hers as midnight struck. It would have felt like a promise for the year ahead. But Peter was here, she reasoned, and it would have been rude to leave him alone. Someone had turned the TV on and the noise of the busy London streets mingled with the noise in the room, and Josephine found herself joining hands with Ben on one side and her father on the other as the countdown began.

THE PARTY HAD BEEN Emily's idea. She had gestured around their large living room, one night leading up to Christmas, and said that they should make use of all this space they had. Michael had gone along with it, but he was reluctant. He wasn't fond of large gatherings of people; he preferred to talk to people one on one. And although that had always been the case, for him, he was aware that it made him seem old and a little boring, and he didn't want Emily to think of him that way. He was careful, sometimes, to divert attention away from the age gap that lay between them.

As the night went on, though, he found that he was enjoying himself. Alex was there, and it had been a long time since Michael had spent time with him. For once, Alex didn't want to talk about Michael's book. Michael brought up the subject early in the evening and Alex batted it away. 'It's a party,' he said. 'Let's talk about it another time.'

Alex and Michael drank steadily, and it felt like old times.

'You're a lucky bastard, you know that?' Alex asked.

'I know,' Michael said, and he meant it. It was easy to take things for granted, to just get used to what you had, but Michael tried hard to remember that his life hadn't always been so easy. 'What about you?' he asked Alex. 'Are you happy?'

Alex shrugged. 'I work hard. There isn't time for much else.'

Alex had got married when they were young, shortly after they'd finished university, but it hadn't lasted. At the time, when he'd attended the wedding alone, Michael had envied Alex for having found someone. It had all seemed so smooth, so simple. They were so young and in love, and their closeness had made Michael feel lonely. But two years later, Alex's wife had left him for another man, and Alex had never had a serious relationship since.

'Do you think you'll ever get married again?' Michael asked. It was the kind of question that was easier after several drinks.

'I don't know. Maybe. I'd like to have a family one day.'

'Yes,' Michael said. 'Me too.'

'What about Emily?'

'We haven't talked about it for a while. She wanted to wait. But soon, maybe.'

Alex lifted his glass then, and touched it to Michael's. 'To family,' he said.

And Michael saw a sadness in his eyes, and changed the subject.

Michael watched Emily darting around. She had invited more people than he'd expected, work colleagues and friends she'd made through Josephine, and he knew that it was important to her that everyone had a good time. When they were first together, they'd had a lot of gatherings like this one and they'd always left Emily so exhausted. There was something in her that needed to please, and he loved that caring side to her but felt it was up to him to make sure she was properly cared for, too. He watched her, constantly moving from group to group, introducing people who didn't know one another, bringing drinks from the kitchen.

He watched Josephine with her father. He seemed pleasant, and Michael was pleased for them, pleased that they had found each other after all these years. They didn't seem quite comfort-able together yet, but that would come with time. There was a similarity to their smiles and their gestures. He wondered whether they had recognised it.

Jack approached Michael and Alex at one point. He shook Alex's hand. 'I'm Jack,' he said.

'This is the writer I told you about,' Michael said.

He saw Alex quietly assess Jack, the way he always did when meeting someone new. 'Jack,' he said. 'It's nice to meet you. Michael said some very complimentary things about your stories.'

Jack seemed wrong-footed then, and Michael thought he caught sight of a slight blush.

'I'm just sorry I couldn't do anything with them. I'm sure Michael explained. But if you ever write a novel, please send it my way.'

'I will,' Jack said. 'Thank you.' And then he moved away, saying that he was going to get another drink, and Michael hoped that he didn't feel uncomfortable.

'He's with Josephine?' Alex asked, once Jack had gone.

'Yes.'

'That's a shame.'

Alex had considered asking Josephine on a date a few years back. Michael hadn't exactly stood in the way, but he hadn't been very keen on the idea, because Alex seemed to be with a different woman every time he saw him, back then. And Alex had sensed Michael's reluctance and stayed away. Michael tried to imagine what kind of a couple Alex and Josephine would have made.

'What do you make of him?' Alex asked.

'Jack? He's great.'

'Hmm,' Alex said. 'There's something about him. He seems shifty.'

Michael laughed. 'That sounds like plain old jealousy.'

'No, I'm serious. He'll break her heart. I'd put money on it.'

Michael shook his head and said nothing.

When midnight struck, Michael and Alex hugged one another. Michael didn't know where Emily was, or Jack, or Josephine. That was one of the reasons why he didn't like the idea of a party — he had wanted to spend the evening with just the people he really cared about. But Emily had said that there would be plenty of evenings like that, and she was right. He felt like he and Alex had reconnected, somehow, and he was pleased.

But when Alex left, less than an hour into the new year, Michael decided it was time to track down his wife. She wasn't in the kitchen or the lounge. He waited until someone came out of the downstairs toilet to see that it wasn't her. And then he went upstairs and saw shadows on the landing.

'Emily?' he called.

There was a pause, then her voice. 'Coming.'

She came out of the spare bedroom. She'd taken her shoes off and she looked small, a little rumpled.

'What were you doing in there?' Michael asked.

'I just needed a minute,' she said, colour rising in her face. 'It's so busy downstairs. I wish they'd all go home now.'

Michael put his arms around her, there on the landing.

'Happy New Year,' he whispered into her hair. 'I wanted to see you at midnight.'

'Me too. I couldn't see you. I'm sorry.' She twisted out of his grasp and went to walk down the stairs.

Josephine was in the kitchen with Peter, and after a few minutes, Jack appeared. Peter stood back as the four of them hugged and wished one another Happy New Year, and then he stepped forward. 'I think it's time I was going. Thank you so much for inviting me.'

'I'll see you out,' Josephine said, smiling.

People started to drift away then, and Michael was pleased. And he could see that Emily was too. She looked tired. As Michael watched her saying goodbye to people and thanking them for coming, he thought back to the conversation he'd had with Alex, about having a family. When they'd closed the door for the final time, he caught her in his arms.

'Let's have a baby,' he said.

'Where did that come from?'

'My heart,' Michael said. 'I love you. Let's make a person.'

CHAPTER TWENTY-ONE

Jack was the first person Emily called; the only person she could call. She was sitting on the bathroom floor when he arrived, the phone by her feet. She thought about him grabbing his coat and his keys and making his way over there, and how she hadn't moved in all that time. How long had it been?

'What is it?' he asked, striding over and crouching in front of her. He was out of breath and his hair was falling in his eyes.

Emily reached across to brush it away but he caught her hand when it was inches from his face.

'Em? Emily! Is it Michael? Does he know?'

Who he was worried for? Himself, Michael, Josephine, or her?

'For fuck's sake, Em!' He stood and began pacing up and down the small room. 'He knows, doesn't he? I knew it.'

'He doesn't know.' Her voice was croaky, as though she hadn't spoken for hours.

'Then what? Jo?'

Emily shook her head and willed herself not to cry. 'I'm pregnant.'

Saying it was like finding out all over again, that morning in the early days of the new year.

'Fuck,' he said. 'I wasn't expecting that.'

She wanted to hit him then. She really wanted to hurt him. Had he really never considered this possibility? For her, it was always there, in the background. She'd carried the fear of it every day since this started. And occasionally, the fear had been tinged with a glimmer of hope, and that was the most terrifying thing of all.

Jack had stopped pacing. He'd opened the window and was taking big gulps of air. She thought maybe he was going to be sick. And then he turned to face her. 'Maybe we can do this,' he said. 'Maybe this is what we need.'

The cold shock of his words gave her the strength to stand. 'What are you saying?'

'Something had to happen, Em. We can't just carry on. We'll have to tell them, and then we can do this thing properly.'

She stood beside him, their backs to the open window, and she could feel the cool January air against her neck. Jack smelled like leather and sweat. She thought about how easy it would be to say yes to him, to try to turn this into the happy moment it should have been. She wanted to touch him, but she felt as though her arms were pinned to her sides. 'There's no way,' she whispered. 'I have to have an abortion.'

Emily was telling herself as well as telling him. She was testing it out, checking whether the thought of it was enough to break her.

Jack grabbed her arms at the elbow, and she looked up to see something new and awful in his eyes.

'You can't just decide that! That's for both of us to decide.'

'Let me go, Jack, you're hurting me!' She struggled to break away but his grip just got tighter. She imagined the marks his fingers would leave, the bruises that would form, change colour, and fade. She wondered where they'd be by the time the bruises had faded.

And then she said the thing they were both avoiding. 'We don't even know if it's yours.' She had never thought that she would be this person. Married, pregnant, unsure of who had fathered her baby.

Jack let go of her. 'Will you ever leave him?' he asked, sinking to the floor. 'Will you ever leave him for me?'

It was the first time he'd actually asked her that, and she was shocked into silence for a few moments. 'Even if I did, what would we do? What about Josephine?'

'I'd leave her.'

'She's my sister!'

He looked up at her, and his eyes were tired. Had she done that to him? Had she worn him down until this was all that was left?

He got up and Emily knew that he was leaving. She knew that she didn't have any right to ask him to stay. She walked behind him down the stairs and to the door, saying nothing, feeling numb.

Before he walked away, he turned back. 'If this is the closest I ever come to being a father, I don't know whether I can forgive you.'

After he'd left, Emily thought about when it might have happened — when the baby might have been conceived. But it was impossible to pinpoint. Had she been pregnant at Christmas? And if she had, had she known, deep down? Had she felt a fluttering? Perhaps. Perhaps she'd known all along, and just pretended that it wasn't happening.

Before she could start to imagine what the baby might look like, she went downstairs, found the phone book, and called the first clinic she saw listed. 'I'd like to make an appointment,' she said, and she was surprised at how strong her voice sounded, how sure. 'For a termination.'

* * *

JACK WAS SURPRISED at how quickly they fitted her in. She had to see two doctors first, but it was a well-worn procedure, and it seemed like a case of going through the motions. When the day arrived, Jack collected her from the house and they took a taxi to the clinic.

'What did you do about work?' he asked. And straight away he wished that he could take it back. It didn't matter; none of it mattered.

'I called in sick,' she said. And then she added, 'Michael doesn't know.'

Jack could read the pain on her face, but he wished he knew how much more there was behind it. Was there was so much pain, stacked up behind her eyes, that it was overtaking her? And was there room for anything else?

'And what about afterwards?' he ventured.

'I'll be in bed for a couple of days. I'll have to say I've got a bug or something.'

More lies. It was what their lives were made up of. Jack wasn't angry with her anymore. At least, he was less angry. He still wished that things could be different, that they could have this child and raise it together, but he understood that they couldn't. He dared to hope that one day this would happen again and it would all be different. One day, when everything was out in the open and the anger and pain had dissolved a little.

In the waiting room, they barely spoke. Jack asked whether she wanted him to go in with her, when the time came, and she shook her head.

'Just wait for me.'

And he felt useless and ashamed, that that was all he could do. So when she went in, after he had kissed her forehead and squeezed her hand and she had nodded to say that she understood, he went out into the car park and wandered around. A little lost and so afraid. He wasn't sure whether the Emily who came out of that room would be the same Emily who had gone in, or whether that Emily was lost to him forever.

The day she'd told him, he could tell that something was terribly wrong just from listening to her breathing over the phone line, and he'd realised that he'd been waiting for that moment without knowing it. Almost holding his breath. Waiting for everything to fall apart around them. He had thought, on his way over to her house, that this day might mark the end of them.

He'd used the key Emily had given him for the first time, and he'd found her sitting on the bathroom floor and he'd sensed her sadness and hoped it was something he would be able to take away. And when she'd taken her time telling him what it was, he had felt a bubble of rage start to build up somewhere inside him and he had worried about what would happen if it burst.

For Jack, it was the second time he'd been given this news. Why was it never the right time? The first time, he'd been nineteen, and the girl had been his university girlfriend. That day, they had both known how it would turn out, that she would end up being treated in a clean, white clinic and that he would wait outside, smoking one cigarette after another and wondering whether it would help if he bought her some flowers.

So maybe that was why, when Emily had told him, he'd dared to imagine an alternative ending, one in which the medical staff involved were there to bring that baby safely into the world. Where he and Emily would take their baby home and learn to take care of it. But it was impossible, he could see that. They didn't even share a home, or a bed.

There, in the car park, Jack thought about whether he really wanted the baby that was being taken from him. All he knew for sure was that he wanted her. That he wanted them to have met when they were free, in other, easier circumstances. That she wasn't married to a man he almost wanted to be. That he wasn't in a relationship with her sister. But he still believed that this situation wasn't impossible, that they could salvage something from it for themselves. Not a baby, perhaps. Not that. But something, all the same. He put aside the knowledge of everything they would have to destroy to get there and concentrated on what they would end up with. He ached for that possibility.

The time passed quickly and Jack was amazed when they said that he could take her home. It seemed too soon, after what she'd been through. It seemed reckless and irresponsible. But this was something they dealt with every day, he reminded himself. How did they do it? Could they shut it out when they went home and turned on their televisions, or was it always there, with them?

Emily was silent in the taxi, but she held his hand tightly as though she would never let it go. Once he'd got her into bed, she seemed peaceful. He stood there, at the foot of the bed, watching her pale face and her flaming hair against the white pillows.

'Can I get you something?' he asked.

'Just some water.'

There was nothing behind her eyes, that afternoon, and Jack wondered again what they had taken from her, in that room.

'Michael will be home soon,' she said, when he handed her the glass of water. 'You'd better go. I'm sorry.'

Emily, he wanted to say, I never meant for it to come to this. I would have given anything for it not to come to this. And if you will let me, I will be here for the rest of my life, and we will fix this. We will do this again, and do it right, and there will be laughter and joy instead of this awful pain.

'Okay,' he said. 'I love you.'

It seemed like so little to offer, he thought, as he let himself out. Those three words that he'd felt for so long but never managed to say, and a gentle kiss. It seemed like he needed to think of something more.

CHAPTER TWENTY-TWO

Michael was trying to write in his study, but he was distracted, worried about Emily. She hadn't been well for days, and she'd been sleeping in the spare room, and he didn't sleep well without her beside him. She seemed distant, and he wasn't sure whether it was the illness or something else. He'd pleaded with her to see a doctor, but she had said that she was feeling a little better each day and that she would be fine.

That Sunday, he'd been sitting in his study for a couple of hours, going over the same sentence in his novel again and again, trying to get it just right. He was nearing the end, and although he'd edited it thoroughly as he'd gone along, he was starting to play around with individual words and phrases. He knew, but wouldn't quite admit, that he was putting off sending it out. He was afraid, now the book was finally so close to completion, of how it would be received.

Michael got up and went through to the spare bedroom. Emily was lying there with her eyes open. There was a book beside her on the bed but every time he went in, she wasn't reading it.

'Can I get you anything?' he asked.

Emily snapped out of whatever daydream she was in and

looked at him. She looked startled to see him standing there. 'No thanks, I'm okay.'

'You're sure?'

'Yes.'

Michael didn't know what to do. They were trapped in this distant politeness, and she was barely eating. He felt more helpless than he ever had before. He decided to go down to the kitchen and make some soup. Sometimes, he found cooking comforting, and he hoped that by the time he'd finished, Emily would have changed her mind about eating.

Once the vegetables were chopped and the stock was made and the soup was simmering on the hob, Michael pulled his phone from his pocket and called Josephine.

'Michael,' she said. 'What a nice surprise. How are you?'

'I'm okay, thanks. But I'm calling about Emily. You haven't spoken to her in the last week, have you?' Asking the question felt strange. There was a time when Emily and Josephine would have spoken every day, even before they lived together. Was it all down to Josephine being with Jack, the fact they saw each other so much less now? Michael wasn't sure, and it gnawed at him.

'No,' Josephine said, and then she paused. 'I've been meaning to call her.'

Michael realised she had acknowledged the same thing he had — she understood something had shifted. He wanted to ask if what she said was the truth.

'She's not been very well,' Michael said. 'She's been in bed. I don't know what to do.' Michael walked over to the kitchen door and closed it. He didn't want this conversation to drift upstairs to where Emily was lying.

'What do you mean? What kind of unwell?'

The concern in Josephine's voice made Michael feel less alone, made him think that things must still be all right between the sisters.

'I don't know, that's the thing. She's very pale, and she's barely eating and not sleeping much. But she won't see a doctor. She keeps saying she's getting better, but I don't think she is. Could you come to see her? See whether she'll tell you what's wrong?'

'Of course I will,' Josephine said. 'Shall I come now?'

Michael exhaled audibly, relieved. 'Yes please,' he said.

* * *

JOSEPHINE HUNG up the phone and turned to Jack. 'Emily's not well,' she said. 'I'm going to go round to see her.'

'Do you want me to come with you?' he asked.

Through her worry, Josephine noticed the compassion in Jack's eyes, and she was grateful that he cared. She thought, however, that he'd probably felt obliged to offer to come. It would be better if it was just her, she decided. She didn't yet know what was wrong. Emily might not want to talk about it in front of anyone else.

'No, you stay here,' she said. 'I'll be back in an hour or so.'

It was cold outside, so Josephine grabbed her scarf and gloves on her way out of the door and pulled them on. In the ten minutes it took her to walk to the house, she felt her face go numb, and she hurried, arriving on the doorstep red-faced and a little out of breath.

'Thanks for coming,' Michael said, when he opened the door.

'Of course,' Josephine said. She was a little shocked at the sight of him, although she did her best not to show it. He looked tired and worried and like he might burst into tears.

'Go up,' Michael said, gesturing pointlessly up the stairs she knew so well. 'I'll bring you up a coffee.'

When she didn't find Emily in her bedroom, Josephine's heart started beating a little faster, and she almost called down to Michael to say that she wasn't in the house. Where could her ill sister have gone on such a wintry day? But then she decided to check the spare room, and that was where she found Emily. She looked thin and small in the big bed, her face so pale and her hair a shock against the white sheets.

'Hi Em,' Josephine said.

Emily raised herself up a little and turned her head slowly to fix her gaze on Josephine, and then she smiled a weak smile that didn't reach her eyes. 'Hi,' she said.

'Michael said you haven't been well. What's up?' Josephine took a seat on the side of the bed, careful to avoid Emily's long limbs, which she seemed to have flung out at strange angles.

'It's nothing really,' Emily said. 'I just don't feel great. But I'm getting better.'

Josephine remembered what Michael had said, about her saying she was getting better, about not believing her. She looked away from the bed, unwilling to let Emily see how concerned she was. It was as though this woman in the bed was not her sister. It was like talking to a stranger. 'Why don't you go to see the doctor? Just in case?'

'There's no need,' Emily said. 'I'm fine.'

They sat in silence for a couple of long minutes, and then Emily spoke again. 'Thanks for coming, Jo,' she said. 'But I'm tired. I think I need to get some sleep.'

And so Josephine stood up and walked to the door, her head bowed. 'I love you,' she said from the doorway.

But Emily had already closed her eyes, and Josephine didn't know whether she heard her.

'That was quick,' Michael said, as Josephine walked into the kitchen. 'I've only just finished making your coffee. Do you want some soup?'

Josephine missed Michael's cooking. When the three of them lived together, he had made them all comforting food on winter nights, and they'd locked the doors and windows against the cold.

'I'd love some,' she said. 'Thank you.'

They sat at the kitchen table, the soup steaming before them.

'I'm really worried,' said Michael.

'I'm not surprised. She's not herself at all. She said she needed to sleep but I think she just wanted me out of the room.'

'Yes, she doesn't really want me there either. If she's like this for much longer, I'm going to call a doctor for her.'

Josephine was glad that Emily had someone to take care of her when she wasn't around. She wasn't sure why she and Emily weren't seeing as much of each other as they used to. Some nights, when she was in the flat on her own, Josephine thought about picking up the phone to call Emily, or even wandering over there to see if she was around, but more often than not, she didn't.

'Is something wrong between the two of you?' Michael asked, as though he was reading her thoughts.

'I don't know,' she said. 'I honestly don't.'

Michael nodded, as if to say he understood. He looked old, Josephine thought. The worry had made him look old.

CHAPTER TWENTY-THREE

After six or seven long days in bed, Emily got up and had a shower. She had lost track of time. The days had blurred and merged in a haze of uneaten food and troubled sleep. Her legs felt weak, unsteady, and when she stepped under the hot rush of water she felt, for a moment, as though she might faint. But she steadied herself, resting her palms flat against the wall, and she washed her hair and her face and her body and emerged from the steam scrubbed and clean.

Emily had decided upon waking that morning that it was time to face things. She had allowed herself to wallow, thinking about Jack and feeling guilty about what they had done. But she had seen the pain Michael was in, not knowing what was wrong with her, and she was worried about what he would do to bring her out of that state.

It was time to face Jack, too. He had left a series of messages on her phone, and she had not listened to a single one of them. So that morning, once she was dressed, Emily sat at the kitchen table and listened to what he had been trying to say to her, deleting each message after she had heard it, as she always did with Jack's messages, fearful as she was that Michael might somehow find them.

Em, it's me. I'm guessing you can't pick up. I just wanted to say that I hope you're okay. God, that sounds so stupid. I know you're not okay. I want to be there for you. Let me know what I can do, and when I can see you.

Delete.

Em, it's me. I don't understand why you haven't called back. I'm worried about you. How are you feeling? I know that Michael will be looking after you, but I wish that it was me.

Delete.

Em, please call me. I feel like I'm going mad. I can't sleep. I'm grieving too, don't forget. I need you.

Delete.

Em, Josephine's just gone over to yours. Michael called and said that he was worried about you. I don't know what to do. Please tell me what I can do.

Delete.

Emily had made a decision while she'd lain there in bed, her eyes on the ceiling. Despite the heartache it would cause, she was willing to end her marriage for Jack. She called him, and he answered on the third ring.

'It's me,' she said. 'Can you talk?'

'I'm in the shop but I can take a break. Are you okay? I've been so worried.'

'A little better,' Emily said. She felt as though her voice might crack, so she didn't say anything for a moment. It was talking to Jack that did it. It was talking to him, and knowing how different things might have been with the pregnancy, if they'd just taken the steps they needed to take a bit earlier.

'I'm ready to tell Michael,' she said.

She heard Jack's intake of breath, waited for him to speak.

'Jack?'

'I'm here. Listen, let's get together and talk about this properly…'

Emily felt a lump start to form in her throat. Was it all bullshit, everything he'd said? Did he not really want this, after all? Had she been taken in, and fooled, by someone who just liked the idea of being with two sisters at the same time?

'If you don't want to…' she started to say.

'I didn't say that. I just…we need to think about this. How best to do it. I've just moved into Josephine's flat, for God's sake. I had no idea you were going to suggest something like this.'

Emily was stunned. She'd thought he was just waiting, for her to agree. All those times, he'd stressed that he wasn't tied in the way that she was. He'd made it seem as though he was waiting, as though he would be ready whenever she was.

'Forget I said anything,' Emily said, hanging up the phone.

Jack called back three or four times, but she didn't answer. And she didn't look at the messages he sent. Perhaps she'd got it all wrong. And that idea was terrifying.

* * *

JOSEPHINE WASN'T sure whether or not Emily was better, or quite what was going on between them, so she decided to turn up unannounced and see how her sister greeted her. She took the tube to Clapham after work, emerged from the station into the crisp air, and called Ben.

'Hey, Jo,' he said. 'What's up?'

His voice relaxed her a little, as it always did. She felt a tug, a wish to see him. He was like home to her.

'I'm on my way to Emily's. Things are weird between us. Have you seen her recently?'

'No, not for ages. But she was acting strange when you came over for dinner.'

'It's got worse. I'm on my way over to talk to her about it. I knew things would change when she got married, but we barely see each other and she never calls.'

'Do you think it's about Jack?' Ben asked.

'What about him?'

'I don't know. It's just, he's the only thing that's changed, isn't he? Yes, she got married, but Michael had been around for so long. Jack's new.'

Josephine didn't know what to say for a moment. She thought about Jack and Emily, about the times they'd all been together.

'I have to go,' she said. 'I'm almost at the house. But can we get together? Just you and me?'

'Of course. I hope it's okay, with Emily.'

Emily opened the door as soon as Josephine knocked, as though she'd been waiting there for her sister. She looked better, the colour returned to her cheeks, but utterly miserable.

'Hi,' Emily said. 'Come in.'

The warmth of the house was such a shock after the cold outside that Josephine felt a little too hot. She pulled at her scarf and shrugged off her coat. She didn't know where to start, now that she was here. She didn't know how to put it.

'Are you better?' she asked.

'Yes, thanks. I'm sorry about when you came over, I was so exhausted. I just didn't want to talk to anyone.'

'That's okay.'

Emily ushered her in to the lounge and they sat down. Once, Emily would have taken Josephine in her arms on the doorstep. Once, they would have laughed and chatted and Josephine would have gone into the kitchen to help herself to a coffee or a glass of wine.

'There's something wrong,' Josephine said. And then she paused, still unsure.

'With you?' Emily asked, her face lined with worry.

'No, that's not what I mean. I mean with us.'

Josephine watched for her sister's reaction. Like everything else, it wasn't what it should have been. She was trying to smile, trying to pretend there was nothing going on.

'I think I know what it is,' Josephine said. 'I'm pretty sure I know what it is.'

'What?' Emily's voice was barely more than a whisper.

'It's Jack, isn't it? It's all been since I started seeing him. You don't like him.'

Emily looked sad, and Josephine was reminded of a time when they were teenagers. Was she thirteen? Fourteen? She'd had this new friend, Kate, who'd moved down from somewhere in Yorkshire. Kate was much bolder than Josephine. They'd started going into town together and Kate had stolen some make-up, and somehow Emily had known. She'd ignored Josephine for over a week. When Josephine had asked her why, Emily had said that she didn't like Kate. That she didn't feel she was the right kind of friend for Josephine. It was the kind of thing a parent would say. Back then, Josephine had laughed and ignored her sister, and later that friendship had fallen apart when Kate had blamed Josephine for something she'd done. Emily had never once gloated about being right.

Since their mother had left, Emily had been more protective over Josephine than ever. She was the big sister, and Josephine had been parentless, essentially. So perhaps Emily didn't think Jack was right for her, and she was doing what she could to disrupt their relationship. It was sweet in a way, Josephine thought, but it was unnecessary.

'I do like him,' Emily said, eventually. But the pause had been too long. It had told its own story.

'Look,' Josephine said. She took a deep breath. She knew that she couldn't take words back once she'd said them. 'You're my best friend, Em. You're my only family. But this is right — this thing with Jack. I love him. And I don't need you to act like an overprotective parent about it. It breaks my heart that the two of you can't get on the way I'd like you to, but I'm not going to end things over it. So you need to start thinking about whether you want us in your life.'

She didn't wait for Emily's reaction. She spun around and went to the door, let herself out. And when she was halfway down the road to the tube station, she realised that Emily hadn't called out after her or tried to get her to stop.

CHAPTER TWENTY-FOUR

Josephine stood outside her father's flat and knocked. It was familiar to her by then, the big door with the row of names and buttons to press, the long corridor with the pristine grey carpet, and then his door, the number nine not quite straight.

She could tell something was wrong as soon as he opened the door.

'Come in,' he said. 'I'll make you some tea.'

'What is it?' she asked. 'Is something wrong?'

Perhaps he was going to tell her he was ill. How would she feel about that, with him having come so recently into her life? She didn't think she would know until he said the words.

'Sit down,' he said.

Josephine wanted to shout at him to answer her question, but instead, she waited and took the cup of tea he brought out to her. She scanned the room for a coaster to stop herself from screaming into all the silence.

When he'd called, Josephine had felt like they'd crossed some invisible barrier, and that he now felt he could ask her over without needing an excuse. But she could see, now, that that wasn't the case. He had something he wanted to say to her. He was nervous, his hands never still. Josephine sipped at her tea. What was it? Perhaps he was going to say he didn't want to continue with this relationship they were building. Just like with an imagined illness, Josephine had no idea how she would feel about that.

'I've got something to tell you,' he said, at last. 'But it's difficult. I don't know how to say it.'

Josephine wondered whether she should say or do something to make this easier. But she didn't know what. She said nothing, kept her eyes on his, and waited for him to speak again.

'It's Jack,' he said.

Jack? What could he possibly have to say to her about Jack? He had only met him once, at Emily's New Year party. Surely he wasn't going to say that he disapproved, as though she were a teenager and he a concerned father. It was much too late for all that. 'What about him?' she asked, and she heard the sharpness in her voice.

'Well, I was in town the other day, and I saw him.'

'He hasn't said anything.'

'Well no, he wouldn't. He didn't see me.'

Josephine felt impatient. He wasn't making any sense. Why would he see Jack and not say hello? But she could see that Peter was finding this difficult. He had left his own tea on the coffee table, abandoned, and he was wringing his hands, looking from them to her, nervously.

'There's no easy way to say it,' he said then. 'He was with another woman. I saw them kissing.'

Josephine's instinct was to be angry. Not with Jack, but with her father. He was mistaken. How dare he assume that Jack would do something like that?

'You're wrong,' she said.

'No. I got a good look at him. At both of them. And…'

She watched Peter put his head in his hands for a moment. 'I'm so sorry, love,' he said. 'The woman he was with — it was Emily.'

Josephine put her hand to her mouth, and in doing so, she

caught the handle of her mug, and it fell. Avoiding her dad's eyes, she watched the mug crack into pieces as the murky liquid dripped from the edge of the table and spread across the wooden floor.

JOSEPHINE WENT straight to the bookshop because that's where Jack was. That's where he'd been heading when he kissed her goodbye that morning; that's what he had said. And Josephine had believed him, just as she had always believed everything he'd told her. Now, for the first time, there was a tiny kernel of doubt, uncurling, growing. And she hated her father for putting it there.

Jack's manager, Tim, was behind the counter, tapping codes into the computer. The bookshop was warm and Josephine unbuttoned her coat as she took in the scene. There were two customers in the shop, both quietly browsing in the fiction section, and a young girl wheeling a book trolley away from the counter. No Jack. But he could be on a break, having a cigarette or in the toilet or reading in the staff room.

Tim looked up and smiled as Josephine reached the counter. 'Josephine,' he said. 'To what do we owe the pleasure?'

'I'm looking for Jack,' she said, struggling to keep her voice from sounding shrill.

Tim frowned. 'He's not in today,' he said. 'I thought he was spending the day with you.'

Josephine was too warm. She pulled her coat off. 'Is that what he said?'

'Well, no,' Tim said. 'I suppose I just assumed.'

'Okay, thanks,' she told him, her voice cracking. Did she have it in her to make a fuss, to shout and accuse?

'Hey, Josephine, are you okay? You look pale.'

Josephine felt weak, and she thought that she would fall, but Tim dashed out from behind the counter and took hold of her arms at the elbows. 'Come into the staff room for a few minutes,' he said, guiding her gently through the door.

The staff room was untidy and cluttered. There was a row of metal lockers against one wall, the kind you see in schools, each one labelled with the name of its owner. Josephine sought out Jack's locker and wondered what was inside. What did she really know about him? She didn't know where he was, what he was doing, who he was with.

'Do you want a cup of tea or something?' Tim asked, looking around for a clean mug.

'I'm fine,' Josephine said. 'I felt a bit faint, but I'm fine now. I'll just sit here for a couple of minutes and then I'll go.'

'You sure?'

She smiled and nodded.

'Don't worry,' he said. 'I'm sure you'll track him down.'

Next stop was Emily's house. As she approached, Josephine felt sick with the anticipation of what she might discover inside. The options weren't good. Either it was true, or her father was lying to her. And why would he? What could possibly be in it for him? He said he'd seen them, that there was no mistaking it. But maybe he'd got it wrong. Misread the signs. Or maybe it wasn't them at all. Josephine hoped with all her strength that somewhere in London there was a couple who looked a lot like her sister and Jack. She remembered the couple she and Michael had seen in Southampton who had looked like them. But there was still the question of why Jack wasn't where he'd said he'd be.

On the front porch, Josephine raised her hand to ring the doorbell and then stopped herself, her arm frozen in mid-air. If they were here, she reasoned, they might not answer the door, and even if they did, they would look out to see who it was first. They would compose themselves, concoct a story. She would have to let herself in. Sneak around her mother's house like a thief. Josephine took the key from her bag and her hands shook slightly as she tried to fit in into the lock. She stopped for a moment and tried to calm herself. On the second attempt, she slid in the key and turned it easily, and she was inside.

Josephine didn't hear or see anything at first, and she wondered what she had expected. She crept into the lounge, and for a second she saw the room as it had been, with the piano in the corner, and she remembered sitting there, practising, while Emily read on the sofa. Then she blinked, and it was back to normal, that old piano long gone. Emily and Michael's wedding photo above the fireplace, and on the sideboard, a framed photo of her and her sister, taken on a beach in Cornwall, their arms thrown around each other and their hair flying. In the kitchen, the tap was dripping intermittently, the drops slowly forming until their weight became too much, and they fell. The sound was a slow torture. Josephine reached over and turned the tap sharply, and the dripping stopped.

She made her way up the stairs. It was on the fifth step that she heard it. Later, she was amazed at the fact that she remembered that small detail. It didn't make it any better or worse, any harder or easier to bear. The sound Josephine heard was faint and muffled, a quiet whimper. By the time she reached the eighth step she had convinced herself that she'd imagined it, but then it was there, again. Slightly louder. There was an urgency to it, and it lay somewhere between extreme pleasure and slight pain. And it was coming from the spare bedroom.

Outside the door, Josephine stopped, trying to regulate her breathing without making any sound. It wasn't too late to turn back, to return to her flat and wait for Jack to come in the door, kiss her and tell her about his day. She thought that, at this point, she could still choose to simply not know. But it wasn't true, not really. That easy state had been robbed from her, and now the only choice she had was between suspicion and knowledge.

Josephine knelt and moved towards the keyhole until she could feel her eyelashes scraping against it. And she saw Emily sitting astride a naked man, her hips thrusting back and forth, the man obscured by the high foot of the bed. She pulled back, instinctively, still feeling guilty for intruding despite the circumstances. One of her questions was answered, for she could see that it wasn't Michael. But was it — could it be — Jack? Her Jack, who brought her a cup of tea in bed each morning and left little notes around the flat for her to find? Who had listened sympathetically when she told him how inferior she sometimes felt around her sister? Josephine turned her head to left and right, trying to get a look at the man beneath her sister. And then she heard a low, lengthy groan and she was left in no doubt.

She pulled herself back from the door and sank down on the top step. She wanted to stay there and give in to her need to weep, but she knew she had to get out of the house. She forced herself back to standing and went down the stairs and along the hall. The door clicked as she pulled it shut behind her, but she knew they wouldn't hear it. She was on the pavement before she knew she was crying and then a wave of nausea crashed over her — hard and unrelenting — and she crouched and vomited violently in the gutter. As soon as she felt strong enough to stand, Josephine rushed back to her flat, not wanting anyone to see what she'd been reduced to.

When she got home, Josephine closed and bolted the door and leaned against it, breathing heavily. She'd almost run there, needing to feel safe. She'd never known pain like this. Not when she'd found out the truth about her father as a child, not when her mother disappeared from her life. She felt ashamed for a moment — that she'd let a man's infidelity cause her pain this deep. That she'd afforded him that amount of power. But there was no room for shame. Just one hurt piled on top of another as she painstakingly went over every second the three of them had spent together. Every conversation she'd had with Jack in which her sister's name had been spoken. She was dealing with a double betrayal. Which was worse? Him, or her. Her sister, her family, her friend. How did she justify it to herself? How did he?

Jack didn't come over that evening, and he didn't call. Josephine couldn't remember whether they'd talked about it; she couldn't connect with the person she'd been that morning, when they might have casually discussed their evening plans. Who was that woman, with the happy relationship? Who didn't know she was being made a fool of. She wasn't ready to confront him, to let him see what he and Emily had done. She ate nothing that night and drank a bottle of wine and pored unhealthily over photos and memories, shifting everything she believed in to make space for this new, awful fact. Sometime in the late evening, she thought to wonder whether Michael could possibly know, and realised almost immediately that he couldn't. He wouldn't stand by and live with something like this, he wasn't that type. But was Josephine? She could be, she decided. She might be.

By the time the sun started coming up on her first full day of knowing, Josephine had resolved that she wouldn't say anything. There would be no confrontation with him, or with her. She would be controlled and calm, and she would let this thing — whatever it was — run its course. Jack loved her, and Emily loved Michael. She believed that. It was a mistake, this affair. Dirty, sordid, without meaning. Josephine would ignore this feeling of cracking in two and wait for it to be over.

CHAPTER TWENTY-FIVE

Emily was angry with herself for letting Jack in again. The previous day, he'd turned up after she got home from school, as she'd known he would. He'd apologised for that phone call when she'd said she was ready to leave Michael and he had stalled. And she'd let him come inside and taken him upstairs and now her certainty that it was over was shaken. That decision that had seemed so clear. Now, she wasn't sure where they were, or what she wanted.

Something was nagging at her, too. After Jack had gone home, after Michael had arrived and they'd had dinner and gone into the lounge to sit down, she'd noticed that one of the photos on the sideboard had moved. It was one of her and Josephine, taken a few years ago on a trip to Cornwall. It was one of her favourites. And it wasn't in the right place. Someone had moved it, put it behind a picture of her and Michael. She'd asked Michael, and he'd shaken his head and said he hadn't touched it. It bothered her.

It was Saturday morning and Emily was moving around the house, trying to find things to do that would distract her for a moment from the mess she'd made. It was impossible, she thought. The web was too tangled. Josephine had come over and said that she loved Jack. Jack might be the one, the love of Emily's life, but it was impossible. She shut herself in her bedroom and called him, arranged to meet him in an hour. Michael was at the library so she didn't have to look at him and lie.

She would let him go. She would let Jack go and she would make her marriage work. It wasn't a bad marriage. And if she respected it and worked at it, perhaps it could be enough.

Outside, it was one of those very cold, very clear days you get when winter is coming to an end. Emily had forgotten her gloves and her hands were numb by the time she reached the tube. But still, she could feel that things were changing, that it would soon be spring, and she was grateful for that. It was a good day to have woken out of the slumber she'd been in for months.

Emily ordered two coffees and waited for Jack to arrive, and when he pushed the door open, her heart jumped a little. She almost panicked and ran past him, out on to the street. But instead, she held on to her chair and she made herself stay very still.

'Hello,' Jack said. He leaned down to kiss her and she turned her face away. If she let him touch her, she knew, she would not be able to go through with this. And she needed to, for all of their sakes.

And then she looked at his face and she knew that he knew why they were there. He looked hurt, and she tried to ignore it, tried to focus on the fact that she was going to prevent them all from hurting so much more in the long run. She was trying to avoid seeing that same look on her sister's face, and on Michael's.

'Don't do this,' Jack said. 'Please.'

'I have to,' she said. 'We have to. Please understand.'

'No. Let me know what I have to do to change your mind. I'll do anything. When you called, Emily, you took me by surprise. That's all. I don't have any doubts. I'm ready to do this properly.'

Emily looked around her to see whether other people were

listening. They weren't. They were lost in their own lives, not caring about hers. Not caring that she was throwing everything away, tearing herself in two.

'I can't do this here,' Jack said. 'Let's go for a walk.'

They left their coffees on the table and she let him lead her to Soho Square. A couple of times, he tried to take her hand in his, and she curled her hand into a fist to prevent him. She didn't let him touch her, but she let him talk.

'Just think about this, Em. We could be together, if we give it some time. I know it won't be easy, but we can get through it together. We'll tell them, just like you said we would.'

'It would break their hearts,' she said.

'But the alternative is to break our hearts. I've never had anything like this. Have you? I don't want to give up on it because it's inconvenient.'

'It's different for me. Josephine is my sister. I love her. And I'm married. I made promises to Michael.'

They sat down on a bench and Jack looked at her for a long time without saying anything. And when he leaned forward to kiss her, she thought she would stop him, but she didn't. It was a searching kiss, one that reminded her of just what she could have, if things were different. She closed her eyes and let it happen, knowing that it wouldn't help her to say goodbye. Knowing she was giving him an extra piece of herself to take away, and wondering what would be left when they had finished.

SHE WAS ABOUT to get on the tube home when she glanced at her watch and saw the date. It was Michael's birthday. She had forgotten his birthday. It was something she couldn't have imagined doing, a few months ago. She had moved so far from the woman she used to be.

But perhaps it was salvageable. Michael had left with his laptop for the library before she had woken. He didn't have to know that she had forgotten. On a whim, she stopped outside a travel agent's and saw images of deserted beaches and city landmarks, and it seemed that perhaps that was what they needed. Some time away in a new and distant place. Together, alone. A week with no work and no distractions. And no Jack. It wasn't what she wanted, but it was what Michael deserved. The very least he deserved. She stepped inside.

When she heard Michael's key in the lock, Emily was icing a cake she had baked for him. 'Happy birthday,' she said, as he entered the kitchen.

She saw his face break into a smile, even before the cake and the holiday she had booked for them. All he really wanted was her. And it was the one thing she wasn't sure she could give him. She hugged him, and it felt strange, their bodies so close. It had been a long time since she'd felt the solidness of him. The scent of him, of his neck, was both familiar and strange. It was like going home, but knowing that you can't stay.

Emily waited until they were eating dinner, their champagne glasses full, to tell Michael about the holiday. 'Can you get a week off work?' she asked.

'I think so. When?'

'Because we're going away. Not for ages. July. I've booked us a week in Barcelona.'

She had booked it to coincide with their first wedding anniversary. It seemed almost impossible that less than a year had passed since they'd made those promises. Could they start again, under the Spanish sun? Could she forget all the mistakes she had made and remember how it had been, before?

'Thank you,' Michael said. 'It's a wonderful surprise.'

* * *

ON THE EVENING of his thirty-eighth birthday, Michael was feeling content, sitting there in his living room with Emily, a bottle of wine and the remainder of the cake Emily had baked on the table. Something had shifted. The distance between him and Emily had shrunk, and they had a whole week in a new city to look forward to. He didn't know what had changed, and he didn't want to dwell on it. It was enough that he'd had this day, with this thoughtful present, and the woman he loved.

Michael hadn't yet told Emily, but that day, in the library, he had finished his novel. He had made his final revisions, and he was happy with it. Before closing down his laptop and coming home, he had emailed it to Alex with a brief note: *Sorry it's been so long coming. I hope you like it.* But he already knew that he had produced something to be proud of. Things were coming together, working out.

He didn't want the evening to end, but by eleven o'clock, Emily said that she was getting tired.

'I'll clear up,' Michael said, picking up the cake tray and gathering their empty glasses.

'No, leave it. Let me do it.'

And so Michael sat in the armchair and let Emily clear things away around him until everything was clean and neat. He was edging closer to forty. He had thought, once, that he would have a child by this age. He had thought he might be a famous novelist. But he'd never thought, back when he was in his twenties and believed that he could have anything he wanted, that he would love someone the way he loved Emily. That he would find someone who would make everything a little clearer, a little lighter.

But somewhere inside, his childlessness — their childlessness — gnawed at him. He felt ready to guide someone through life, now. He felt ready to see what a combination of himself and Emily might look like, might be like.

It wasn't the right time to bring it up, he knew that. The last time he had suggested it, Emily hadn't really said yes or no. And things had been very uncertain for a while, and they were only just starting to turn around.

So perhaps he would mention it in Barcelona. Michael imagined them there, lying close in bed with the sheet thrown off because of the lingering heat of the day, and he imagined whispering to her. *Let's have a baby.* At New Year, she had brushed him off. He would ask her again, make her understand that he was serious, that he was really ready.

Michael imagined how Emily might look, towards the end of a pregnancy. He closed his eyes and envisaged them on the sofa in this very room. Her, glowing and rounded, and him, resting his ear against the hardness of her swelling belly, and then turning his head to whisper secrets to his baby through her skin.

And then he tried to picture the baby that would emerge, their baby, and he wondered whose eyes it would have, whose bone structure, whose lips. He considered the responsibility that he would feel, of having someone to take care of forever, of having someone rely on him in order to learn how to walk, and talk, and how to be. He wasn't so naïve as to believe that he wouldn't make any mistakes, but he promised himself that any false moves he made would be made out of loving too much, and not too little.

Michael moved from the armchair to the sofa, stretched out, and closed his eyes again. In as little as a year, he thought, their lives could be completely different. There could be a new life. And this house that was too big for the two of them would be altered to accommodate a new inhabitant, and there would be cupboards full of toys and books and all the equipment that went along with having a baby.

He dared to imagine a son, skinny and quick, who he would play ball with in the daytime and read to at night. Who would come to him with questions about things he'd seen on television and heard in the playground. Who would trust that his answers were correct. He imagined a daughter with Emily's fiery hair and her pale, freckled skin. He would teach her to write, showing her how to hold a pencil — not too tight — and sit patiently while she learned to form the letters in her name. He would teach her how to tell the time and tie her shoelaces. He would teach her to swim, letting go of her slippery limbs and waiting — breath held — ready to catch her if she started to struggle.

And that is how Michael fell asleep that night, on the sofa with his head full of thoughts of the future. When he woke, more than an hour had passed, and the house was in darkness. He made his way upstairs, still half-asleep, and climbed into bed beside Emily. And curled around her as though he were her shell.

CHAPTER TWENTY-SIX

Lying beside Jack, Josephine dreamed about her mother. It was to be expected really; her mother had been much on her mind since she'd started spending time with her father.

Josephine had found photos of her mother, Alice, aged twenty or so, when she was a child, and was astonished by how beautiful and elegant she was. This woman, who was the only parent Josephine and Emily had ever known, who cooked and mentored and cleaned and disciplined and advised and clothed the two of them, had once been something entirely different. It was a shock, although it shouldn't have been

In the dream, Alice was younger than Josephine had ever known her to be. Younger even than Josephine was now.

'Mum,' Josephine called out when she spotted her.

They were in a park on a warm spring day and it was bustling with bodies, alive with music and talk.

Alice turned at the sound of Josephine's voice, and then she laughed and began moving further away. She was wearing a red dress Josephine had never seen. It was loose and flowing, skimming the ground. Her feet were bare. Her blonde hair long and loose.

'Mum,' Josephine called again, a little louder. She quickened her pace, worried that she'd lose her mother in the crowd.

This time, Alice didn't turn. Josephine broke into a run, and as she dashed forward, keeping an eye on the red flashes of her mother's dress, she started listing the questions she'd ask her once she caught up. Everything felt fuzzy and muddled, and she couldn't make her thoughts line up straight.

'Did you ever love my father the way you loved Emily's?' Josephine shouted. And then, as she waited for her mother to turn, she caught her foot against a tree stump and stumbled, fell. She scrambled to her feet but Alice was no longer in sight. Josephine ran faster, her breath coming hard and shallow. She pushed people out of her way and they fell to the ground like dominoes.

'Did you ever love me the way you loved Emily?' she screamed into the crowd.

She woke up sweating and cold.

'Jo? What is it?' Jack's voice was full of what sounded like real concern.

'Did I scream something?' Josephine asked.

'You were screaming. I couldn't make out any words. Bad dream?'

Josephine turned to him. Her eyes were adjusting to the dark and she could make out parts of his face, but his eyes were in shadow. 'I can't remember,' she lied. She felt her heartbeat start to return to normal, but she was a long way from feeling calm.

Jack sat up and pulled her across to his side of the bed, held her tightly in his arms. And for a moment, Josephine felt like it might be all right. She felt like she might be able to forget.

When Josephine's alarm woke her, she reached out for Jack and felt cold sheets. Before getting in the shower, she went downstairs and found him sprawled out on the sofa, dressed, asleep. It had happened before. She knew he didn't always sleep well, but it was something she couldn't easily relate to. On weekend mornings, she would often sleep until ten or eleven, and, on waking, would find that Jack had already been out to get a paper, and eaten breakfast, and sometimes tidied the flat.

But why had he got dressed? Had he been out, or planned to? She felt a surge of panic, knowing what she knew, until she remembered that Michael was at home, so he couldn't possibly have been with Emily.

Josephine saw her laptop on the kitchen table as soon as she entered the room. She kept it in the living room, in its case. What had Jack had used it for, in the early hours of the morning? Then Jack appeared, his face creased from the sofa cushions, just as she was pouring out water for her coffee.

'Do you want one?' she asked.

He shook his head. 'I need to get going.' And then he gestured to the sofa. 'I couldn't sleep.'

Josephine saw that his eyes landed on the laptop and then looked away, uncomfortable. As soon as she heard him pull the door closed behind him, she took her coffee and the laptop into the living room and opened up Jack's emails. She scanned his inbox for her sister's name, and then she went to sent items. And that's where she found it.

Emily, I can't sleep. It's worse than ever. The only times I sleep soundly now are when I'm beside you. I keep picturing you with him, and it doesn't seem like that's where you belong. It may be selfish and stupid of me to put this down in writing, but I don't feel like I have any choice. I love you, Emily. That's what it comes down to in the end. Jack.

So it wasn't a fling. It wasn't something insignificant, something small. Josephine felt the tears hot on her cheeks, pushed the heels of her hands against her eyes as if to try to force them back inside.

There was a bus that went to the end of her father's road. It took longer than the tube, but Josephine preferred to watch where she was going, rather than being stuck underground among the morning commuters. She didn't open her book and she didn't check her phone for messages. She just sat on the top deck beside the window, watching the houses and shops rush past, hoping to find her father at home. If she didn't do this now, she knew that she might back out, change her mind.

Peter answered the door seconds after she rang the bell. Perhaps he'd seen her get off the bus and make her way towards his house because his face didn't match the surprise in his words.

'I didn't expect to see you again so soon,' he said. 'Come in'.

Josephine stepped inside and followed him into the living room. She took her coat off and hung it on the back of a chair. 'You were right,' she said. 'And I'm ready to listen now.'

Once they were settled in the lounge with mugs of coffee, Peter looked at her with sympathy in his eyes.

'Listen,' he said, 'I told you what I saw, there's nothing else. But it didn't seem like a one-off to me. It didn't seem like a fling.'

'It isn't,' Josephine said. When she closed her eyes, she could see the words of the email behind her eyelids. She started to cry. She wasn't quite comfortable enough with Peter yet to cry in front of him, but there was no stopping it.

'Oh love,' he said. 'I don't want to see you hurt. You know, I've been thinking about this a lot since I saw them. I stayed with my wife for years when I knew I didn't love her anymore, and it wasn't fair. Don't let Jack do that to you. Give yourself a chance to be happy.'

Josephine nodded through her tears. He was right. She couldn't let it go on like that, couldn't pretend anymore. She could feel some of the sadness inside her turning into rage.

CHAPTER TWENTY-SEVEN

Michael and Emily were eating breakfast when he asked her. Toast spread thickly with jam, mugs of tea. Winter sun was streaming in through the kitchen window and lighting up Emily's face, and he could see some lines around her eyes and her lips that he hadn't noticed before. She looked beautiful. And suddenly, he wasn't sure what he was waiting for.

'What do you think, Em, about trying for a baby?'

He saw Emily wince, and he wished he could take the words back. He'd thought everything was okay, and he wasn't ready to find out it wasn't. He kept his eyes on her, watched her fumble for the right thing to say.

'I'm not sure I'm ready,' she said, and shrugged her shoulders.

Michael saw the shrug for what it was: an attempt to appear casual. She was trying not to rock the boat, not to worry him. But her eyes were pure panic. I know you, he wanted to say. Why won't you tell me the truth?

'Do you think you ever will be?' he asked. The last time, he'd let her shrug the question off, but they couldn't go on like that indefinitely.

'I don't know,' Emily said, then. 'How do you know, for sure? It's not the kind of thing you want to make a mistake about.'

Michael thought about that. It felt like something he'd always known, that he wanted to create a family, but when he searched back, he saw that it wasn't quite like that. When he was young, in his early twenties, he'd had a string of casual relationships. He'd moved easily from one to the next, never settling down, never feeling anything much stronger than affection and lust. And back then, he hadn't known, had he? Back then, if one of those women, whose faces he couldn't quite make out in his mind, had come to him and said that she was pregnant, he would have been terrified. But he didn't think it was an age thing. He thought it was a person thing. Ever since he'd been with Emily, he'd felt sure. Even when they'd been in the early days of their relationship, an unexpected pregnancy wouldn't have fazed him.

So what did it mean, for him and Emily, that she still wasn't sure? After they'd been together for so long, and exchanged vows, and promised to live their lives side by side. Part of him didn't want to dwell on it. But there was a bigger part that knew they'd reached a crescendo of sorts, here, and he needed to shine a light into the dark corners, even if he didn't know what he might find there.

It was Michael's turn to shrug. 'I think you just know when you know,' he said.

Emily smiled a half smile. She didn't want to hurt him. He could see that. And that was good. But it wasn't enough to keep him satisfied. Not anymore.

'Emily,' he said, and even then, he wasn't sure he was going to do it. Even then, he might easily have called a halt to it, and gone in another, less heartbreaking, direction.

'What?' She looked uncomfortable. It was right, he thought, that she was a little uncomfortable.

'Do you still love me?'

Emily took a sharp breath in, and Michael forced himself to

keep looking at her. It was his last chance to really look at her without knowing the answer to that question. If he was going to lose her, he needed to memorise her face, her expressions, her movements. The wait for her to reply felt endless, and he wondered how she could be so cruel, so reckless with his heart. She knew how he felt, after all. He had never wavered.

'I think I do,' she said. Her face was flushed red, and he had a sudden urge to slap her. It shocked him. It shocked him into action; he stood and scraped his chair across the kitchen floor, and in the hallway, he put on his coat and his shoes, and he walked out of the front door without looking back.

Michael didn't know where he could go. He was so far from his family. Emily was his home, his everything. Walking out on her left him without options. So he walked, tears building and then falling, his head down against the wind. He walked to Clapham Common, and he sat on a bench, his fingers frozen. He watched a young family who were feeding bread to the ducks. The children, two boys, were about two and four, he guessed. They were bundled up in puffy, waterproof suits covered in brightly coloured stars. Their cheeks were pink. Michael watched as their father watched them, reaching out to grab his younger son whenever he got a little too close to the water. Their mother was laughing, but she looked tired and cold. After a few minutes, they turned around and walked away, and Michael imagined they were going home, to sit in front of the fire or perhaps to eat a roast chicken.

It wasn't so much to ask for, to have a family, Michael thought. When he was too cold to sit any longer, he set off for home. Because there was nowhere else. And because Emily hadn't said no, after all. She was in the kitchen when he got there, emptying the dishwasher, and he stood in the doorway and waited for her to acknowledge him.

'I'm sorry,' she said, without looking his way.

'I need you to think about what you want,' he said. 'I need you to make a decision, and let me know.'

Emily met his eyes and nodded. 'I will.'

* * *

EMILY AND MICHAEL avoided one another for the rest of the day. It was easy enough to do, in a big, empty house like theirs. She didn't know what to do or say, so she did load after load of washing, cleaned the bathroom, wiped the surfaces in the kitchen until the house looked cleaner and brighter than it had in a long time. She wasn't sure what Michael was doing. He drifted from room to room, rootless and lost. And then he went to his study and closed the door, and she hoped he was working on his novel, and not just sitting there, hurting.

Had she done the wrong thing, answering his question the way she had? Sometimes there was no right answer. She could have lied, and made him happy, and been miserable herself. As it was, she had half-lied, because she hadn't quite been able to bring herself to shatter her marriage. And even that had been enough to wound him. She could see in his eyes, when he came back from his walk, that he was horribly sad. Emily tried to trace back through their relationship, to identify where it had gone awry. Had she been wrong to go on that very first date with him? To let him start to leave a toothbrush and some clothes at the flat she shared with Josephine? To let him take over the food shopping and cooking until she began to expect to smell dinner when she opened her front door? Had she been wrong to accept his proposal of marriage? She'd had doubts on the wedding day, after all, but it was meeting Jack that had concretised it all. It was falling in love that had made her realise that what she had with Michael was something else, something less.

She hadn't seen Jack since she'd ended things with him and vowed to focus on her marriage. And now, so soon, she'd set something different in motion, spun things an entirely different way, and she had no idea what Jack would think. It might be that he had accepted things, by now. It might be that he didn't want her. That risk was a big one, but Emily had known, that morning at breakfast, that it was just no good, all this pretending and compromise. It simply wasn't going to work. And that was true whether Jack was waiting for her or not.

In the middle of the afternoon, Emily's phone rang, and she jumped at the shrill sound. When she looked at the screen, she saw her sister's name there, and felt that stab of guilt that had become so familiar.

'Hello?' she said.

'Emily, it's me. I need a favour. I want to talk to you and Michael about something. Could we come over, tonight, for dinner? I can bring something.'

'Tonight?' Emily was stalling for time. Because it was impossible, wasn't it, to sit in a room with Jack and Josephine and Michael, with things as they were? But she couldn't think of a single reason to say no. And she couldn't bear to refuse her sister a favour, after all she had done to her.

'No need,' she said. 'Come at seven.'

It was only after they'd hung up that Emily thought to wonder what Josephine might want to talk to them about. She hoped it was good news. She'd always hoped for good things for Josephine, even as she was actively sabotaging her sister's happiness. Emily went upstairs and stood outside Michael's office door, building up the courage to knock. She could hear the click of his fingers on the keyboard, a flurry of tapping and then a long silence. She waited for one of those silences before knocking and going into the room.

'Josephine called,' she said. 'She asked if her and Jack can come for dinner tonight. She wants to talk to us.'

Michael looked at her, his gaze even. 'What did you say?'

Emily smiled a little tightly. 'I said yes. I didn't know how to say anything else. But look, you don't need to do anything. I'll go to the supermarket now and buy the food, and then I'll get it ready. I'll just do something simple. And we'll just get through it, and tomorrow we'll talk, okay?'

Michael nodded and turned back to his computer screen. Emily wondered about his book. She hadn't asked much about it. She'd wanted to wait until it was finished before reading it. Would she ever get to read it now? Would he ever want to know what she thought of it? And would she be able to bring herself to read all those words he'd strung together, over the months and years he'd loved her?

Despite seeming like an obstacle to overcome, the dinner gave Emily plenty of reasons to stay busy for the rest of the day. She went to the supermarket around the corner and struggled back with four heavy bags. And then she made a vegetable soup, and a lasagne, and a chocolate pudding. She put white wine in the fridge to chill, and she set the table. And all the time, she thought about what she would say to Michael the next day, how she would break the news that would rip them from one another. Without knowing how Jack now felt, she thought it might be better to leave her infidelity out of it, for now. To tell Michael that she had just fallen out of love. She could picture the way his face would change when she said it, and she felt her stomach twist with dread. But it was one of those things she couldn't avoid forever, and she'd put it off long enough.

When the doorbell rang at seven, Michael still hadn't emerged from his office, and Emily had started to feel sick with worry. What were they doing, hosting a dinner party when they were in the middle of this crisis? Why hadn't she said it wasn't possible? She started to go to the door, but heard Michael on the stairs, and by the time she reached the hallway, he was at the door. She stood back, listening to him greeting their guests, waiting to hear a crack in his voice. But there was nothing. When Josephine and Jack came inside and removed their coats, Emily tried to smile at them. Jack looked at her, and she thought she saw a warning in his eyes. But she wasn't sure what he was trying to tell her. He looked sad. They all looked sad.

'Hi,' Emily said. 'Come through.' She turned and they all walked into the living room in a strange little line. Nothing felt right, or normal.

'Can I get anyone a drink?' Michael asked.

'Yes please,' Josephine said. 'I'll have a glass of wine.'

And then she looked over at Emily and her eyes were flashing with anger. And Emily knew that this was not a dinner party at all, but a reckoning.

CHAPTER TWENTY-EIGHT

Josephine watched as her sister brought out bowls of steaming soup, her hands shaking slightly. There was something going on between Emily and Michael, she thought. They weren't looking at each other. Usually, he watched Emily almost constantly. And tonight he was looking anywhere but at his wife. Michael was her concern in all of this. She wasn't the one who was breaking his heart, but she was the one who was going to set things in motion. And he didn't deserve what she was about to do.

'So,' Josephine said, letting the silence gather and grow. 'I said I wanted to talk to you about something, right? Anyone want to guess?'

Emily didn't answer. She was looking down at the food in front of her, very still.

'What's going on, Josephine?' Michael asked. 'Are you okay?'

'I'm not, Michael,' she said. 'I'm not okay. Emily knows why I'm not okay.'

Michael turned to face Emily, but Emily kept on looking down, her hair obscuring her face. Jack cleared his throat, and Josephine's head snapped round to him.

'Oh, Jack knows too, of course,' she said. She took a long slug of wine and leaned back in her chair. 'Anyone care to fill Michael in? Anyone want to tell him why I'm not okay?'

'Jo,' Emily said, her voice a plea.

'Don't you dare call me that.'

Michael reached across the table and put a hand over Josephine's. 'What's going on here?' he asked.

Josephine envied him the time he'd had of not knowing. She felt like she'd known forever. The knowing was sitting inside her stomach, getting heavier and heavier. She felt like it was dragging her to the ground.

'Is there more wine?' Josephine asked. She didn't wait for an answer. She stood and went through to the kitchen, opened the fridge. Inside, she saw little hints of Michael and Emily's lives together. The strong cheese they both liked, Michael's Greek yoghurt, a leftover portion of pasta. She took the open bottle of white from the door and filled her glass almost to the brim.

When she returned to the dining room, Michael was sitting up very straight in his chair. As if asserting his authority, claiming his territory. Not for long, she thought.

'Josephine,' he said. 'Just tell us what's going on here, please.'

No one had touched the soup. In the middle of the table, Emily had placed a basket of crusty bread and a butter dish. The bowls had stopped steaming, and Josephine wondered whether the soup would burn Emily, if she picked up her bowl and threw its contents in her face.

'It's your *wife*,' Josephine said, looking at Michael and stressing the final word. 'Your wife has been fucking someone else behind your back.'

Michael's face was pure shock. He turned to Emily, as if he were asking her to deny it. She looked up at last.

'Don't do this, Jo,' she pleaded. 'Not like this.'

'Oh, not like this?' Josephine asked. 'Forgive me, Emily, but I don't know how you're supposed to react to your sister fucking your boyfriend. Tell me, what's the etiquette here?'

* * *

HOW LONG HAD JOSEPHINE KNOWN? Jack tried to think back over their last few days together, to search for any indication. But there was nothing. So she'd held this inside, hidden it. And now she was letting it out. Jack could take it, but he didn't know whether Emily could. He knew that looking over at her could make things worse, but he couldn't help it. He had to know how she was faring. Not well. Not well at all. This was the first time they'd been in the same room since she'd told him it was over, and he still didn't believe that it would stick.

'Jo,' Jack said, 'maybe we should go.'

Josephine laughed, and it was a strangled, sad sound. The saddest laugh Jack had ever heard.

'I'm not going anywhere with you,' she said.

And that was when he really knew that it had all fallen down around them. That this was really happening, that Josephine was putting a lit match to their relationship, and to her sister's marriage, and to this foursome they'd become.

Jack turned his head when Michael stood up.

'Emily,' Michael said, his voice full of quiet fury. 'What the hell is going on? Tell me this is some kind of joke.'

Jack looked at Emily intently, waiting for her to speak. He longed to hear her voice, to hear her admit that she loved him, that the two of them would stand and walk out of the wreckage, hand in hand. If only he'd agreed when she suggested telling them, none of them would have had to go through this ordeal. At least, not like this.

'It's true,' Emily said, her eyes on her husband. 'I'm so sorry, Michael.'

'And what about me?' Josephine asked in a clipped, controlled voice. 'Where's my apology?'

Emily turned to her sister and Jack could almost see the years that existed between them, the years and years of closeness. That intimacy was like an old wall that was crumbling. 'I'm sorry,' Emily said. 'Of course I am. We both are.'

Despite it all, despite everything, Jack felt a rush of joy to hear her refer to the two of them as a 'we'.

'You've slept together? You and Jack?' Michael was struggling to come to terms with the truth of it.

'How long?' Josephine asked. 'That's what I don't know.'

Emily looked over at Jack, and there was a plea in her eyes, but he wasn't sure what it was. Did she want him to take over, to speak for them, to answer the questions they had? Or did she want him to lie to them, to try to minimise it, to make out that it was less than what it was?

And where did they stand now? He wanted to know. He wasn't one of the wronged parties, but he wanted to stand up and scream that he needed to know whether there was a chance for them, still.

* * *

MICHAEL FELT like he was falling. Tumbling, the world off its axis, slightly skewed. It was strange, he thought, that people talked about falling in love, when this — this kind of betrayal — felt much more like a fall.

'How long?' he asked. There had been silence since Josephine asked the same question, just a lot of heavy looks between one person and the next.

'Months,' Emily said. 'Almost since we met.'

Michael made an involuntary choking sound. Again, he didn't know where to go. In the kitchen, he got a glass out of a high cupboard, turned the tap on and waited until it ran very cold. He drank a full glass of water, then another. He'd drunk a couple of glasses of wine, and he felt a little fuzzy, and he wanted things to be sharp and clear again. If this was the end of his marriage, of his great love, he wanted to remember it. He wanted to ask why, but he didn't know whether he could bear to hear the answer. Jack was younger than him, he was more attractive. He knew these things. But there must have been more than that, for her to throw away their life together, and he wanted to know what. And at the same time, he didn't. He could hear shouting coming from the dining room. Josephine's voice, loud and furious, all the composure she'd shown earlier disappearing. He went back.

Josephine was crying, her face reddened and her words shaky. She was telling them that she had loved Jack, that she had really believed it was something real. Jack's face gave nothing away, but Emily's was pure pain. And Michael knew she wouldn't do this lightly. She wouldn't hurt him, and her beloved sister, unless it seemed like the only thing to do. Unless she couldn't help it because she was in love.

'Do you love him?' Michael asked, bracing himself for her answer.

Emily looked at Michael, and then at Jack, and Michael saw that Jack was gazing intently at her, desperate to hear her answer. So he loved her, too. It was so obvious, now that he knew. How long had he been blind to this?

'I do,' Emily said. 'I'm sorry. I do.'

'I hate you,' Josephine said into the silence of the room. 'I hate you both. I could never, ever have done anything like this to either of you.'

Michael smelled burning, and Emily must have noticed it at the same time, so they both rushed to the kitchen door, and when their hands touched on the doorknob, Michael felt that her skin was cool, and instinctively he wanted to pull her to him, into his arms. But she flinched at the touch and pulled away. The kitchen was full of smoke, and Michael pulled the lasagne out of the oven while Emily opened a window and waved the smoke away from the smoke alarm with a tea towel. And he wanted to say 'Look how it works with us — how we work together well', but he knew he was too late to plead his case.

Michael was thinking about what Emily had said. That it had been going on for months. How had they missed it, he and Josephine? How had they not seen?

'At Christmas?' he asked Emily, and she nodded.

'When I was writing in Yorkshire?' Another nod.

'I can't tell you it didn't mean anything,' Emily said, quietly.

'Because it did,' Michael said. 'I can see that now.'

* * *

When the smoke had cleared, Emily walked back out of the kitchen. She wanted to ask Josephine what she was still doing there, now that she'd exploded their lives like that. But that wasn't fair, because it wasn't Josephine who'd planted the bomb. She was just the one who'd lit the fuse. And if Josephine left, what would happen next? She'd made it clear that she wouldn't be leaving with Jack. Emily didn't know where they were all going to go, now that they were all broken apart. Would Michael leave too, that very night? Would Emily be left alone in that big house, with the people she loved the most scattered outside, along with the certainties she'd built her life upon?

Michael went upstairs without a word, and Emily heard him moving things around. Packing. Her heart ached for him. And for her, too.

'How does this feel, Jack?' Josephine asked. 'To be here with both sisters. To have slept with everyone in the room?'

'Stop it, Jo,' Jack said, and Emily saw Josephine flinch at the sharpness of his words, even now.

Jack lit a cigarette and Emily longed to ask him for one, but didn't dare. She didn't dare to look at him.

'Josephine,' she said. 'What can I do?' She moved to sit beside her sister and reached to take her hand, but Josephine pulled it away.

'Do you think we can just move past this?' she spat. 'Like the time you lost my doll or when you ruined my favourite dress in the dryer?'

'Of course not,' Emily said. 'But I'll keep trying. Whatever it takes.'

'You know, when Mum first left, I was so sad about it, but I kept thinking at least it wasn't you. At least I still had you. I was so sure you'd never leave me behind.'

'And I wouldn't!'

'But what you've done is so much worse,' Josephine said. 'It's unforgiveable.'

Emily stole a look at Jack and saw that he was looking out of the window. But she knew he was listening. She was glad. She needed him to understand what they'd done. What they'd broken with their carelessness and their selfishness.

Emily heard Michael on the stairs and she waited for him to come into the room and tell her he was leaving. But he didn't. The next thing she heard was the door opening and closing. Not a slam. He was too dignified for that. Just a quiet exit. It didn't feel like the end of a marriage, she thought. But she supposed it wasn't. The marriage had ended long ago, when he wasn't looking. This was just the aftermath. Had he packed an overnight bag or a big suitcase? Would he go to Alex's, or up to Yorkshire, to his family? But it wasn't her business. After years of having access to information about what he was doing and thinking and where he was going, she was cut off.

'I'm going, too,' Josephine said. She turned to Jack. 'Don't you dare to come to the flat. Not tonight, not ever.'

'Josephine,' Jack said, his voice gentle. 'I'll need my things.'

'Fuck you,' Josephine said over her shoulder as she left the room. 'You can get new things.'

When the door closed again, Emily looked over at Jack. The silence stretched out and she felt as though there was no way to break it.

'I don't have anywhere to go,' Jack said.

Emily wanted to ask him to stay with her, but she couldn't. Not that night. She shrugged her shoulders, as if to say that she didn't know what the answer was.

'You can't stay here,' she said.

'But, can I ever? Have you changed your mind?'

Emily knew what he was asking her. Now that Michael had gone, could he, Jack, take her husband's place? And she didn't know what the answer was. She didn't know what to tell him, or what she had left to give, or when she would feel stronger and more able.

'I don't know, Jack,' she said. 'I don't know.'

CHAPTER TWENTY-NINE

Emily had been up all night. She supposed that all four of them had, and she tried to picture them, all in different rooms of different houses when they were usually to be found in pairs, all unable to find any rest. But other than Josephine, she didn't know where they had been. In the early hours of the morning, Michael had sent a message asking to see her, and she had said yes. She had decided that she would do as much as she could for him, to make all this a little easier. She was glad that he'd asked to come over early, because she didn't know how much longer she could stay awake. She felt weak, and brittle, and she thought she might break if he touched her.

Emily didn't know whether Michael would use his key to let himself in, or knock on the door like a stranger, a visitor. She hoped, in a way, that he wouldn't knock, and yet she didn't want to be surprised by his presence, to find him suddenly there in the room, before she was ready. As it happened, Michael knocked and then opened the door, as if to warn her that he was coming. He'd done the right thing, the fair thing, like he always did. Even though she could no longer expect that of him. And Emily was grateful for those seconds, during which she rubbed her face and smoothed her hair and brushed uselessly at her wrinkled dress.

He looked handsome, and tired. It was strange, Emily thought, how you stopped seeing the people you loved, the ones you saw every day. How you stopped noticing them. She saw Michael then as though it was the first time, and she saw a man who had been damaged.

'I was so worried,' she said. She wanted to get up from the sofa and put her arms around him, but she held herself there, determined not to do one more unfair thing to this man.

'Emily,' Michael said. 'Tell me none of it's true.' He was still standing in the doorway, and the sun was shining through the bay window on to his face, illuminating him. He was unshaven and his clothes — the same clothes he'd been wearing the night before — were crumpled. He was a man who had not been home. Perhaps he was a man who no longer had a home.

'I can't,' she said. She couldn't quite make eye contact with him, and so she was grateful for the sunlight that was obscuring his eyes, but then he crossed the room and sat down beside her, and she had to catch her breath when he reached to take her hand.

'Can we fix it?' he asked. 'Do you want to try?'

Emily was amazed that he was asking this, that he was hinting at a willingness to forgive her, but at the same time, she wasn't. It was the same Michael after all, her Michael, who had told her, time and again, that he would do anything to stay with her for the rest of his life.

'I don't think so,' she said. 'I love him.' It was hard to say, but she owed Michael the truth. It was the very least that she owed him. She'd known for months that it was Jack she wanted — since that day Michael had returned from his trip to Yorkshire.

She couldn't know for sure that she and Jack could actually make it work, out in the open and with no secrets. There was so much they'd never had, or done. A lazy Sunday at home, a Christmas, a trip to the supermarket. She wouldn't know until they tried it. But that wasn't a reason to stay with Michael. It was a risk she would have to take, the risk of ending up with neither of them. She had hurt Michael enough.

'Why?' Michael asked.

Emily winced. Of course he wanted the whole story, the whole truth, and she had promised herself that she would answer any questions he had truthfully. But was it the right thing to do, when she knew that the answers would only hurt him more?

'Come on, Em, I need to know. For my peace of mind.'

'I don't know,' she said 'It isn't rational, is it? Love.'

'Did you ever love me?'

Emily hated the pain she could see in his eyes. 'I thought I did. I think I did. But then Jack came, and I knew it was different again.'

'The way you feel about him is the way I feel about you,' he said.

She thought that was probably true. She had always known that Michael adored her. In the early days, he'd been so serious, so quickly. She'd just been swept along.

'So what, then? Do you want a divorce?'

Emily snapped her head up, stared at him. She hadn't thought ahead that far. It was too fast. In the space of a day, things had shifted to the point where she was no longer allowed to touch him, where they would no longer live together in this house, where they would never kiss again. And she knew that it was her fault, and that she had brought them to this sorry place, but she couldn't think about divorce yet.

Emily thought of her mother, who had loved a man, and married him, and had him taken from her by death after just three short years, and she knew that she had never deserved a man like Michael. She and Jack were two of a kind; they had both lied and cheated to get what they wanted. And maybe he would cheat on her, too, and she would learn exactly how Michael was feeling at that moment. Or maybe she would cheat on him, maybe she would spend her life going from man to man, never settling for what she had, never really being happy. But she didn't believe it, not really. She had to believe that it would all have been different if she had met Jack first. If there had been no Michael.

Emily looked up at Michael, forced herself to meet his eyes. 'I don't need a divorce. It's up to you. Whatever you want. I'm so sorry, Michael.'

And there it was, less than a year after their wedding day. The end of their marriage. Despite the anxiety she'd felt as the wedding approached, Emily had never really thought she would lose him. That she would push him away.

MICHAEL HAD SPENT the night before that meeting with Emily thinking up ways that he could hurt her with words. He knew her weak points, her insecurities, and he had planned to pounce on them, exploit them, hold them up to the light and make her feel ashamed.

But when he had walked into the room and seen her sitting there, looking scared and small and startlingly beautiful, he had known, at once, that he would not say any of the things he had planned. And so he had to improvise, and he found himself asking her to take him back. So he was the weak one, in the end.

It wasn't until she said sorry that he really believed it was over. That sorry was a final one, and a heavy one — she was apologising for the affair, and for hurting him, but she was also saying that she was sorry for marrying him, for being with him for all those years when he was not the right man. He wanted to ask her whether she'd known, all along, that he wasn't the right man. Or if she'd only realised it when the right man had appeared before her, at her sister's side, as though she had conjured him up. He wanted to ask her that, but he didn't.

There were a lot of things Michael didn't say, didn't ask. It struck him, in that room, that they might never talk properly again, and that there were thousands of things he had never talked to her about, never would. He knew her, of course he did, and yet how could it be that he'd never asked her how she would describe the smell of a thunderstorm? Or how she felt when a song came on the radio she hadn't heard since her childhood? She was lost to him, and there was so much left for him to discover, and he'd thought he had a lifetime to explore her.

When Michael left the house, he looked back at it, still shocked that it would no longer be his home. He didn't know where he would go, where he would live. He got on a tube to King's Cross, bought a ticket to Leeds and boarded a quiet train. He would spend some time with his family, let his mother fuss over him.

But as Michael approached his destination, he imagined telling his parents the whole story, telling them that she had left him for someone else. And he imagined the way they would all say spiteful things about her that he wasn't ready to hear, and the way the news would spread around the village like a rash, and he would receive pitying looks from everyone he passed on the street. There's the Spencers' youngest, they would say. Come back from London because his wife's walked out on him. As much as he needed to be near the people who loved him, he could not bear all of that. He wouldn't tell them — he would dress it up as another research trip, would say everything between him and Emily was fine.

But how long could he spin the trip out, and what would he do after that? Michael tried to pull himself together. He would find a flat in London, start again, live the way he had lived before he met Emily. It would feel like his life was going backwards, with him living alone and staying out late with friends when he had hoped to be embarking on family life. But he had no choice.

Michael wondered whether there would be another woman in his future. He knew that he wouldn't be ready for it for a long time, but surely one day he would. And would it be too late, then, to think about starting a family? Had he missed his chance? Perhaps.

Michael called his mother when he was at the station, waiting for a taxi to take him home. He said that he was sorry to turn up unannounced, but that it had been a last-minute decision, and she laughed, and told him not to be silly, he would always have a bed there, just as if she knew that that was exactly what he needed to hear.

When he got to the front of the queue, Michael got in the waiting taxi and settled down to look out of the window at the scenery he knew so well.

'Visiting?' the taxi driver asked, eyeing Michael's case.

'Yes, my family are up here.'

'I see. Staying long?'

'I'm not sure yet.'

The driver made a sort of grunting noise and sat a bit further back in his seat, and that was the end of the conversation. Michael opened his window a crack to smell the fields and trees that made him feel like he was home. It had been cold and lifeless the last time he'd been back, but now it was turning to spring, and there was a gentle breeze and everything smelled fresh and new.

Michael had brought Emily up here a couple of times, and she had stood in his parents' garden at night looking up at the stars, amazed at how clear the sky was away from the pollution of London. But after a couple of days, each time, she had been restless and ready to get back. She had said that being out in the countryside made her feel lonely. He had said that he found it much lonelier to stand in a crowd of people he didn't know in the middle of a city, and Emily had given him a funny look. She had always lived in London. It was something she didn't understand.

Maybe he wouldn't go back to London, Michael thought. Maybe he would set up closer to home, find work on a local paper and have a roast dinner every Sunday with his family. He'd been tied to London because Emily had never wanted to live anywhere else. And now he wasn't tied to anything. But there was something depressing about the idea of living up here alone too, the idea of coming back home as though his time in London had just been a phase, something he needed to get out of his system. It was the living alone he didn't like, of course, regardless of the location. Michael found that he had to keep reminding himself that it was just him now, that his life was no longer bound up with hers. He couldn't imagine it, but perhaps a time would come when that seemed natural and right.

Up in his room, he called Josephine. She was the only one who could understand, he thought. The betrayals they had both suffered, although not identical, were close enough. She had lost a lover and a sister. He had lost a wife and a friend. Michael weighed their losses against one another for a moment, tried to decide whose was greater. But it didn't matter because there were no winners.

'I'm sorry, Michael,' she said. 'I'm sorry for how you found out. That was cruel of me. I was just so angry with them.'

Michael didn't blame her and he told her that. Her breathing was shaky, and he thought she might be crying.

'How long have you known?' he asked.

'Not long. I tried to pretend it wasn't happening for a little while.'

Michael thought about times the four of them had been together, tried to focus on looks that had passed between Jack and Emily. Searching for clues. Perhaps, if he and Josephine sifted through it all, they would be able to work it out, track it back to its origin. But what was the point? Would it help them?

'Do you hate her?' Josephine asked.

'I don't know,' he said. 'Do you?'

'I want to.'

Michael didn't know what that meant. He suspected she meant that she couldn't. He felt sorry for her, casting around for a hatred she couldn't feel. 'What will you do?' he asked her.

'I'll just carry on,' she said.

'But, without them?'

'Without him. I don't know about her. It depends on what they do now. I can't imagine being in her life while he's still there. But if she ends it, and he disappears, I don't know. Would you have her back, if that happened?'

Michael thought about that, wanting to answer truthfully. 'I don't know,' he said. And then, more quietly, 'I might.'

They could both forgive her, Michael realised, that's what they were saying. As long as Jack was out of the picture, they could go back to the way things were. Michael and Emily, and Emily and Josephine. And no Jack. Were they wrong to feel that? Did it make them weak? Maybe it was that weakness in them that had allowed her to do it to them. Maybe she had known, all along, that they'd let her.

Suddenly, Michael remembered those days Emily had spent in bed, that distance that had sprung up between them, and saw it in a new light. And there was no stopping the memories, then. He thought of the day he and Josephine had spent together at Christmas, while Jack and Emily did some last-minute shopping. He thought of the time he had spent up in Yorkshire with his family, Emily alone in the house. He tried to close his mind to the slow torture of it all.

CHAPTER THIRTY

J ack turned up on Emily's doorstep two days after he'd left. It had pained him to stay away so long, but she hadn't called or messaged him. Did the fact that Michael knew, that he'd left, change anything? Did it change things enough? He wasn't sure. All he knew was that he had to see her, even if it was only for a minute or two; even if she ended up turning him away.

She didn't, though. She opened the door looking pale and tired and looked at him as though she'd known he would come and had been waiting for him to appear. Not grateful, not happy. Resigned. She pulled him inside wearily. He wanted to ask her dozens of questions, but he didn't dare.

Jack leaned in to kiss her, fully expecting her to push him away, but she didn't. She tasted just the way he remembered, and the relief of being with her again was almost enough to make him weep. They went upstairs, to bed. It was only after that Jack realised — something in the way Emily touched him had changed. She wouldn't let him hold her anymore. When they had sex, Jack had felt as though she was taking something from him, and after-wards, she retreated into silence, turned her back. There was an anger to her, a bitterness. Jack felt the small life they had snuffed out in the air around them. He tasted it in their mouths when they kissed.

'You can't stay here,' she said, into the silence between them.

'Emily...'

She turned to face him, and he took her face in his hands and kissed her again.

'What are we going to do?' he asked.

'I don't know. I love you, but everyone is so hurt. I can't bear what we've done.'

Jack dressed hurriedly, resentful of having to do so. This was not what he wanted with this woman, these snatched hours and hasty retreats. Couldn't she see what they could have? This was not what he wanted at all.

Jack walked out the door, not really sure where he was going. Not wanting to face the tube at rush hour but knowing it was too far for him to walk all the way home. He passed a taxi rank, and he watched the people climbing into the waiting cars. Some with luggage, some in pairs or groups. And he wondered whether any of them were truly happy. Whether any of them had found what he'd found, with Emily, and could hold on to it, show it off to the world. He didn't think so. The faces were glum, subdued. Everyone in a hurry to be somewhere else when he just wanted to go back to where he'd come from, and stay there.

Eventually, he joined the queue and waited for a cab, too tired to negotiate his own way to his friend's where he'd been staying. And once he got there, he let himself into the flat with his spare key and grabbed a pen and some paper. For the rest of that evening, Jack tried, for the first time, to pin down Emily on the page. He wrote a story with her at the centre, in the limelight. And him? He didn't put himself beside her, or even on the sidelines.

In the story, Emily was alone in the world. She had no family, no lover, no friends. She moved through space and time seamlessly, gathering up objects and ideas as she went. Meeting people, touching them, but never taking any of them with her.

Jack wrote feverishly, and he didn't stop until the story was finished. And when it was, he read it back, making small changes here and there. It was almost dawn when he was done. A thought came to him, the kind of thought that only comes in those lost, night-time hours. He thought about sending it to Michael, to see whether he would recognise his wife in the character Jack had created. He was convinced that, in a way, he knew Emily better than Michael did, despite the years Emily and Michael had spent together and the vows that bound them. He got as far as opening up his emails, but he didn't send Michael the story. Not because it would be cruel, but because he knew Emily would think it unforgiveable.

Despite the late hour, Jack could not sleep. He lay in bed, warm beneath the covers, watching the sun come up through a crack at the side of his curtains. He thought about the child that they had not had, the future that was not open to them, the past they did not share.

The next day, on his way to work, Jack called Josephine. He didn't think she'd answer, so he was surprised when the call connected. She didn't say anything, just waited for him to speak.

'Josephine, it's me, Jack. Listen, I know you probably hate me...'

'I do.'

'Can I come, to pick up my stuff?'

Josephine made him wait for her answer. 'Not yet,' she said, eventually. 'I'm not ready to see you. I'll let you know when.'

It was a step forward. Jack had thought she might have thrown his things away, or burned them. He'd been staying with various friends and acquaintances, pulling a small suitcase with him everywhere he went. He'd bought a few clothes and a pair of shoes. He was making do.

Jack was standing outside the bookshop, about to go in, when he decided to make another call.

'Jack?'

Jack was even more surprised when this one was answered. 'Michael,' he said.

'What do you want?'

Jack wondered where Michael was, and also how he was. He'd admired this man, he'd liked him.

'I'm sorry,' he said. 'It's not enough, I know. But I'm sorry, and so is she. We didn't mean for it to happen.'

'You don't speak for her,' Michael said, and he hung up the phone.

* * *

'SHALL we go out and drink until we're sick?' Ben asked.

Josephine laughed. It was Friday night and she'd planned to get an Indian takeaway and drink wine in front of the TV. But now here was Ben on her doorstep, with a bunch of tulips and a hug that actually lifted her off her feet and made her remember who she'd been before this heartache.

'Okay,' she said. 'But I need a shower first.'

'I can wait.'

Josephine didn't spend long deciding what to wear, didn't put on much make-up. Jeans, a black top. Red lipstick. She had always been fairly confident about how she looked. The break-up had knocked her, of course, but when she made herself think about it rationally, she could admit that she was in her twenties and there would be other men, even if right now she couldn't imagine being ready for them. What there wouldn't be was other sisters. That was a thought that nagged at her at least once a day. As she always did, she pushed it away. Later — she'd deal with it later.

Ben whistled when she appeared in the doorway of the living room. He'd helped himself to a beer and put the tulips in a jug.

'Let's go,' she said.

There was a tiny fizz of excitement in her belly, for the first time since Jack. A night of drinking and dancing was just what she needed.

'Will we dance?' she asked, as she pulled the door of the flat closed behind them.

'Hell, yes,' Ben said, taking her hand and twirling her around there in the hallway.

Ben took her to a bar she'd never been to, on a back street near Covent Garden. They sat on high stools by the bar and drank cocktails and in between they went outside to smoke cigarettes, and Josephine found herself laughing at Ben's silly stories and jokes the way she always had.

'Have you seen her?' she asked. There were four cocktails in her system, and her resolve to avoid talking about it had weakened.

'Once,' Ben said. 'She called round. She wanted to tell me her side of it.'

'And?'

'I let her in, I listened. But then I told her I couldn't under-stand. I couldn't just tell her it was okay.'

Josephine wanted to thank him. For taking sides. For taking hers. But it seemed so childish. 'I can't forgive her,' she said, instead. 'Not yet.'

Ben shrugged. He finished his drink and signalled to the barwoman that they would like another. 'Then don't,' he said.

Later, much later, Josephine was coming out of the toilets and a man grabbed hold of her hand. She spun around, pulled away, but he held on tight. 'Can I buy you a drink?' he asked.

Josephine looked at him. He was older than her, wearing a suit. He'd come straight from a city job, she thought. He was drunk, and he thought it was his right to simply take hold of things he liked the look of.

'I'm fine, thank you,' she said. Her voice was cold, but her head spun, and she knew it was time to go home.

'Just one drink,' he said, letting her go but continuing to stare at her.

And then Ben was at her side. 'Leave her alone,' he said, and the man stood up, and Josephine felt the tension in the air and turned to look at Ben.

'Let's go,' she said, pulling Ben by the hand.

Outside in the street, she became aware of how drunk she was. 'I need to go home,' she said. She was close to tears.

'I'll take you,' Ben said, holding his arm up for a taxi.

Inside the car, the radio playing love songs and the heating on high, Josephine cried. 'We didn't dance,' she said.

'There'll be other nights,' Ben told her.

And she believed it. She could see ahead, through the tears and the fog and the relentless pain. There would be nights out, with Ben, with other friends. There would be dancing.

Back at her flat, Ben made coffee and opened a big bag of crisps. They sat side by side on the sofa, not talking much. Josephine's pain had more or less disappeared for the evening, but it was back, rolling over her like an enormous wave. She knew that she couldn't numb it with alcohol forever, knew that she would have to face it, experience it, bit by excruciating bit.

'I loved him,' she said, into the dimly lit room. 'I was so happy. And she's got Michael. Why would she take him? She already had everything.'

'It's not fair,' he said. 'None of it's fair.'

It was almost three o'clock by the time Josephine stood up to go to bed. 'Ben, will you stay? Just tonight?'

'Of course,' he said.

She found him a blanket and a pillow and he made a bed for himself on the sofa, his long legs hanging uncomfortably off the end.

The next morning when Josephine woke up, she forgot everything for a moment, and when it all rushed back to her, along with a dull headache, she was reassured to find Ben there. He, at least, was where she had left him.

CHAPTER THIRTY-ONE

Josephine's father had been good to her since everything had turned upside down. He called regularly to check how she was and offered to take her places. As a result, she'd seen much more of him. Josephine wondered whether the situation reminded him of the affair he'd had with her mother.

One Sunday in early May, she asked him about their relationship for the first time. They were walking down Portobello Road, looking at the antiques and the jewellery, his arm linked comfortably through hers.

'Tell me about how you met my mother,' she asked.

Peter turned to her. 'Didn't she tell you?'

'Yes,' she said. 'But it's not the same thing. I want to hear about it from you.'

'Well, you know, she worked in the library, and I used to go in there every now and again to pick up books for the boys. They both read so much we couldn't buy books fast enough, and we didn't have that much money. And one morning I nipped in there and I saw her. She was helping an old lady who'd run up some fines and was very upset about it, and I suppose I saw how kind and patient she was with her. She must have noticed me looking over because she looked up, and she had these incredible pale blue eyes.'

Peter was silent for a moment and Josephine let him remember. She'd waited a long time to hear this story from him, and another couple of minutes weren't going to make any difference.

'My wife and I were going through a tough time. The boys were hard work and I was working long hours and we just weren't making the time for each other. And it was so long since she'd really looked at me that, when your mother looked at me that day, I was lost. I put my books down and left because I was scared of what I might say or do if I stayed there any longer.'

He paused. They'd reached a coffee shop with an upstairs terrace. 'Shall we get a drink up there?' he asked.

'Yes.'

Josephine enjoyed the feeling of the sun on her arms and her face as they took their seats at the table and gave their orders. She thought about Peter seeing her mother in the library that first time, about her seeing Jack in the bookshop. 'Go on,' she encouraged, as soon as the waitress had left their table.

'Where was I? Oh yes, I'd left the library. Well, I went back, didn't I? Couldn't help myself. I'd been thinking about her every day. But the next time I went she wasn't there, and I was so disappointed. That's when I knew I really felt something for her. It was crazy, we'd never even spoken. So I kept going back and I got to know which days she worked, and I thought she must have noticed me coming in all the time and trying not to stare at her, but she was always very friendly. It went on like that for a few weeks. Then I decided I'd have to get up the courage to approach her, or it would go on forever. So one day I went up to the counter with a couple of books, and my hands were shaking, I was so scared, and I asked her whether I could take her out for dinner when she'd finished her shift.'

'What did she say?' Josephine had been holding her breath.

'She said she had a baby to get home to, but that she was free on Saturday afternoon if I'd like to take her out then. Her mum would look after Emily. So that was our first date, and she told me that she'd been waiting for me to ask her out for weeks.'

'Did you tell her that you were married?'

Peter hung his head. 'Not at first. And when I did, she was furious. But it was too late by then, we were both in too deep.'

The waitress brought over their coffees, but neither of them looked at her. They were lost in the story.

'I thought you were going to say "in love",' Josephine said.

'I thought I was in love; we both said we were. But when it came to the crunch and I had to decide whether to leave my family, I just couldn't do it. The boys needed me. I couldn't leave them.'

'What about me?' Josephine had stopped being angry with him for not being there while she was growing up. There didn't seem to be any point, not when it couldn't be changed or righted. But she still wanted to know.

'The truth is, you were less real to me. You hadn't been born yet. The boys were there, running around, asking me to fly kites with them and play ball. I know it wasn't the right thing to do, leaving Alice on her own like that. I know that. I wanted to be with her, I was crazy about her. I suppose I was too cowardly to go through with it. And it was all or nothing, for her, so then we cut all ties.'

It was painful to hear it, but it eased a pain in Josephine too. All her life, she'd had an idea of her mum and Emily's dad having a pure, fairy-tale love, and of her mum and Peter having a sordid affair. But the way he spoke about her that day, Josephine believed that they had cared for one another, that she had been conceived out of tenderness, if not love.

'Why did you divorce, in the end?'

'I think we'd fallen out of love a long time before, and it just became more and more apparent after the boys left home and started to set up their own lives. As they needed us less and less, it was just the two of us left, you see, and we didn't have anything to say to each other. We used to have these awful evenings in front of the TV, hardly a word passing between us. And still I left it for too long, I was still too cowardly. I think she was relieved when I finally said I thought we should call it a day. I think she'd been waiting for me to put a stop to it.'

'Does she know about me?'

'Yes, I told her about Alice and about you. And she said she'd known all along. Not about you, of course, but about the affair. Sometimes we're not as good at keeping secrets as we think we are. She encouraged me to get in touch with you.'

'She sounds nice,' Josephine said.

Peter sighed, took a sip of coffee. 'She's a lovely lady. She just wasn't the right lady for me.'

That evening in her flat, Josephine tried to concentrate on her book but found herself mulling over what Peter had said. He'd had an affair, and her mother had slept with a married man, and she didn't think that either of them were bad people. She thought perhaps she was to Jack what Peter's wife had been: lovely, but not right for him.

Josephine thought about those long nights Peter and his wife had spent watching the television in silence. Is that what she and Jack would have come to, in time? If Peter had been true to himself, he would have left his wife for Alice. Instead, he had led half a life, with a woman he didn't really love. And Jack had been true to himself and gone after Emily. And so perhaps it would have been wrong if it had turned out any other way. It was just so painful to be the one who wasn't loved.

Since that night, Josephine hadn't seen Emily or Jack. She was torn between wanting to know whether they were trying to build a life together and not being ready to hear. Emily had sent her a couple of text messages, but she hadn't replied. The messages had been so polite and apologetic that they had made Josephine sad. They were the kind of messages you sent to someone you barely knew. Perhaps that's what all this had cost them as sisters. Perhaps, if they wanted to have a relationship with one another again, they would have to start from scratch. Although they wouldn't be starting out on equal footing, would they? Josephine had been wronged by Emily, and there would never be any way to even that out.

Josephine hadn't seen or heard from Michael either, since that desperately sad call he'd made the day after it all came out. She decided to phone him. They could help one another through the pain of all this, she thought, and they should.

'Jo,' he said, picking up after the second ring. 'Give me a couple of minutes.'

She heard the sound of him making his way upstairs.

'Sorry about that,' he said. 'How are you?'

'I'm okay. Are you? Where are you?'

'I'm at my parents' place. I needed to get away for a bit.'

'What did they make of it all?'

Michael didn't reply, and for a minute Josephine thought she'd lost him, but then she heard him take a deep breath. 'I haven't told them, Jo. I can't. That's why I had to come upstairs just now to talk to you. I just don't want them to know.' He broke into quiet sobs.

'Oh, Michael. You should tell them. They'll support you. My father's been great.'

Neither of them said anything for a few moments, but the silence was not uncomfortable. Josephine liked knowing that he was there, at the other end. It made her feel less alone. She waited patiently for him to compose himself.

'I know,' he said at last.

'When are you coming back? We should get together, if you want to?'

'I'll let you know Jo, okay? I'll let you know.'

He hung up and Josephine stood there, the dial tone buzzing in her ear. His last words had sounded hollow, insincere. It would be understandable if he didn't want to see her, if he wanted to cut all ties with Emily's family. But she hated to think of him up there, pretending everything was fine, grieving in private.

Josephine put the kettle on to make a coffee, but when she went to the fridge, she found that she'd run out of milk, so she flicked the kettle off and picked up her keys and her purse and went out in search of a shop that was still open. And as she was coming out of the shop, trying to balance things in her hands, she saw them, in the distance. Emily and Jack. They were walking hand in hand, their heads close together. Josephine froze, hoping that they would not turn and see her. And they didn't. They were absorbed in a conversation, deep in their own world.

Josephine hurried home, feeling cold. It was bound to happen, she told herself, at some point. And yet she hadn't expected it, so soon. She was jealous of Michael now, all those miles away from the mess. She felt like she was standing in the middle of a pile of broken glass, picking her way out carefully, trying to avoid being cut. They had looked like any other young couple, clinging to one another, making their way home. No one who saw them would know what their love had cost.

CHAPTER THIRTY-TWO

Jack wanted to move in, but Emily wouldn't let him. He wanted to know why she was holding back, now that they were free to be together. He wanted to ask if it was because of the abortion; if that had changed the shape of things. But she let him spend most nights there, and for now, at least, that was enough. Jack had started to learn the things he had always felt locked out of, her daily routines and her sleep patterns and her bad habits. And with everything he learned, he thought, he loved her more.

Emily would leave banana and satsuma peelings on the kitchen worktops, and it would just remind him, when he got home, that she was there, smelling of fruit, her fingers sticky. She would take long showers in the mornings, combing conditioner through her hair and leaving it for two minutes before rinsing it out. Sometimes he would make an excuse to go in there, brushing his teeth or looking for something in the bathroom cabinet, just to watch her. He had a key to the house, so that he could come and go. It was enough.

Jack had told his boss, Tim, the whole story, and Tim had rolled his eyes and refused to take it seriously at first, seeing it as just another romantic mess that Jack had got into. But Jack had felt Tim's attitude changing the more he'd talked about Emily. Tim must have seen the look in Jack's eyes when he talked about the plans he wanted to make with her, the places he wanted to take her, and the family he wanted to have one day.

'You're actually in love, aren't you?' Tim asked.

It was the end of a long day, and Jack had turned the sign on the door to closed, and they were cashing up. 'Yes,' Jack said. It felt good to say it, and to mean it, and for it not to be a secret anymore.

'Poor Josephine,' said Tim. 'I liked her.'

Poor Josephine. She had disappeared from their lives, but Jack knew that that was not a permanent thing. She was Emily's sister, and he knew that Emily was worried about her, and about Michael, and about the damage that had been done to them. Jack thought about calling Josephine again, but what was there to say? He didn't think she would want to hear more apologies from him, didn't think they would make any difference to her now. No matter how sorry he was, he had still left her on her own. He had still taken her sister away from her.

For Jack, the worry was always with him. The fear that, one day, Emily would decide that it was too awful, this thing that they had done, and that it would be over. She would never be happy until things were resolved. So that night, on the way home from work, Jack went over to see Josephine.

'What do you want?' she asked, when she opened the door.

She looked almost the same, he noticed. But there was no denying that she looked a little more tired, a little more sad. He felt ashamed.

'Can we talk?' he said. 'Can I come in?'

Josephine didn't say anything, but she stepped back and he took that as an invitation to come inside. In the living room, there was a book open on the arm of the sofa and a plate of half-eaten food on the coffee table.

'I'm sorry to interrupt your dinner,' he said.

Josephine shrugged, her arms folded.

'Look,' he said, taking a seat in the armchair. 'I know you don't want me here. But I'm worried about Emily. Do you think things will ever be all right between the two of you?'

'Does she know you're here?' Josephine asked, her tone flat.

'No.'

There was a silence and Jack didn't know how to fill it. Should he ask her again?

'What do you expect?' she asked, finally.

'I don't know. I just hate the fact that I've caused this when you used to be so close.'

'But you have.'

She wasn't making this easy for him. And why should she?

'Maybe I shouldn't have come here,' he said.

'I can't just pretend it never happened. Did you think I could? Did you think the three of us would sit around having dinner together? And maybe with Michael too? Just like old times.'

There was a bitterness in her that Jack had never seen before. 'I'm going to go,' he said. 'I'm sorry.'

She didn't stand up, and he let himself out. He wouldn't tell Emily about this, he decided. He would have, if he'd been able to make a difference, make things slightly better, but he feared he may have made things worse.

Would it always be this hard? And, if it was, would they become exhausted and eventually give up? Would it all be for nothing, in the end?

As Jack turned the corner and Emily's house came into view, his phone rang. It was his mother. 'Mum?'

'Jack,' she said. 'How are you?'

He thought, for a moment, about telling her how he was. About the mess he had made of things. About the fact that he was in love. 'I'm okay,' he said. 'How are you?'

He thought he heard her crying, then. But he couldn't ask her what was wrong. He wasn't in her life.

'I miss you so much,' she said. 'Do you think we could meet up sometime? Just the two of us?'

It wasn't quite what Jack had hoped for. She wasn't leaving John, but she understood that he wouldn't come home. She understood that if they were ever going to be mother and son again, it would have to be on neutral ground. Jack felt something break inside him, something that he'd built up so he couldn't be hurt again the way he had been as a child. He was standing at Emily's door, and he sank down and sat on the step. 'I'd like that,' he said.

He hung up, searched in his bag for his key. He would take Emily to meet his mother, he decided. He could see them getting on, teasing him and laughing over cups of tea. She would be the first woman he had ever introduced to her, the first woman he'd ever wanted to.

They would take things one step at a time, Jack thought. First, his family, and then, in time, hers.

EVERY MORNING, Michael remembered it all over again. It was as though his brain couldn't retain the information while he slept. He would wake, and turn over, reach out for Emily. And then he would open his eyes, and see that he was in his childhood bedroom, and he would remember. Some days it came crashing back, making him gasp, and other days it came in bits and pieces, like a terrible jigsaw that he'd piece together to reveal the awful truth.

Because he hadn't told his parents what had happened, Michael went on long walks and told them that he was calling Emily. He would wander around those lanes and paths he knew so well, sometimes climbing over fences and venturing into fields, all the time dreading his return to the house when they would smile and ask how Emily was, what she had been up to. Michael invented dinners and drinks for her, nights in with Josephine, long days at work, yoga classes. And all the time, he pictured her in their house with Jack. In their bed.

Had Jack moved in? Had Emily cleared the shelves of Michael's clothes, making room for Jack's? Did Jack sit in his armchair, read his books? Did he put the rubbish out, mow the lawn? Was Emily's life essentially the same, just with a different man in Michael's place? Or was everything different? Perhaps they stayed up all night, perhaps they wandered around the house naked, perhaps they sat together on the sofa, holding hands.

Michael borrowed his Dad's car and went for a drive, trying to outrun his thoughts. He headed for a long, flat stretch of road with barely any traffic. It was where his father had taught him to drive. And he put his foot down and felt the exhilaration of speed.

That morning, Alex had called, and Michael hadn't picked up. He'd listened to the message afterwards.

Michael, it's me. I've finished the book. Sorry it's taken me a while. Anyway, listen, it's perfect. So much better than I'd imagined. Not that I didn't expect it to be great. You know what I mean. So I'm going to start sending it out. They'll be falling all over themselves to publish it, trust me. We might have to go to auction with it. So give me a call, okay? And congratulations.

He waited to feel proud, relieved, happy.

Michael drove on. He put the radio on and tuned it to a station that was playing requests. He listened to the messages — apologies, declarations of love, wishes for happy birthdays and anniversaries. And he felt alone. He looked at the road, stretched out in front of him until it eventually merged into a point on the horizon. There wasn't another car in sight. He wanted another car to come into view, to pass him, to convince him that he was really there.

When Michael started to cry, he thought about pulling over, but he didn't do it. He drove faster, letting the tears spill down his neck. He imagined accelerating and accelerating until he hit something or went off the road. He imagined his family or the police calling Emily to say that he'd been in an accident, that it was serious. He wondered whether she'd come. And then the sadness overtook him completely, and he could hardly breathe, and he was gulping back huge sobs, and he had to pull over. He parked the car and took his seatbelt off, and he pulled his knees to his chest and wept, there on the side of the road. He didn't want to go back and he didn't want to go on.

Emily had called Michael the day before, and he had looked at her name flashing on his phone, unable to reach out and answer the call. He'd expected her to leave a message — he'd looked forward to hearing her voice, anticipated listening to it over and over — but she hadn't. And now it haunted him, wondering what she had wanted. Wondering whether she had changed her mind about it all, and she was asking him to come back. Or whether she wanted to ask him for a divorce, after all.

When he got back to his parents' house, Michael parked the car in the drive and let himself in the back door, hoping that no one would hear him. But his mother was in the kitchen, and she asked him whether he wanted a cup of tea. Michael knew that his eyes were red and his face was tear-stained, but all of a sudden he wanted to sit with his mum and drink tea, as if his life wasn't falling apart. They sat down at the kitchen table once she'd made the drinks, and she looked hard at him, unflinching. Michael met her gaze, bit the inside of his cheek to stop the tears from starting again.

'What is it?' his mother asked. 'There's obviously something wrong.'

Michael wondered how long she'd known, whether she'd

always known, since he'd arrived. Mums knew, didn't they? Mums could tell. He wasn't ready to speak, and she asked her next question, and he could hear in her voice how hard it was for her.

'You're not…ill?'

'No,' he said, her worry freeing his tongue. He couldn't let her think that.

He knew that there were many parents who would assume their child's partner had done something immediately, but his had never been like that. They liked Emily, and they'd always trusted his judgement with her, and shown her the greatest respect. He had a choice. To tell her the truth or to make up something lesser, to ease her mind.

'We've got a few money problems,' he said, trying to think fast. 'Neither of our jobs pays particularly well, and I haven't published a book for so long…'

His mum's face changed, her eyebrows drawing together. 'But there's no mortgage on that lovely house, is there?'

There wasn't. It was true that they didn't earn a great deal, but they'd also been very lucky. They paid Emily's mum a very reasonable rent.

'We've spent more than we should have on our credit cards, that's all. But we'll work it out.' Michael wanted to shut the conversation down. He hadn't considered the questions she would ask.

'I'll talk to your dad, see what we can do,' his mum said, patting his arm.

Michael felt tears start to creep up on him again, at her kindness. Of course she would offer to help, if she could. Michael cursed himself for not thinking of something better than financial difficulty.

'No,' he said, a little sharply. 'It's under control. It's almost sorted.'

He stood and left the room, feeling his mum's worried eyes on him as he went.

'You know,' she called out when he was at the bottom of the stairs, 'you can come to me, to us, about anything. You can always talk to us.'

Michael didn't answer. He couldn't. Upstairs, he closed the door to his room and sat down on his bed, his body shaking with sobs. He thought about being a child, about how he had taken every little problem to his parents, believing they could solve them. And they had. And now here he was, back in his childhood bedroom, lying and hiding and pretending because he was ashamed of the truth.

Michael thought about writing Emily a letter. It would be easier, he reasoned, to put it all down on paper. That was what he did, after all, what he was good at. And then she would know, at least, how he felt. Whatever she decided to do, at least she would know. But when he tried to start, he had a vision of Emily reading the letter, with Jack standing behind her, reading over her shoulder. Would they mock him, together? Would they be that cruel? He thought they wouldn't, but he wasn't sure enough. That image of them made him forget what he was thinking and he couldn't write a single word.

He thought about calling her. He had the perfect excuse: he could return her call from the previous day. And maybe he could get her to agree to them meeting again, face to face. And if not that, he could just listen to her smooth voice, and be calmed. But then he had the same vision, of Jack standing beside her while they spoke, leaning in close to catch Michael's words.

And so, in the end, Michael didn't write a letter and he didn't make a call. Instead, he went to the bathroom and washed his face, and then looked at himself for a long time in the mirror above the sink. He remembered sitting on the side of the bath, watching his Dad in the mirror while he shaved, asking him questions. And he remembered looking at himself in this mirror the morning he'd left home to go to university and wondering how he would be different when he came back. And now he had his answer. If he could have seen himself like this, back then, what would he have done? It wouldn't have seemed worth going through it all, just to end up like this.

On a whim, he went back down the stairs and reached for the keys he'd only recently replaced in the basket where they were kept.

'I need to borrow the car again. Is that okay?'

His mum nodded. 'Of course. Will you be back for dinner? I'm doing a chicken.'

Michael nodded. 'I will.'

CHAPTER THIRTY-THREE

When she first got the call, Emily didn't feel sad or surprised, because it couldn't be real. And yet there was Michael's mother, on the other end of the phone, her crying mixed with a low crackle on that long-distance line. Emily couldn't connect the words she had heard with her life. They just didn't fit. It was telling Jack that made it real. But she didn't call him straight away. She moved around the house, picking up things that Jack had left lying around and putting them back where they belonged. She emptied an ashtray, sorted out the recycling.

She tried repeating the words inwardly, to make herself believe them. Michael was dead. That's what she had said, his mother. He'd had a car crash, come off the road and hit a tree. She stressed that it was an accident, but Emily couldn't stop hearing the words 'no other cars involved'.

Emily picked up her phone to call Jack. He'd gone out for a drink with Tim, his boss. He was almost always the last person she'd called, and yet, she found she'd forgotten how to bring up his number. She didn't know it by heart. What did that say? She knew Michael's. Her fingers were clumsy, too, as if she was wearing gloves. Eventually, she managed to make the call and when he answered, she said his name. The rest of the words got stuck in her throat.

'Emily, what is it?'

Emily tried to speak but found she couldn't.

'Em, what? Shall I come?'

'Yes,' she said. It was the only word she could manage.

Jack was there within a few minutes, and when she saw him, she could believe for the first time that it was true. Here was her lover, knowing that something was terribly wrong, pulling her off the sofa and into his arms, and her husband was dead. She knew, of course she knew, that it was all a result of the mess she and Jack had created.

'It's Michael,' she said. 'He's dead.'

Emily watched Jack's face twist into an expression she'd never seen before. She watched him let go of her and sink down to sit on the sofa. Did he know, as she did, that this spelled the end of them?

There would be questions, she knew. It had been clear, from speaking to Michael's mother, that she didn't know what had happened between them. She thought of Michael, passing his days up there with his family, keeping it all locked up inside.

'I'll have to tell people,' Emily said. 'His friends, people his mother wouldn't know to call.'

'I can do it, if you like,' Jack said.

Emily recognised that he wanted to do something to help her, but she couldn't let him. How could she let this man she'd left Michael for pick up the phone and tell the people who loved him this news? She found a pen and paper and started making a list. His friends, from university and work and a handful from school. Couples they knew. His boss. And Josephine, of course. When she had finished she looked through it again. It looked too short. Not enough people to fill up a life.

'You don't have to do that tonight, Emily,' Jack said.

But she did. She could see that he was trying to protect her. But she felt like asking him to leave. She felt dirty, just being in the same room as him.

Emily left Josephine to the very end. It was nearing two o'clock when she dialled her sister's number. She had no idea whether Josephine would answer, or would see Emily's number there, and let the phone ring. Or if she would be fast asleep, locked in the peace of not yet knowing. While she listened to the ringing, Emily silently urged her sister to pick up. She needed her, then. She didn't have any right to ask anything of her, but it didn't stop her from aching with that need.

'Hello?' Josephine's voice was thick with sleep. Emily pictured her, lying in bed, reaching out for her phone, with no idea of what was to come.

'Jo, it's me. I have to tell you something.' Emily wished, more than anything, that it wasn't true.

'What is it?' Josephine sounded clearer. The mention of bad news, so often delivered in the dead of night, had woken her.

'It's Michael... He's dead.'

Emily listened to Josephine breathe. And then, suddenly, her sister's voice was back on the line, sharp and strong.

'How? Suicide?'

It was Emily's turn to be shocked.

'No! A car accident.'

'What happened exactly?'

'They don't know,' Emily faltered. 'He hit a tree.'

Josephine was silent, but she might as well have screamed at her sister. Emily knew just what she was thinking. You did this. You. Did. This.

'I have to go,' Emily said, when she couldn't stand the quiet any longer.

LATER, when she was lying in bed, her body turned away from

Jack's, Emily closed her eyes against a rush of images, but the darkness only intensified them. Michael, at the book signing where they had met, his glasses slipping slightly down his long nose as he read. Michael, standing at the altar on their wedding day, his hands clasped behind his back and a nervous smile on his face. Michael, pouring drinks for Jack and Josephine at dinner. And then Michael's face blurred into Jack's. His features sharpened and the weight dropped from his frame. But Emily concentrated on picturing him, on banishing Jack's image, and Michael was there again, distinct. It wasn't as easy to erase Josephine's silent accusation.

Sleep would not come, and so she wandered through the rooms of the house without turning on any lights. She walked through the home that she and Michael had made, and he was everywhere in it. The heavy oak dining table and chairs that he had chosen, the Victorian novels on the bookshelves, the bottles of French wine. This house would never belong to her and Jack. It was why she'd held back from letting him move in. Michael would always be there, behind and beside and inside them.

Emily didn't know how to grieve for him. Grief should be straightforward, shouldn't it? Mostly pain, a little anger, maybe fear. No relief.

* * *

JOSEPHINE STAYED UP THAT NIGHT, after Emily's call. For her, there was no space between hearing and believing. Was she wrong to conclude, so quickly, that he had done this on purpose? The last time they'd spoken, he had sounded like he was drowning, and she hadn't done anything to save him. A car accident. A tree. She didn't know what would be left of his body for them to bury or burn.

They had been damaged by the same event, her and Michael. And yet here she was, getting by and, gradually, getting better, and he was gone. She had envisaged them spending more time together, when he got back to London, helping one another through it. Their wounds gradually fading, healing. She had already begun to depend on the help she had anticipated from him. She felt ashamed for being angry, for feeling betrayed.

Josephine got out of bed and moved around the flat, opening the windows. It was the start of summer, and the flat felt hot and stuffy. She could barely breathe. She lit a cigarette and smoked it hungrily, flicking ash out of the living room window.

She tried to imagine what Emily expected from her. She had lost her husband, but Josephine still couldn't be a sister or a friend to her. Not now. She had Jack beside her, after all, and it meant that she couldn't have anyone else. Josephine wondered how the news would affect them. Would it break them? It wasn't the sort of thing you usually had to handle in those early days of love.

Josephine sat quite still while the sun came up around her, and the room was slowly filled with light and air. She didn't notice it happening, she was so caught up in her thoughts. She jumped when her phone rang, hesitated before reaching for it. Could something else have happened? Could there really be more?

'Josephine, it's Sarah. I just got to work, I heard about Michael.'

Josephine pictured the news travelling around the corners of London that Michael had been a part of. Tearing through his office, his life, creeping from friend to friend.

'I wanted to check on you, see how you're doing.'

Sarah knew the whole story, because Josephine had told her, in those days after it all came out, when she had laid low and cancelled lessons. But Josephine didn't know who else knew. Would they be secretly holding Emily accountable, blaming her as Josephine had, or would she be the poor, grieving widow? Josephine didn't know what she hoped for.

'Thanks for calling, Sarah. It's such a shock.' It was the kind of thing you said. But it wasn't all that much of a shock for Josephine, not really. She had known that the repercussions of this would be vast and terrible. She had known that, to a greater or lesser extent, Michael would be destroyed.

'We're all so sorry, of course. Do you want me to come over after work?'

Josephine thought about that, about having someone else in the flat and having to talk about it. People could be bloodthirsty, she thought. They always wanted to know how, and where, and when. When really the only question was why. 'No, it's okay. I'm okay.'

'Well I'm thinking about you, and Emily. If you see her, could you tell her?'

'I will.'

Josephine cried a little. There had been so much crying, and yet, there was always more. She cried for Michael, and for his family, who were nice, ordinary people, and who didn't deserve this. And she cried for Emily, who had lost everything, now. Surely she and Jack couldn't survive something like this? She cried for herself, for the sister and lover she'd lost. And the friend.

And after the crying, Josephine pulled herself together and called Michael's mother. She said how very sorry she was, and talked of how she had loved Michael, of how good he was. She said that she was thinking of his family, and asked if there was anything she could do to help. And when she hung up the phone, she felt like she had done something real and good. And she hoped that, in a day or two, she might find the strength to call Emily too. Hoped they could begin to get past this wall of pain. Where would they end up, if they did?

CHAPTER THIRTY-FOUR

Michael's parents were travelling down to London to help with the funeral arrangements, and Jack understood that he needed to disappear from the house, at least while they were there. On the day they were due to arrive, he packed up the things he had started to leave there — a couple of pairs of jeans and some T-shirts, a book, his laptop, his toothbrush. It could be that, in a couple of weeks or maybe a little longer, he would be putting these things back, or it could be that he was clearing them out for good. Emily hadn't said much about the two of them since she'd heard the news, and why should she? She had to bury her husband.

And so Jack packed his things into a rucksack and took the tube back to his friend's flat. His friend was out at work, so he opened all of the windows and let the air circulate. It was a warm, sunny day. A day for having drinks or a picnic in the park. He and Emily had not had a summer. Their relationship had started as the previous summer ended and he had started to think that this summer might be theirs. But he hadn't known, then, what was coming, and now it seemed destined to be a summer of grief and loneliness.

When Jack had explained what had happened, Tim had given him a few days off. And Jack had been grateful that they were friends because he couldn't face working, but how could he explain this situation to anyone else? But that morning, he thought about calling Tim and saying he was ready to come back. Emily had all the arrangements to make, and he couldn't help her, so he was at a loss. Tomorrow, he decided, he would go back to work tomorrow.

He made himself a coffee and picked up the stack of paper lying on his coffee table. It was Michael's novel. What would happen to it now? He'd read it as soon as Michael had sent it, and he'd been awed. He started to read it again, intending to stop after the first chapter. But he sat there, absorbed, until he'd finished it for a second time. And Jack was still awed, but this time the experience of reading it was entirely different.

There was no escaping from the fact that the author was dead. Jack had searched for clues to Michael's state of mind as he read it, and all indications pointed to the fact that he was content. He'd finished writing it before he knew about Jack and Emily, of course.

The first time Jack had read Michael's words, he had tried to avoid thinking about the lead female character as Emily. But he had known that she was, at least in part, based on this woman he and the author loved and shared. He couldn't help but compare her to the Emily he'd written himself.

And what he learned, from doing so, was that they loved her in different ways. While Jack was running after her, trying to grab hold of a loose piece of clothing, terrified of losing hold and losing sight of her, Michael walked beside her, in step with her, secure in his belief that she was his. While Jack wanted to spend every second with her, Michael was more trusting that, if they had to be apart, she would come back to him. What they had in common, of course, was their idolisation of her, their true devotion.

Jack didn't believe Michael had loved Emily more than he did, but he could see that Michael had loved her more considerately. And yet he had lost her, and Jack hadn't, at least not yet. If she hadn't stayed with the man who loved her so generously, what hope did he have of keeping her? His love was possessive, demanding, all-encompassing. And he knew, in that moment, that he would lose her as a result. If he hadn't lost her already.

All the rest of that day, Jack fought against his desire to call Emily, to check that she was all right, to check that she was still his. She had asked him not to. She had dreaded this day, in which she would answer Michael's parents' questions and choose his coffin and plan his funeral service, and yet she had asked him to leave her to it. Perhaps, he thought, she didn't see him as a support when she had to deal with the most difficult things, but rather as a burden. He wasn't sure whether it was too late for him to change, to somehow morph into the kind of man that she needed.

The next morning, Jack got up and went to work. As he walked through the door, Tim flashed him a supportive smile, and Jack knew he had made the right decision. Another day of silence and contemplation would have been too much. He took his place behind the counter, kicked at the legs of his high stool.

'How are you doing?' Tim asked. 'You didn't have to come back yet, you know.'

'Thank you, but I wanted to. I'm fine. I knew him, and I liked him, but I haven't lost someone close to me.' I'm about to, Jack thought. I'm about to lose the most important person of all.

'So how is Emily?'

How was Emily? Apart from the previous day, Jack had been by her side since it had happened. He had watched her cry, he had watched her throw a wine glass at the wall and then sweep up the pieces, pricking her finger with a piece of glass. He had watched the faraway expressions in her eyes that told him she was thinking of Michael, remembering. She was like a woman who had lost her husband. She was grieving. Jack hadn't dared to ask her whether she regretted everything that they had done to him. Would she take Michael back now, if she had the chance?

'She's okay, you know.' Even as he sat there and spoke about her, Jack could feel her slipping away.

She called him that afternoon, asked him if he'd like to come over after work. Michael's parents were staying at the house, but they were going out somewhere. It was like it had been before, Jack thought, sneaking around and grabbing opportunities to see one another when they could. 'Yes,' he said. 'Of course I'll come.'

He tried to establish whether there was a message in her voice, whether she was going to tell him, that night, that it was over. He heard nothing. But he knew that didn't mean the message wasn't there.

Jack stopped on the way to the house to buy Emily flowers. And when he handed over his money, he began to think of all the things he would do, if he was given the chance. All the things he'd never done for her that he desperately wanted to do. He had never surprised her with a weekend away, or met her at school and taken her to the theatre. He had never asked her to stay with him forever. All the things that Michael had done, that Michael had had all those years to do.

When Emily opened the door, he kissed her. He expected her to resist but she didn't, and he put his arms around her, pinning her arms to her sides. He kissed her the way he had kissed her the first time, when he had needed to show her what he felt, needed to convince her that he was worth the risk. He hadn't expected to have to convince her again, so soon. Jack moved her gently until she was standing with her back to the wall, started to kiss her more urgently, and Emily responded, pulling at his clothes and her own. He undid a couple of buttons at the top of her dress and licked the skin between her breasts, tasted its saltiness.

Jack looked at her clean white skin and her clear wide eyes.

'What?' she asked, in a whisper.

'I feel like I'm losing you,' he said. And then he pushed himself into her, not wanting to hear her reply, and she turned her face to one side but didn't let go of him.

'WHAT NOW?' he asked, afterwards.

'We'll have dinner,' she said.

And then, he thought. What then? They both knew that wasn't what he'd meant. Jack had a cigarette and Emily told him about the plans they had been making for the funeral, and he didn't know how to tell her that he couldn't bear to hear it.

'Will you come?' she asked. She turned to him, knife in mid-air, in the middle of chopping vegetables. It was as though the question had come from nowhere, taken her by surprise.

'I'd like to,' he said. 'If you think it's all right.'

'Yes. He liked you. He'd want you to be there, I think. Well anyway, I want you there. But we can't sit together.'

No, he thought, they couldn't sit together. It would be indecent, disrespectful. He would sit somewhere near the back, trying to pass as one of Michael's acquaintances, trying not to be seen. He would watch her, up there in the front row, with no parent or partner by her side, and he would hold on to his seat to stop himself from going to comfort her when he saw her shoulders shaking. And when they all gathered, afterwards, for food and drinks and memories, he would be polite and offer his condolences to the family and he would hope, quietly, that when the room cleared and only he was left, she would still want him.

They didn't speak much while they ate. Jack had no appetite but he forced himself to eat, and when they were finished, he took the plates and cutlery and stacked them in the dishwasher. He wanted to do more so she would think of him as helpful and supportive, but when he looked around the kitchen he saw that everything was in its place, neat and clean.

'They don't know about you, his parents,' Emily said, when he returned to the living room.

'No.'

'I didn't tell them about you. And I don't think Josephine will. They're so terribly upset. I don't want to complicate it.'

'It's for the best,' he said. He didn't say he understood that she wanted them to see her in a certain way, and that telling them about all that had happened would make that impossible.

'Have they said much, about the crash?' Jack asked.

'Just that they think it was a terrible accident.'

'And what do you think?'

'I don't know. I know he was desperate. I can't help but wonder whether he was sending me a message.'

Jack didn't ask what the message was. He had sensed it too. He felt like he could hear it sometimes, being whispered, when he was trying to get to sleep. Michael's message to the two of them. His final plea.

When Emily started looking at her watch, Jack got up to leave. He didn't want her to have to ask him. He kissed her, and in that kiss, he tried to convey what he wanted and needed from her.

'It's going to be on Friday,' she said, when they were standing at the door.

Friday. They would lay him to rest and it would all be over.

'I'll see you then,' he said. And he walked away, feeling her watching him go.

CHAPTER THIRTY-FIVE

Emily woke to bright sunshine on the day of the funeral, and it didn't seem right. She wasn't ready to say goodbye to him. Josephine had called the night before and offered to go with her. It was more than Emily had expected, more than she deserved. And so it was that she travelled to the undertaker's office in a taxi with Michael's parents and her sister. Emily and Josephine sat in the back of the car, close but not quite touching. Emily wished she could let her sister know how much it meant to have her there.

They took turns to see him, laid out in the coffin, and when it was Emily's turn she could barely look at him, and she wanted to open a window, to let in a little air and a little light. She leaned against the wall, next to the door, feeling as though she might faint. From where she stood, she could see the bridge of Michael's nose and his lips, but not his eyes. And she was too cowardly to step forward, to face him, even in death.

She had let Michael's parents choose everything for the ceremony. So when it was time for the hymns and the blessings, she had forgotten what was coming, and she felt adrift. She felt Josephine's glance rest on her at one point, and it felt like fire.

When they walked out of that dim, cool chapel, the sunshine

hit them like a slap. People gathered in groups, and Emily made out, through her tears, a handful of people she didn't know, and she wondered what they were to him. Were there any old lovers in that crowd? Had any of them known him the way she had? She saw Jack, of course. It was the first time she had seen him wearing a suit, and he looked awkward, like a child dressing up as someone else. She noticed the way he tried to blend in, and she saw the tears in his eyes, and she wondered who they were for.

There was an endless stream of people who wanted to talk to her, it seemed. Emily took their warm hands in hers, and thanked them for coming, and said that he would have been pleased. She didn't know whether he would have been pleased, but it was the right thing to say, and she could see in their kind smiles that they were truly sorry for her. She wanted to let them all know that she didn't deserve their sympathy, but it wasn't about her, that day.

Michael's mother came to her, later, when they were back at the house drinking toasts to his name. 'It's such a tragedy,' she said. 'He had everything, here with you.'

Emily couldn't contradict her. What was the harm in her believing that he'd been happy until the end of his life?

'Will you be okay?' the older woman asked, and Emily nodded, feeling that she couldn't accept this kindness that she was so undeserving of.

If you knew, thought Emily, if any of you knew, everything would be different. And yet Josephine knew, and here she was, standing by Emily's side. They hadn't spoken much, but it was enough to have her there. 'Thank you,' Emily said, turning to her sister.

'I loved him too,' Josephine said.

At one point, Emily wished they would all leave her house. She felt suffocated, trapped. There were people everywhere she turned — eating, drinking, talking about him. She felt as though she would never escape it, as though this was her punishment for what she had done to him. But gradually, they drifted off, leaving her with dry kisses and dirty glasses. Michael's parents left for Yorkshire, wanting to get back to their own beds on that most awful of nights. And before she knew it, Emily was left almost alone. Josephine was still there, gathering up plates and glasses and running water to wash them.

Emily wondered where Jack was, and just as she thought it, she heard someone coming down the stairs from the bathroom, and it was him. She told herself that she would stop him if he touched her. And so, when he came into that empty room and reached for her, she turned away, and she curled her hands into fists and clenched them tightly, until her nails made angry indents on the skin of her palms.

Strange as it was for the three of them to be left in that house together, Emily recognised that neither Jack nor Josephine wanted to leave her there alone. And so they passed the night there together, in the living room. A collection of long quiet hours. Night found its way into the room and kept falling, and no words were spoken. Emily sat beside Josephine on the sofa, and Jack folded his long legs into the armchair.

And Emily did take some comfort from having them there, but she was preoccupied with thoughts of her uncertain future. She would let Jack go, even though it would break her to do so. And Josephine? Well, that day had allowed her to hope that Josephine might be back in her life.

THAT LONG NIGHT after the funeral, Josephine stayed by her sister's side. She thought of the time she had spent alone with Michael's body earlier, at the funeral parlour. She had been led down the corridor and ushered into a small room with pink flowers fading on the walls, and there had been no smell and no sound, and she had wished for a more suitable resting place for him.

Josephine had approached the coffin, but what she saw inside had nothing to do with Michael. He was smaller, almost lost. He was lying awkwardly, and his wild black hair had been tamed, smoothed. 'Michael,' she had sobbed, the words spilling out. 'I wanted to help you through it. I don't know who to call now, when I'm lonely. I'm so sorry, Michael, and I hope they are, too.' And then she had wiped her eyes and leaned back against the wall until she was ready to leave the room.

Josephine thought about going back to her flat, but she couldn't bear to leave Emily and Jack there, together. She didn't want Emily to look back on this night and regret spending it with her lover. Josephine had a feeling she wouldn't see Jack again, but what that meant for her and Emily, she wasn't sure. In a way, she thought, they were grieving for more than Michael that night. They were grieving for each other. For the relationships that had been destroyed.

At times, they stood up and wandered around, stretching their legs. And that was how Josephine ran into Jack, in the kitchen, when she went to fetch a glass of water. He turned when he heard someone approach, and she noticed how his expression stiffened when he saw it was her.

'What happens now?' she asked.

'I don't know, Josephine. I just don't know.'

She thought he was probably talking about his relationship with Emily. She wasn't sure what she had meant by her question. They returned to the living room, Josephine in front, Jack a few steps behind. And Emily looked up when they took their seats, her eyes confused, as though she'd just woken from a dream.

All of a sudden, Josephine wished desperately for one of them to say something. To honour Michael in some way. She felt certain that, if they didn't, it would mean that they intended to keep this thing going. That they intended to skulk away together to try to build a life out of this bitterness and regret. They would learn that love isn't enough, she thought, not when this is what it costs.

Slowly, morning came. Josephine was relieved that that awful day was over, that she had refused to give in to sleep and had faced it until the very end. That it had been defeated, finally, and replaced by a new day in which Michael would not be buried. She would go to the common, she decided. She would take a blanket and a book and she would surround herself with sunshine and with life. But first, she would have to leave this house, the house of her childhood. And it might be for the last time. She would not leave until Jack did.

Jack stood, when it was nearing seven, and he walked to the sofa where Emily and Josephine were sitting. 'I'm going to go,' he said.

Josephine looked from him to her sister, saw Emily's tight little nod, understood that something inside her sister was breaking.

'Goodbye,' Jack said.

Neither of them stood, and he walked over to the door, his head hung low.

'Jack,' Emily said.

He turned, and Josephine recognised the hope in him. But Emily didn't say anything more, and after a moment of pure silence, Jack left the room. Josephine listened out for the click of the front door, and took a deep breath when she heard it.

Josephine didn't turn to Emily, but she could feel her sister's small, controlled sobs. Emily's shoulders were shaking slightly. It seemed like such a small thing to do, to turn and put her arms around Emily and console her. But it was an enormous gesture too, and Josephine couldn't do it. She had stood beside Emily at the funeral, and she had spent the night beside her, and she couldn't do any more.

There was a gap in the living room curtains, and a thick slice of light was shining through it. Josephine could see tiny dust particles dancing in it. The light divided the room in two, fell, and landed on the sofa between the two sisters. It was like a chasm that could not be crossed.

Josephine slipped out quietly, without saying goodbye, and sat on the tyre swing, her feet in the dust. She felt hot and dirty in yesterday's dark funeral clothes. Josephine kicked at the dust until she scuffed the pointed toe of her new black shoes. Then she walked down the side of the house, out on to the street, and into the bright June morning.

ACKNOWLEDGEMENTS

This novel will always be special to me, because it was the first one I wrote. I can't thank my editor Kate Evans at Agora Books enough for helping me to shape it into something so much better than what I initially presented to her. Huge thanks also to Sam Brace and Peyton Stableford at Agora Books for their involvement in the whole process.

I'm so grateful to the authors who took the time to read my debut novel, Missing Pieces, and said lovely things about it: Sarah Pinborough, Fiona Mitchell, Amanda Berriman, Tamsin Grey, Christina McDonald, Jane Shemilt, Luke Allnutt, Laura Marshall, Clare Empson, Joanne Sefton, Louise Beech, Francesca Jakobi. Even typing all those names, I still don't believe it.

I owe an enormous debt of gratitude to the bloggers who reviewed Missing Pieces so kindly and thoughtfully. And to everyone at The Motherload and in The Motherload Book Club (especially Kate Dyson, Alison McGarragh-Murphy, Clara Wilcox and Gabrielle Clapp) and Late Nite Mummies Club who read it and cheered it on.

Thanks to writing friends who've answered questions, read through things and kept me sane. Gillian McAllister, Rachael

Smart, Rebecca Williams, Lia Louis, Steph Chapman, Hannah England. You're all so invaluable. Thanks to Melissa Febos for reading and critiquing it kindly so many years ago.

Thank you to the friends who read this book when I first wrote it: Gavin Schaffer, Suze Wilding, Steve Arnold, Liz Jones, Kyla McDonald and Tara McDonald. And the friends I talk to every day about writing and mothering and everything else: Jodie Matthews, Lydia Howland, Deb Chambers, Abi Rowson.

Thank you to my parents and my in-laws for always being supportive. Thank you to my husband, Paul, for working so hard to allow me to pursue this dream. Thank you to my children, Joseph and Elodie: you never let me write but you give great cuddles and occasionally go to sleep.

MISSING PIECES

LAURA PEARSON

1

5TH AUGUST 1985

21 DAYS AFTER

The coffin was too small. Too small to contain what it did, which was not only Phoebe's body, but a large part of Linda, too.

At the funeral parlour, a man touched Linda's arm and asked, gently, whether she wanted to see Phoebe, and even as she was nodding her head, she knew that it was a mistake.

'Are you sure?' Tom asked.

Linda knew that this was a decision she couldn't unmake. Knew, instinctively, that she was wrong. She would wish, later, that she hadn't seen their daughter like that, because no matter how peaceful she looked, she was still gone. Knew that the memory of her lying there, surrounded by silk and dressed too immaculately, would interfere with the memories she held of Phoebe laughing and running. Alive. And still, she nodded her head and followed the man down the corridor towards a lifetime of regret.

Linda looked back, once, at Tom and Esme. They were standing hand in hand, quite still, dark heads bowed. Esme's fringe needed cutting, and it was covering her eyebrows and, when she looked down at the thick carpet, her eyes too. This is my family, Linda thought. This is what's left of my family. And then she looked down at her swollen belly, touched it as her baby flipped over like a fish, felt nothing.

When they reached the room, the man told her to take as long as she needed. He opened the door for her and then disappeared down the corridor like a ghost. And Linda approached the coffin slowly, looked in at the girl who couldn't possibly be Phoebe. Who was too small, and still, and quiet, to be Phoebe.

And Linda felt like getting inside it, curling up with her daughter and going to sleep.

But the coffin was too small.

2

13TH AUGUST 1985

29 DAYS AFTER

Linda set her hands on her rounded stomach, interlaced her fingers. Tom was beside her in the sparse, white waiting room, and neither of them reached for a magazine, and neither of them spoke. The receptionist was eating her lunch, and the smell of her egg sandwiches made Linda feel sick. She unlaced her fingers and gripped the sides of her chair, willing the waves of nausea to pass. She'd given birth to both of her daughters in this hospital, had sat in this room waiting for numerous scans, and she'd always found it cold. That day, though, it seemed stuffy. She thought about standing and opening a window. She lifted her thick hair from the back of her neck, rooted in her bag for a band to tie it up.

When her name was called, Linda stood. Tom held out a hand for her to take, but she didn't reach for it, and he let it drop, followed her down the corridor. When they opened the door, the doctor stood and offered them a kind smile.

'I'm Dr Thomas,' he said.

'You were here when Phoebe was born,' Linda said. 'I remember.'

He smiled again, but didn't confirm or deny it. He saw

hundreds of babies being delivered, Linda told herself. He wouldn't remember hers. She sat down on an uncomfortable blue plastic chair and crossed her legs. She couldn't look at Dr Thomas, and she couldn't look at Tom, and so she set her eyes on the abstract painting that hung on the wall to the left of Dr Thomas's head. Every time she blinked, she kept her eyes closed for a fraction too long, trying to ignore the strong smell of ammonia that hung in the air.

'I heard about your daughter. I'm so sorry.'

Linda wanted to ask why he didn't say Phoebe's name.

'Thank you,' Tom said. 'It's been very hard.'

Since Phoebe's death, almost everything anyone said seemed ridiculous to Linda. She wanted to shake Tom, to punish him somehow for reducing their pain like that.

'Of course,' Dr Thomas said. 'That's why we wanted you to come in today and have another scan. The stress of something like this can be very tough on a baby. We just wanted to have a look and check that everything's all right. Try not to worry, though, I'm sure it will be. Now, Linda, would you like to get up on the bed?'

Linda did as she was told. As she pulled her legs up, the paper that was covering the bed tore a little, and it sounded loud in the quietness of the room. Six weeks ago, they'd come here for her twenty-week scan. Esme and Phoebe were being looked after by Maud, their next-door neighbour. Tom had closed his travel bookshop and they'd driven to the hospital, and Linda had felt a clutch of excitement in her throat, like she had on the day they'd run away from their families, when Esme was growing inside her. On the way to the appointment, Tom had turned the radio up loud and they'd sung along, the car windows open and the breeze whipping Linda's dark hair against her face.

It was hard to reconcile that memory with the question that wouldn't go away. The question that had come to Linda, formed and ready to be spoken, a few nights before. That was rising up in her throat, like bile.

'Dr Thomas?'

He turned to her, and she met his eyes for the first time.

'Yes, Linda?'

'Is it too late to have an abortion?'

Linda heard Tom's intake of breath and saw the flash of shock that Dr Thomas tried to hide. She wouldn't back down, or retract the words. How could she? How could she be expected to have this new child, and love it, when her love for Phoebe had brought her to this? When she could barely take care of her remaining daughter, barely look Esme in the eye?

Dr Thomas cleared his throat and the sound brought Linda back into that room, and she glanced at Tom. He was looking at her like he didn't quite recognise her. Squinting slightly, as though trying to work out whether he'd seen her somewhere before.

'It is too late,' Dr Thomas said. 'But if you don't think you can care for this baby, there are options we can discuss.'

'Adoption?' Linda asked.

She considered this, briefly. Going through the labour, feeling the baby emerge from her like a miracle, and then handing it over. Would she hold it first? Would she be told the sex, be given a chance to think about a name? No, she decided. That option wasn't for her. But before she could speak, Tom spoke for both of them.

'No,' he said, his voice soft but firm. 'We're having this baby, and we're keeping it.'

'Let's get this done,' Dr Thomas said. 'And then we can talk some more.'

He smeared the cold jelly on Linda's stomach and she almost laughed at the tickling shock of it. She waited to be told what she knew, that the baby was fine. She was aware that Tom was worried that her grief, her refusal to eat properly, and her inability to sleep, had caused the baby harm. But she could feel it moving, turning and probing. And more than that, this baby was a part of her, and she felt sure that she would know instantly if there were anything wrong. Just as she had known, that night, that something had happened to Phoebe.

And so, when the image appeared on the screen and Dr Thomas said the heartbeat was strong, Linda wasn't surprised. But she saw Tom, saw his hand fly to his mouth in pure relief, saw the love in his eyes that was ready and waiting. It was simpler, somehow, for him.

Despite what Dr Thomas said about it being too late, she knew there were ways to rid yourself of a baby. Ways that women had relied on for centuries. Painful and dangerous ways, but possible. But she wouldn't do it, because of Tom. She closed her eyes briefly, tried to imagine herself as the mother of a newborn again. Tried to imagine them being a family of four again. But it didn't feel right, when Phoebe wasn't one of them.

'Well,' said Dr Thomas, 'everything looks fine here. Come and take a seat at my desk again, when you're ready.'

He wiped the fluid from Linda's belly and she pulled her clothes back into position, pushed herself up and off the bed. Tom waited until she was ready. When she stood, he placed a hand on the small of her back and guided her the few steps back to the waiting chair. Linda anticipated a lecture, a talking to about how she would get through this. How other women had. You don't know, she wanted to scream. She wanted to open the door and let her voice bounce and echo along the empty white corridor. None of you knows.

'I'd like you both to think about having some counselling,' Dr Thomas said.

'It won't change anything,' Linda said.

'Not the situation, no. But I really think it might help you to come to terms with things. To accept what's happened, and start to move on. I'm not asking you to make a decision today. Just think about it.'

Linda took the leaflets he was holding out to her, and stood, ready to leave. When she was at the door, she felt Tom's breath on her neck, and she was sorry, for a moment, that they were leaving together. That they would have to suffer the car journey home, and then the evening, and the days and weeks to come in that too-empty house, with the words she'd spoken hanging there in the air, like a threat.

Tom didn't speak until he was behind the wheel with his seatbelt on. He reversed neatly out of the parking space, and Linda watched him, waiting for the accusations and the blame. He was handsome, this man she'd chosen. His profile was strong. They were both still young, him thirty and her twenty-eight, and yet small flecks of grey were starting to show in Tom's neat, dark hair. Once, he'd mentioned colouring it, and she said that she liked it as it was, and Esme commented that he looked like he'd been caught in a tiny snowstorm, and he left it. Tom must have felt her eyes on him then, and he glanced at her. It was his eyes that she'd noticed first. Green in some lights, grey in others. Kind, open. There was kindness in them still, she saw, even though she expected to be met with disgust.

When Tom did speak, it wasn't what she expected at all.

'I do understand,' he said, his voice calm. 'I lost her too. Just—'

His voice cracked, and Linda watched his face, saw the tears welling.

'—Just try not to shut me out.'

'I'll try,' Linda said, because she wanted to offer him something other than hurt.

THAT NIGHT, after Tom fell asleep, Linda lay awake beside him, listening to the occasional sounds of people and cars on the street outside. Sometimes, even before Phoebe's death, Linda woke up wondering how she'd ended up here, in an unassuming semi on a residential road in Southampton, so far from home. The night before she'd left Bolton with Tom, they had sat in his car with a map of England spread out on their laps. Linda's eyes were drawn to the edges, to the places beside the sea, and she'd pointed at Southampton, smiling. She had known almost nothing about the place. Her grandparents had holidayed there once. It was where the *Titanic* had sailed from. Linda had pictured a crumbling sort of house by the sea. Fish and chips, walking along the beach, her hair salty, being lulled to sleep by lapping waves. And when they had arrived, and it was nothing like she imagined, she hadn't cared much, because it was still a fresh start, a new life. But almost a decade had passed, now, and that freshness had long since faded.

Linda was aware of the sound of her breathing. She watched the clock crawl through half an hour, and when it got to one o'clock, she sat up carefully, trying not to wake Tom. She took her white cotton dressing gown from the hook behind the door and left the room, looking back once to check that he hadn't been disturbed. He was lying on his side, his breathing deep and slow, his mouth open.

She didn't turn the light on in the kitchen. After almost eight years in this house and two babies, she knew her way around in darkness. The kitchen had always been her favourite room. When they had come to look at the house, weary with unsuccessful viewings and the knowledge that they couldn't afford the kind of place she would choose, Linda had gone to the kitchen first. She'd looked around, at the drawings on the fridge that were held in place by colourful magnets, at the old pine table in the corner still messy with breakfast crumbs. The walls were painted a bright yellow and the cabinets were a pale wood, chipped and marked in places. It was the kind of room where a family gathers at the beginning and end of each day. And she'd known, then, that it didn't matter that the bathroom was small and the garden was a bit wild. This was the house where she would have her family.

For a while, Linda stood at the window, watching the stillness of the dark garden. It was mid-August, late summer, and although she was hot with the weight of her pregnancy, she wasn't ready for the season to change. Because when that summer had begun, she'd still had Phoebe. And it still seemed impossible that she was gone for good.

Linda opened the narrow cupboard in the corner of the room, stared at its contents. And then she took out the bottle of vodka and unscrewed the cap. She did it quickly, as though afraid of being caught. The bottle was three-quarters full, and she calculated that it had probably been there since the previous Christmas, when they'd had a party for some friends and neighbours. That night, she'd taken the drinks Tom had handed her, and she remembered feeling light-headed, feeling that the room was spinning slowly, as girls in bright dresses darted in and out of the small groups that had formed. She remembered catching sight of Phoebe, and dropping to her knees, catching her youngest daughter's wrists and kissing her forehead. Phoebe had wriggled from her grip, dashed off after her sister and the other older girls, and Linda had poured herself another drink.

Now, alone in the dark while Esme and Tom slept upstairs, Linda longed for the edges to blur a little, to take a break from the heaviness of her thoughts, and alcohol was the only way she knew. She lifted the bottle to her lips, tipped it, gulped. The baby inside her kicked, a quiet protest. And Linda tipped the bottle again, swallowed, and put it back in the cupboard. She sat down at the kitchen table, waiting for something to change, for some of the darkness to lift.

WANT TO HEAR MORE FROM LAURA PEARSON?

Sign up to Laura Pearson's Book Club to get:

1. An exclusive author Q&A with Laura and topics for your book group;
2. Details of Laura's publications as well as a sneak peak at her next book, and;
3. The opportunity to receive advance reader copies and win prizes

Interested? It takes less than a minute to join. You can get your Q&A and first newsletter by signing up here.

Connect with Agora Books
agorabooks.co

facebook.com/AgoraBooksLDN

twitter.com/agorabooksldn

instagram.com/agorabooksldn

Printed in Poland
by Amazon Fulfillment
Poland Sp. z o.o., Wrocław